STORM CHILD

Mikyla Baggström-Wild

ISBN: 9780646818672

In complete dedication to Stephen, Dom and Farryn—
for refusing to abandon me through my rotten first draft and endless indecision with everything which came afterwards.

"Damaged people are dangerous. They know how to make hell feel like home."

- Unknown

ONE

THE ESCAPE

She was on hyper alert.

Each silent, calculated step that she took, still felt to her as though it was taking too much time. Time she knew she might not have. Her ink-like eyes fixated, unblinking, on the sash window at the end of the silent, darkened hallway. It seemed distant and eerie in the grey light.

Careful to keep her breathing even and controlled, she tightened the straps of her backpack and shifted her focus back to her footsteps. She edged past bedroom door after bedroom door, listening intently for even the slightest of pin drops— any signal that a weakened floorboard might so much as murmur under her weight and alert somebody below to her presence.

She was completely exposed. There were no unlocked rooms to slip into, no cupboard doors to climb inside. Nowhere that she could hide if she was caught. But she wasn't fazed. She had done this before.

1

She flinched as an indistinct shadow threw itself across the bare wooden floorboards only paces ahead of her, catching her by surprise. Her pulse quickened as she looked to the window, seeking its creator. It was nothing but the branch of a tree in the moonlight.

She let out a low snarl and clenched her fists, silently cursing the tree and then herself. Her mind flickered back to the weather broadcast she had caught earlier in the week, predicting this exact storm, on this exact night; the thunderous wind, the vicious downpour of rain— the louder, the better.

Her hands reached out to the window as she stole the last two strides, closing the distance between them. Reaching her fingertips into her pocket, she slid out a small, silver butter knife. She had spent *weeks* working to steal this from the kitchen downstairs. She had had eyes on her at all times, day after day, year after year. This knife was her holy grail. Bringing the knife to her lips, she opened her mouth and secured it between her teeth. The smooth steel felt unsettling against the enamel of her incisors.

The latch that locked the window was old and out-dated. The paint was ancient and cracked as though nobody had opened it in years. It had been painted perhaps once, a long time ago and then left to decay. She looked out of the window into the heavy storm. She felt her heart interrupt the smoothness of her breathing, edging it out in a troubling rhythm. She focused and took a deep and forceful breath— taking back control.

Gripping the latch, she pressed her knuckles against the window for leverage against the lock, twisting her hand gently. The rough coat of paint cracked only slightly, but the lock remained stuck in place. Biting down on the knife, she gripped the latch tighter and pulled hard, jerking it out of place. It groaned with the new and unknown friction, sending small flakes of white paint onto the window sill below. She

2

paused briefly, pricking up her ears to listen for any movement that wasn't her own.

Forcing the end of the knife between the two wooden window frames, she began prying the two apart, just enough to wriggle her fingertips underneath. It was lighter than she had anticipated, and the strength she used to hoist the frame upwards was too much; it moved fast, but it did not move quietly. The wood screeched against itself as it screamed upwards, filling the hallway with deafening thuds as it jolted slightly from side to side on its way up.

She froze, her eyes wide. She knew instantly that she had been heard. She immediately dropped the weight of the window, yet it remained in place. Grabbing it hastily, she yanked the window down, careful to stop it before it slammed closed and sliding it carefully into place.

It was in this moment her fears were confirmed. A door from downstairs crept open, dragging rudely across the floorboards. A singular pair of heavy, shuffling footsteps echoed from the bottom of the stairs. With adrenaline still surging through her, she gripped the knife as her pupils dilated in panic. She sprinted back down the empty hallway, keeping to the edges of the floorboards. She slicked herself right up against the wall, wrapping both, shaking hands around brass handle of her bedroom door. She closed her eyes, holding her breath as she sent an urgent prayer to a god she didn't believe in that she would make it inside unseen— a god that was on her side it seemed, as the handle turned with quiet ease. She slipped inside the room, swallowed by complete darkness.

Her nose pressed against the wood as she stared through the keyhole of her door. She watched as the dark figure came to a halt only a few feet away. There was nothing but silence bouncing of each surface around her, except for her heartbeat pounding in her eardrums. It was so deafening that she wondered for the smallest of moments if it was audible to anybody but her. Gripping the knife by her side, she backed away from the door and found the bed behind her, sliding her backpack off and tucking it underneath her bed. She crept under the scratchy, woollen blanket and stayed as still as death.

There was a sudden rattle of keys and a door across the hall flew open, hitting the opposing wall with a loud bang.

She flinched. Feet moved quickly.

Struggling to listen through her pounding ears, she could barely make out the exchange of muffled voices followed by a loud hiss. A door slammed shut and dead air ensued for no longer than a moment. In this quiet moment, her thoughts turned to him. She thought about the life he would have without her, her without him. Her stomach tightened involuntarily.

The same heavy footsteps approached her door, tearing her from her thoughts and casting two dark shadows through the crack between the door and the floorboards. She squeezed her eyes shut in fear, expecting her door to be thrown open recklessly just like the one before. Had they noticed the window had been pried open? Had they spied the tiny, fallen paint flakes?
She waited in silent panic, praying she would not hear a key slide into the brass keyhole of her door. That alone, would give her away. Her door was not locked— and both her and the figure on the other side knew without a doubt that it should be.

She heard nothing, yet the shadows remained; listening but not moving. It felt like a silent battle. Her, willing the shadows to leave while they searched for a reason to push forward. She struggled to remain present. Her mind snaked it's way around itself, mimicking the sounds of disembodied footsteps and whispers, lying to her like it always did.

After what felt like an age, the wooden floorboards creaked slightly as the weight beyond the door shifted and the

4

shadows vanished, footsteps retreating back down the stairs from where they came. The door from below was dragged back over the floorboards, closing with an echoed thud that bounced from wall to wall.

Snarling into the lightless oblivion above her, she threw off the covers and rose off the bed, forcing herself to regain composure. Tucking a stray curl of dark and wild hair behind her ear, she picked her backpack up, swinging it once again over her shoulders. She made her way back over to her bedroom door and pressed her ear against the door briefly to check for movement outside. Hearing nothing but the sound of an empty hallway, she returned the knife to her mouth. She had now lost her patience. She had to get back to that window.

Noting the still silence, she slid her door back open, crossing the rugged wooden threshold of her doorway. This time, she moved fast with steady purpose. This time, the knife slid easily beneath the window as she jacked it up. Taking note of her previous mistake, she lifted the window gently up over her head.

The icy assault from the wind was instant. Chills ran through her, causing her entire body to shudder involuntarily. Her wild hair flew up around her face and gave no signs of settling as long as the wind kept up its reign. Doors in their frames quietly rattled around her and she was acutely aware of her time running out.

Climbing up onto the window sill, she reached her hands through the rusted iron bars and jammed the knife into one of the four screws holding the grille in place. She steadied the knife with both hands, twisting it with as much strength as she could find on such an awkward angle, and to her silent pleas— it slowly gave. She immediately got to work on the remaining screws as the grille began to come loose.

As it finally came free, she gripped the bars as tight as she could with both hands, her arms straining under the weight

5

of the iron. She warred with herself momentarily, wondering whether to risk putting herself off balance in the wet by throwing the grille away from the weatherboarded house or just to simply let it drop. She attempted to steady herself as she perched between the window and the storm, but her toes began to slip, making her mind up for her. She let the bars fall from her hands onto the wet grass, two storeys below. She cringed immediately, squeezing her eyes shut as she heard them scrape down the side of the house before connecting with the second set of bars directly below with a loud clang before landing on the grass with a soft thud.

She scrambled out over the ledge of the window— just as she thought she heard a whisper. She spun around, turning her back to the growling storm. The hallway sat, still as empty as ever. Her heart sank.

Using one hand to steady herself, she slid the window back down with the other. It was almost symbolic, she thought, as she closed the window on a life she knew she would never return to. Her skin prickled and her eyes stung as she struggled to wrestle her thoughts away from him. She would have to learn to accept that she was not his choice; that she would be alone from this point forward, just like she had been before him. Her chin wobbled. She grit her teeth and gripped the window's ledge with both hands as she lowered herself down.

Her biceps burned. The rain continued to pound relentlessly against her back and her bare feet slipped as they struggled to find grip on the saturated weatherboard house. Her shoes had been taken from her years ago and locked away, along with all the others. Looking down, she lined her toes up with the iron grille directly below her, identical to the one she had just dismantled. Her toes didn't quite reach— an inch or two shy. She took a deep breath, preparing herself to let go of the bars nonetheless.

Without warning, a light turned on above her. A square spotlight illuminated the wet and muddy grass below. She looked skyward to the source of the light. There could be no mistaking the missing grille through the window from the hallway. She had been caught.

Quickly glancing back down at the grass, she let go of the ledge, kicking off from the side of the house with enough force to throw her body far enough to avoid landing on anything that wasn't grass. Her hands sunk deep into the mud as her bare feet slammed into the ground, sending a sudden and savage burning shock up her legs after having dangled them in the air for so long. She forced herself to stand on shaky legs as the harsh wind continued to throw the rain hard at her face, stinging her ice-cold skin as each sharp drop connected.

This was it. She was free.

And she ran, headfirst, into the storm.

TWO

BAREFOOT AND BRALESS

Skin on skin; that's all she craved.

But none of this *love* shit.

As Kora lay still in a soft, white duvet in a king-sized bed, she looked down and watched the Thursday morning sunlight that had crept in through the blinds above her head as it played on her toes. It felt warm, but in a different sense, she still felt cold.

Feeling the blankets stir, she shifted her gaze to the sleeping man beside her and held her breath, silently hoping he would not wake. Not this early.

Not ever, would suit her even better.

The stubble on the sleeping man's chin was somewhat attractive to her but as she adjusted her body and propped her head up to look at him properly, she could feel a touch of heat across her throat where the same stubble had grazed her. It was uncomfortable. Painful but familiar. She found herself glaring at him, resenting him for it.

She rolled onto her side and eyed the small, white bedside cabinet beside her. It had one small drawer; a drawer that begged loudly to be opened. Kora was never one to deny her own curiosity. She slowly dragged it open and peeked inside. It was empty, almost. All that it contained in the far corner, was a ring box.

Her heart stuttered in her chest at the thought of what might be inside. She bit her lip and took a deep breath, taking back control of her heartbeat. She tried to bring her thoughts back down to a more logical playing field. She held her breath and opened the small black box, only to find it emptier than the drawer had been. Clenching both her fists, she silently cursed at herself for being so stupid as to get her hopes up. She returned the box to the drawer and closed it without a sound.

Turning back to face him, she wondered what would happen if he happened to wake, what kind of man he would be, sober. Would he offer her an awkward cup of coffee but not entirely mean for her to accept it? Or would he make some polite excuses about the time, about how he had to leave for work— hiding the ever-present tan line on his left ring finger? Or perhaps he would turn out to be more of the relaxed, morning sex and "let me make you breakfast" type.

She hoped she wouldn't have to bother finding out. She liked to throw people away as it suited her. She grew tired of them quickly, especially when they were no longer of any use to her. She had no-one and she wanted no-one. She was empty and hollow— just the way she liked it.

She watched him for a little while longer. Watching his eyelids, each pupil moving simultaneously behind them in no particular pattern, watching the soft rise and fall of his chest, listening to him breathe. To the outside world, it might have looked as though she was admiring him, staring at him longingly, perhaps even lovingly— but that could not be further from the truth. She watched him only to be sure of his sleeping state.

Content with his unconsciousness, she slipped gracefully out from underneath the covers and sat on the edge of the bed in nothing but her black lace panties. Looking down at her thighs she absentmindedly thought about how soft her skin looked in the mornings. It was like a secret, dusky mocha velvet she kept hidden from the harshness of the world, and it was only hers. Kora ruffled her collarbone-length, onyx curls with her fingers. They were still damp and the ringlets only tangled around her fingertips, so she left them.

She arched her back slowly, lifting her arms above her head and moving from something somewhat non-committal, into a sleepy, full-body stretch. Nothing in the world could feel better in that moment, as she felt her bones crack. She counted each one, letting out a long, slow breath as she relaxed. Her eyes lazily grazed the beige carpeted floor. She spotted her jeans over by his sliding wardrobe door and gave herself a sleepy smile.

Perfect placement.

Standing up, she let her head adjust to the sudden change in altitude as the blood rushed through her body. She swayed slightly as her vision darkened at the edges, if only for a moment before the light fought off the static eclipse and her vision returned to normal.

She carefully tiptoed over his leather belt as she made her way over to her jeans. Instead of picking them up, she wrapped her fingers around the edge of the wardrobe door and quietly slid it open. A small collection of collared shirts and dull-looking business suit jackets hung lifelessly above some dress shoes and some runners. A black leather watch box sat empty on a shelf, aside from a pair of plain, silver cufflinks. Nothing of any interest to her.

Disappointed, she closed the wardrobe door and reached down, picking her jeans up off the floor. She dragged the black denim over her toes and up over her legs. She was slight in build but her jeans were tighter. Upon reaching almost to her hips she gave a little jump, giving herself just enough momentum to get her jeans past the crease and curve of her backside.

The light seeped in through bold wooden blinds. It stained the far wall and carpet with glistening stripes— too bright for so early in the morning. There was another door across from where she stood that led to an ensuite. Behind the door, a two-person spa bath beckoned, still filled to the brim from the earlier hours of her late night rendezvous, but by now the water would be glacial, and the bubbles, nothing but ghosts.

Taking one last quick look at the naked, sleeping stranger sprawled across the bed, she crept barefoot and braless out of the room.

Her head began to pound. Last nights empty wine glasses sat guiltily across from some type of brown prescription pill bottle. The label had been torn half off and small, white pills had been carelessly spilled on the gloss black stone kitchen counter next to her handbag. She eyed the pills as she walked around the counter and into the kitchen. She opened the refrigerator doors, curious and thirsty.

The refrigerator, much to her surprise, was almost bare.

Two different brands of bottled beer and some aged cheddar sat on various shelves but it wasn't until she spotted the expensive, vintage merlot sitting in the refrigerator door that she truly rolled her eyes. This man had worn a mask. He dressed himself up with beautiful words and a pretty suit but had no real idea about class and definitely no real idea about how to hide it.

Forgetting about her thirst, she walked back around the kitchen counter, letting the refrigerator door close on its own. Collecting her nude camisole from over the back of a barstool, she slipped it over her head. The thin straps lay loosely on her shoulders as she continued to look around the apartment in search of what she really wanted.

Kora couldn't remember the last time she slept on her own. Why would she, when she could sleep in soft, expensive sheets with people too caught up in a world of money and the illusion of escaping monotony with it? She secretly laughed at them, albeit deep down there was a pang of hunger and jealousy, as she knew it was still a world she would never really get to be a part of.

She wandered towards the fireplace. The modern, featherstone bricks triggered flashbacks of last night, like film clips flooding her mind, and she let them.

The memories hit her in sudden but broken fragments. The man from the bedroom in his navy shirt, two buttons laying undone; complaining in notably slurred speech about his long work hours in the flickering low light; about the early starts and the late nights, how much it had cost him; his friends, his freedom, his wife. She remembered his eyes, how they travelled from her lips, to her chest, to her hips. How she smiled sweetly as his head tilted back in the ecstasy of a welcome distraction from the world as she straddled him on his cream leather couch. How the fire warmed her back as her fingertips played with the silver buckle of his leather belt, teasing him, watching him salivate over her.

Her memory was blurred and hazy, and she squinted as she tried to force herself to remember more, begging the fragments to come back and fill in the blank spaces. Where did he take off his jacket? Where did he empty his pockets? She looked around in frustration, the stubborn silence of the living room not giving her any more than what it already had.

She could hear traffic in the distance. It was already getting late.

Grabbing her handbag from the counter in the kitchen, she slung it over her shoulder and turned to head down the hallway towards the front door but as she did so, the pills that lay sprawled across the countertop caught her eye. She stopped, gripping the strap of her handbag just that little bit tighter. She noticed somewhere in the back of her mind that her hands were clammy.

Fuck it, she thought, and leaning over, she scooped a few of the pills up. She laid them out in the palm of her hand and inspected them. Shrugging, she popped just one in her mouth and let the rest fall into her bag. She didn't know what they were but what she did know, is that she didn't really care. She hated to leave a house empty-handed.

Once again, she turned to leave and strode back down towards the hallway. Her black wedge heels and faux leather jacket lay carefully underneath a black wooden console table by the front door. It seemed odd to her that in her drunken stupor she would be so tidy with her things— especially her heels after kicking them off. They weren't expensive and if she were honest, she wasn't exactly the tidy type. Nonetheless, she began to slip them onto her feet. Her toes pushed against something sharp and uncomfortable. Confused, she put her foot back down on the floor and tilted her shoe to look inside. It rattled.

Keys.

She rolled her eyes, smiling to herself as she reached in and pulled them out.

Drunk Kora, you beautiful bitch.

She must have picked them up last night and placed them there, keeping them from being lost in her morning search, somewhere that her sober self would find them. She almost laughed at the thought of her drunken antics.

Placing her handbag down on the console table, she glanced at the front door, taking note of the locks; a steel deadbolt and a push-in lock. Inspecting the set of keys she picked out the only two that were on the same keyring, and carefully pried each of them off the metal ring. She placed them on the table side by side. Digging around in her bag, she pulled out a small silver container. She pried the lid off, revealing grey modelling clay that she had pressed flat. She picked up each key, pressing it into the clay until there was a clear impression of each.

With a slight smirk, she slid them back onto their keyring and left them laying on the console table, seemingly untouched.

She looked back down the hallway. An eerie silence seemed to bounce off every angle of the cream walls and she couldn't decide if it was the closed-in space between the hallway walls that gave it such a feeling of dead air, or whether it was all just her own mind.

She gathered her belongings and crept out of the front door, closing it carefully behind her with a small click. She mentally took note of the two, large, silver numbers that clung to the wall next to the apartment door before she left. Thirty-three.

The elevator ride to the ground floor of the apartment building made Kora feel uneasy. The doors closed after a loud buzz and the floor jolted. In the dim light, she distracted herself by staring at her reflection, involuntarily picking out things about her face she didn't like. Her jet black curls looked more wild than usual and noticing this, she ran her fingers through them quickly, flattening them, then scrunching them to give them a little more attitude. They ended up looking almost exactly the same and so she gave up, her eyes travelling back to her face in the strange light. If she changed the angle of her head slightly, the light in the elevator made her nose look thinner, her lips full, poutier, but her eyes never changed— they were forever just empty sockets of darkness.

The elevator slowed to a stop and buzzed loudly. The building foyer was small and simple. There was no fancy decor, if only for a wall of grey, numbered post boxes and two large, glass front doors. Wasting no time, she pushed through one of the oversized doors and stepped out into morning sun and the musky city air.

She would be back.

THREE

SAFE HOUSE

"Alright. Who have we got?"

"Kora Brookes, ten years old. Mother deceased— drug overdose. Her father has recently been imprisoned, life sentence."

"How long have we got her?"

"This one could be another lifer."

The two women sat together at a small cubicle desk looking over a thick folder full of paperwork. The first, a Child Protection caseworker with short, platinum blonde hair pinned back out of her face and the other, Naomi Kennedy, a Foster Rehabilitation Specialist. The caseworker slid an open file across the desk to Naomi.

Both women's eyes lingered on the two photographs that had been paper-clipped to the pages. Faded photographs of a young girl about five or six with short, dark curls. One was taken of the girl sitting alone on the beige carpet floor of a bedroom, smiling at the camera. It was immediately clear that the girl's surroundings in the photo were the main cause for concern. The room she was sitting in was dark and dishevelled. A thriving patch of mould could be seen growing along the wall trimmings and the floor was scattered with rubbish and dirty cutlery. In the second photograph, she sat on her father's lap at a small, rectangular dinner table. He looked as though he'd been hit by a truck. His eyes were unfocused, encompassed by yellowish rings and accompanied by deep purple bags underneath each one. There was a brown leather belt hanging loosely around his bicep. Heroin, presumably. Her eyes were red and puffy as though she had been crying.

"She was brought in this morning," the caseworker explained. "Police were alerted a few days ago by her school. Teachers claimed Kora has displayed continuously odd behaviour. She's mostly quiet and keeps to herself, a little jumpy, but recently she's been becoming increasingly prone to violent outbursts. It's also noted that her personal hygiene was lacking and she seemed to have stopped showering."

Naomi frowned as she continued to flick through the paperwork laid out in front of her as she listened.

"After an incident at school," the caseworker continued, "where she attacked another student, the school counsellor questioned her and found significant signs of physical abuse — bruising and such. That's when the police were alerted. Her medical assessment taken later on also showed definitive signs of sexual abuse. It's a wonder this wasn't picked up earlier," she shook her head sadly.

"Why's that?"

"Her medical history has a record of her hips having been cracked apart."

Naomi visibly cringed, adjusting her black, thick-rimmed glasses.

"The father?"

"Yes."

She picked up another file and began to flick through the pages, still frowning as she did so. She was usually only called, as a rule, when there was a significantly difficult case

16

— usually one of severe circumstances or psychological damage and desperate need for rehabilitation. This case definitely seemed serious, but something didn't quite add up.

"What makes you think she could be a lifer?"

"Her psychiatric assessment."

"Oh?" She questioned.

"All the information is there in that folder you're holding, but you'll understand once you meet her."

"What exactly *did* the evaluation show?"

The woman with the bright blonde hair shifted uncomfortably in her seat.

"The psychiatrist came to the conclusion that Kora shows early signs of developing an antisocial personality disorder and," she paused for a moment, pursing her lips before continuing, "she also shows signs of conduct disorder, which we well know could develop into sociopathic tendencies."

Naomi stopped suddenly, raising an eyebrow behind her glasses.

"At her age?"

"I'll introduce you."

Leading her out of the cubicle and down a long corridor, they arrived at a frosted glass windowed room with a lilac door. The door looked slightly out of place in such a professional office environment as all of the other doors in the building that they had passed were a stark white, and the walls a dull grey. Stickers had been stuck to the inside of the frosted glass windows and a green crayon had been dragged across the lower panel. This was clearly a room for children.

"Remember— be stern with her. What you say, goes." She warned, checking her watch.

Knocking quietly on the door as a warning that she was entering, she reached to her belt and unclipped an ID badge with her name, photograph and a black, magnetic strip running down the side. She placed it inside the slot of the security lock fastened to the door and swiped downwards, clipping it back onto her belt. The security lock beeped and a small, green light flashed. She pulled down on the handle and pushed open the door. The woman peeked her head around the corner as she entered, smiling brightly before stepping inside the room.

"Kora, this is Naomi."

Kora sat on a bright violet sofa, red-eyed and chewing on one of the sleeves of her striped button-up sweatshirt. Immediately, Naomi noticed how thin she was. Kora looked up and stared at the new woman for a second, her dark, sunken eyes taking in her features. Kora instantly seemed fascinated by Naomi's immaculately straight, ashy hair and thick glasses. She looked over her outfit, from her ruffled blouse, to her rose gold bracelets, down to her matching, shimmering sandals. It seemed almost as if Kora was assessing her, before returning her hollow eyes to Naomi's face and finally greeting her with a tiny smile of her own.

The caseworker piped up brightly, "You'll be staying with Naomi for a little while. She takes care of other children too, so you'll be able to make some new friends and you'll get to do loads of fun activities. Isn't that exciting?"

"Some of the other children are the same age as you, too," Naomi added, smiling.

"I'm going to leave you two alone together for a few minutes, just you can get to know each other a little bit." She turned to leave, giving Naomi a small nod as she closed the door behind her.

Kora's smile faded as she glanced down at Naomi's ID badge which hung from a lanyard around her neck. She squinted, as if struggling to read the small letters and numbers from her short distance away. She frowned suddenly, and her childlike demeanour held a hint of hostility. She rubbed her eyes with her sleeves. She looked exhausted.

"Hi, Kora," she spoke softly, walking over to the sofa and sat in the empty space, facing her. Kora, still frowning, looked at the floor.

"It's been a long couple of days, hasn't it? Would you like to come home with me and get some rest, maybe eat some food? Watch TV?" She paused, receiving no answer. She tried again. "What shows do you like?"

Kora glanced at her from out of the corner of her eye.

"You can't be my friend."

Taken aback by this response, her smile instinctively faltered for a second. Was her frown more of a scowl? Had she misread this child already?

She made a playful face at Kora, attempting to keep the conversation light-hearted.

"Why not? I bet we'd make great friends!"

"You can't do anything for me."

Kora jumped off the couch and sat in the corner of the room on the floor next to her backpack. Naomi noticed how full it looked and assumed it was the bag she used for school. The zips had struggled to close, and a small pencil case poked out of the top, decorated with a picture of a fox.

She tried a more honest approach.

"It might take some time, Kora, but I'm going to try to make you as happy as I possibly can."

Kora ignored this, continuing to fidget with the straps on her bag.

There was a knock at the door. A small beep was heard and the door swung open. The caseworker and her big, fake smile had returned.

"How are you getting on?" She asked.

"I think we'll be alright. What do you think, Kora?"

Kora didn't even look up.

"Great!" she clasped her hands together, simultaneously giving Naomi a sympathetic smile. "Let's grab your things and get you all ready to go."

Kora hugged her backpack to her chest as the three of them walked out to the car park together. Kora in front, and the two women behind, speaking quietly between themselves.

"She hasn't been prescribed any medication just yet, so you won't have to oversee that she takes anything. She has enough of her own clothes in her backpack to last her a few days but a clothing grant for her has been approved so feel free to take her to get her whatever she needs, whenever you see fit. I'll check up on her in a couple of days to see how she's adjusting and we can take it from there."

"Of course, thank-you."

She handed Naomi the folder containing Kora's files and turned to Kora with a bright smile.

"Bye, Kora! I'll see you in a couple of days. Have fun!"

Kora hid her face behind her backpack and turned to face the car door, not saying a word.

Smiling, Naomi shrugged and pressed the button on her car remote to unlock her red hatchback. Hearing the doors unlock, Kora, quicker than lightning, opened the back door and scrambled inside, closing it behind her. Naomi turned to the caseworker.

"I'll be in touch."

"See you."

They nodded goodbye and went their separate ways. Naomi couldn't help but feel like Kora's caseworker couldn't wait to palm her off to somebody— *anybody* else. She sighed. Some people just weren't cut out for this type of job.

Upon reaching the car, Naomi walked around to Kora's door and opened it. Kora didn't even look up. She bent down and flicked the miniature lever on the inside of the door before she closed it; the child lock. Anti-social behaviour was incredibly common in this type of situation. She knew that making Kora feel comfortable would take some work and she would take it one step at a time, as she always did with all of the children she took in.

Jumping into the driver's seat and closing the door, she glanced in the rearview mirror at Kora. Much to her surprise, she was staring straight back at her. They held eye contact for a few seconds and Naomi smiled, expecting her to look away.

She didn't.

Naomi's skin prickled with unease and the feeling caught her by surprise. She looked away, shaking off the feeling. She felt silly. She placed the stack of Kora's files in the passenger seat and inserted her keys into the ignition, bringing her little car to life. They pulled out of the carpark and away from the building, beginning their journey.

Quickly glancing at Kora again in the mirror, she was relieved to see her staring out of the back window instead of into the mirror. She knew it was silly to let a child make her feel that way. Kora's demeanour hadn't come across as anything other than what was expected of a child put in her position but the earlier conversation regarding this little girl being diagnosed as a sociopath still lingered in the back of her mind. Shaking off the unease for the second time, she decided instead to make conversation.

"Do you want to hear about the home?"

Kora continued to stare out of the window in silence.

"There are three other children in the home," she explained, not truly expecting an answer. "Two girls and one boy. One of the girls is around your age and the other girl is a bit older, Claire. She's seventeen."

Checking her side mirrors and quickly glancing behind her on the freeway, she flicked her indicator on to change lanes. It was then that Kora surprisingly spoke up.

"Where are their dads?"

A moment of silence ensued as Naomi stared at the road ahead, confused for a moment. Usually, if anything, children ask about their mothers. She thought about how to answer her question in the right way. The question itself was innocent enough, albeit carried a heavy weight behind it.

"Some of them don't have dads, sweetie. We try not to talk about our families with others in the home, just in case it makes the other children upset."

"But I won't get upset."

"Yes, but the other children might."

"Not me."

Naomi sighed quietly to herself. Bringing a new child into the home was always a bit of a juggling act. On one hand, she wanted the new child to feel as welcome as possible to make the transition smooth and comfortable for everyone. Unfortunately, more often than not, the new addition to the home would start out unruly, undisciplined and difficult, upsetting the children who already lived in the home and who had already adjusted to their new life. It was completely normal for them to react this way to such a drastic change, considering all of the children she took in were uprooted suddenly from troubled homes, however, she was furiously protective over each of her foster children and it was always difficult for her to see one upset the rest.

"Now, Kora, I'd like to explain a few rules before we get back to the house. These are rules that everyone follows and I'd like you to do the same, okay?"

Hearing this, her face changed, growing dark. She scowled out of the window. This reaction didn't sit well with Naomi and the small, niggling, uncomfortable feeling returned as she continued.

"The first rule is the first thing we will do when we arrive, and that is that we are going to put your shoes in a special cupboard. You are allowed your shoes when we go out on day trips, but otherwise, you are not to keep them. Do you understand?"

Kora gave nothing away. Naomi chalked this up to stubbornness.

"The second rule is that we do not touch the other children. This means that we don't touch them with our

22

hands, our feet or our mouths. We do not hit them, we do not hold on to them or hug them, and we always, always listen to each other. If another child or adult tells you to stop, you stop what you are doing immediately. No exceptions. We must respect each other."

Out of the windows of the car, the houses began to seem few and far between. They drove straight through suburbia and more towards the outskirts of town, but Naomi gave away no tell-tale signs of stopping. Kora had been picked up from Pearl City, but the nearest rehabilitation home was the home run by Naomi, and it was an entire city away— Almost two hours drive.

"As for the third rule, this one is the most important. We don't tell people where we live. If a stranger or even somebody you know asks you where you live, you are not to tell them. This is what we call a *Safe House* which means nobody is to know the address. I need to know that you understand this, Kora."

She looked back at her through the rearview mirror for a response.

"Can you nod for me to let me know that you understand?"

Kora with her ever-present scowl, nodded grumpily.

"That's good, thank-you. Now the fourth is easy and pretty straightforward. If you need something, if you have any questions, if you're unsure about anything or if you see something you don't like, maybe somebody breaking the rules, you come to either myself or Claire straight away. Nobody is to take matters into their own hands under any circumstances. Understood? We're here to help you and we want everyone to feel safe and happy."

Kora sat still, surrendering nothing.

Over an hour passed, and she had not once so much as stirred in the back seat. Eventually, Naomi pulled off the

23

freeway, and after a few minutes, they turned into a quiet street. Kora sat up straight, pressing her nose to the glass as the car suddenly pulled into a long gravel driveway. Tall trees surrounded the surprisingly large property, giving it an eerie feel and as the two-storey house came into view, the first things Kora noticed were black, iron bars guarding each window.

Naomi jumped out of her skin as Kora let out a feral scream. She had taken off her seatbelt and moved across to the opposite door, pulling violently on the car door handle to no avail, thrashing wildly about like a caged animal.

"Kora! Stop!"

She quickly slammed on the brakes and took off her seatbelt. She spun around, managing to grab hold of both of Kora's wrists. Kora screeched again and lunged forward, snapping her teeth at her face, barely missing.

From inside the house, a tall, slender young woman with fiery auburn hair and freckles to match came running out to the car to help Naomi. She opened the car door and picked Kora up, wrapping her arms around her tiny body as she continued to struggle, growling, but the girl held her secure. Naomi got out of the car, shaken, grabbing Kora's bag from the backseat.

"Claire, take her inside."

As Naomi watched her carry Kora inside, she turned back to the car and collected the paperwork that had been strewn all over the passenger seat in the commotion. She picked up one file in particular that caught her eye.

Prone to extremely violent outbursts.

It was becoming all too clear to her that somebody had poisoned something deep inside this child.

FOUR

ENGRAVERS' LTD.

The sunlight glared off every outside surface at Kora and she glared right back.

The streets smelled of warm rain, which still dressed the pavement from the previous night. The scent wore a metallic hint. Spring in the city was always temperamental this way. It could be smooth and summery or it could be painfully arctic, but the only thing notable that never changed is that it was seemingly always wet. There was something that felt almost nostalgic to her about the way old rain glistened in the light but she decided that it was not a feeling she liked, and so she unburdened herself from it and began walking.

With each dull click of her heels on the concrete, the city noise grew louder as it came to life. Shop owners dragged their desperate signs full of cheap humour and bad puns outside to lure in the days' customers. A dark green and grey garbage truck roared and screeched inconsistently a few hundred yards away and in-between the ruckus and every so often, somebody would walk out near the edge of the footpath and either holler or whistle obnoxiously at passing and oncoming taxis. She forcefully drowned it all out and stared at the pavement as she walked.

The further she walked, the city quickly turned from high-end to low, and fourteen blocks downtown from where she woke, she made a turn down a crumbling brick alleyway with a rusted pawn shop roller door taking over the corner. The city had its own secret maze, and although it was filled with paths and alleys; shortcuts from one road to the next, this particular alleyway snaked around several tall, unkempt buildings. Some which she knew only as the city's more *affordable* housing units.

The alley came to an abrupt end with a large gate which opened up wide enough to fit trucks through. The gate was closed and locked, with a large, rusted padlock hanging from the opening. The wire fence that sprawled across from brick wall to brick wall had curled up slightly at the bottom. Without skipping a beat, she dropped to her hands and knees, lifting the gate up further with one hand and crawling underneath it. The concrete hurt to crawl across and she found herself gritting her teeth as little stones dug into all of the soft points in her knees. The sharp pain, surprisingly, almost unbearable.

Once she had made it underneath the broken fencing, she stood, relieved, brushing herself off. She began to make her way down the wide concrete berth between the rows of dirty, brick buildings. With each step, she counted the endless, old warehouse roller doors on each of the buildings under her breath but stopped counting as she approached one that was open, pushed only half-way up. Looking behind her, she counted the doors again, up to the one that sat open. Eight doors. This was the one. Sure enough, there sat a bold plaque screwed into the old bricks to her left, reading *Engravers' LTD*. Ironically, engraved.

She lifted up her hand, balled up into a fist ready to bang on the door for attention but hearing noises inside, she

26

quickly changed her mind. She grinned, relaxing her hand and slowly ran her fingernails over the rivets of the metal door, making loud, echoed clicks with each one.

The noises on the other side of the door stopped, and somebody cleared their throat.

This was the sign she wanted.

"Theo," she cooed. She was met with silence.

She sighed dramatically and turned her back to the garage door and leaning against it. It groaned, even under her slight weight.

"Theo, come out and play with your baby sister," she called out, playfully. Her voice was husky like a crackling fire, yet soft and feminine. She let her dark tresses fall to one side of her face, and began playing with a lock, wrapping it around her fingers.

"You are *not* my baby sister, Kora." A voice snapped back.

She rolled her eyes.

"Don't be like that. We grew up together, what else could I ever be to you?" She paused. "You don't want anything else from me, you made that pretty clear."

There was silence, and for a second she fought the urge to storm off. Would he feel guilty if she left on that note? Guilty enough to call her back?

His voice interrupted her thoughts, although softer this time.

"You can't come around here no more. You gotta go. Enough is enough."

Stung, she growled, spinning around and ducking under the garage door.

Theo stood, six foot four and looking every part the concerned, handsome older brother. But even a stranger could tell that he was not. His hair was much lighter than Kora's and his eyes were a cerulean blue while hers were a dark brown; almost black, matching her tiny, dark freckles sprinkled across her cheeks and nose.

He had been leaning against a stack of boxes but now that she had entered the cluttered warehouse, he stood alone, looking apprehensive. She watched his jaw muscles tense as he laid eyes on her for the first time in what could have been weeks, but she wasn't counting. It wouldn't do her any good to count days.

His eyes involuntarily flickered to a corner of the room and then back to her, the movement so fast that she almost didn't catch it. Almost. Her eyes followed where his had gone and she spied two black rubbish sacks in the corner on their own and she knew instantly that her belongings were inside. Almost everything she'd ever owned, in two black trash bags.

"I'm not even worth a box, Theo? Really?" Her voice was laced heavily with malice.

Theo looked down at the floor guiltily, clearly wanting the interaction to be over as soon as possible.

"Why can't I be here?!" She took a small but menacing step forward. "*You* don't want me here? Is that why?" She glared at him, allowing him a chance to retract what he had said.

He looked up at her, seemingly finding his strength. He stood a little bit taller and broadened his chest, showing no sign of changing his mind— so she decided to change it for him.

"Is it that you don't want me to get caught sleeping here and get you into trouble? Or is it that you think that you just get to throw me away when you're done with me?"

He took the guilt-ridden bait she dangled in front of his face. She knew Theo, and above anything, she knew he couldn't stand to be the bad guy. Not with her. It was sweet, really.

"I'm not throwing you away. I just... I just wanna keep my job this time. Some of us actually want to build a life out here."

"And I don't?!" Visibly upset, she broke eye contact, looking anywhere but at him.

Theo sighed, feeling her pain.

"You just..." He faltered, searching for the right words.

"Look, I know you ain't here that often, but things go missing almost every time you show up and it's not like my boss don't notice, Kora. The woman down at the pawn shop goes broke returning things to us that she buys from you. And who knows what else you sell her!" He threw his hands up in the air, exasperated. "My boss thinks it's *me*. I gave you the address of my contact for a new passport so you can make something of yourself too. I can't do anything more for you. I'm trying to sort my life out and you're just these little breadcrumbs that lead straight back to trouble. I can't mess this up again. I'll lose everything."

Kora looked up at him, her eyes on fire.

"But you're happy to lose *me*."

He looked up at the concrete ceiling and closed his eyes, vexed.

"I already lost you," he growled. "You left me alone in that foster home and let me fend for myself. I waited a whole year to get out and find you and I did, but look at you. You never grew up, Kora. It's been three years and it's like you're still trying to escape."

She hissed as rage burned throughout her chest.

"I tried to get you to leave that house *with* me, and you made the decision that I'd do it alone. Alone for a year. And now what? You find me and slowly decide that because now that we're not stuck in some shitty foster home together that you don't even have to *like* me anymore?" She zeroed in on him. "Is that what eleven years of therapy taught you about *family*?"

She was fired up but he stared bravely back at her.

"There is no *with you*. It's only ever for you or against you. You'll find somebody else to take my place. You always do. I can't be skipping my meds and getting into trouble with you no more. I'm done. I can't even find a place to live. I'm lucky Der lets *me* sleep here let alone you."

Her eyes narrowed and she felt the overwhelming sense of searing rage inside her chest grow, making it's way up to her throat.

She tore her eyes away from him and paced around, looking at the contents of the room in an attempt to distract herself from her own temper. Ultimately, her intention wasn't to infuriate him and being as hot-headed as she was, she knew if she didn't reroute this conversation, then infuriating him is exactly where she would end up no matter who was in the wrong.

He *had* given her the address of a shifty ex-convict he had kept in contact with since he had been in prison, yes. The same ex-convict he used to sell stolen car parts to from the cars he and Kora used to steal together— the entire reason he had gone to prison in the first place.

Expensive car parts had never been difficult to steal. Theo had started an apprenticeship as a mechanic straight out of the foster program in a small garage predominantly used for importing and replacing car parts. He had always had an unparalleled passion for cars and knew every inch of every vehicle that came through. It wasn't long after he had found her again that he had stopped taking his medication. They had spent their spare time concocting plans to turn the garage into their own little chop shop right under his boss's nose. They bought cheap, malleable car parts to replace undamaged parts on expensive cars— all without their owners having even the slightest of inklings, as long as what *was* damaged, was replaced or repaired. The prison sentence should have been much heavier than it was, but nothing would ever be as heavy as the guilt Theo carried. His shoulders had been rounded ever since he was released, and Kora knew it was the weight of it all. The deaths that had occurred from the cheap parts crumbling to bits in the middle of highways or in road accidents haunted him into the dawn of most mornings. Most of the blame had fallen on Theo's shady contact, who, according to the news reports, was somewhat of a "seasoned pro". Kora, however, had evaded police questioning and her name had been on a list ever since.

In the most spoilt, childish way, she felt like pouting. Theo was no fun now that he was back on his medication. She missed her carefree partner in crime.

But she had kept the address. She needed forged documents just to apply for a job, let alone a house. Nobody would hire her with her background. She had never been to school, she had never been released from the foster program, she had never had a job, though not for lack of trying. It was almost as though she had never existed. Employers took one look at her vacant list of previous employment and shook their heads. If they so happened to do a background check, a big red flag would have popped up beside her name along with the word *fugitive*.

Thinking about it only baited her temper further, wondering how Theo expected her to pay for an entire set of forged documents legitimately, without being able to find a job to pay for them.

The warehouse had changed since the last time she had been there. It had been cleaned up, reorganised. Stacks upon stacks of cardboard boxes, filled with trophies, bracelets, watches and various other collections of metallic goods were usually piled up on top of one another like a bad game of Tetris. Now they sat labelled and tidily shelved, separated into what she could only assume were the trophies and other miscellaneous items that had already been engraved, and the ones that were not. The new set up had cleared what little space there was in the already cramped area. All Theo's work, she assumed.

The workbench itself, old, wooden and worn, had not changed. Deep grooves wounded the flesh of the oak from the damage of day to day life. Steel shavings sprinkled like fallen metal snowflakes across the top, covering the bench and the machinery. The engraver was new, foreign to her and similar to the old one, but the key cutting machine was the same, like an old friend. Careful not to stare at it for too long, Kora ran her fingers over the marks on the bench top, still trying to dull her anger for the sake of Theo's.

Ever since she could remember, she had always been acutely aware of other peoples' thoughts and feelings. Whether it was reading what was already scrawled across their faces, or finding what was buried beneath a slight crease on their brow or twitch in their forefinger. Like flexing a muscle, she seemed to be able to anticipate others' thoughts, even before they had completely registered with the person themselves. The small movements of their tell-tale body language, the unsure, momentary pauses before speaking; she saw it all and not only did she see it, but this was her playground.

She stole a glance at Theo. His hands were balled into fists in his pockets. His eyes, cast down at the concrete floor, held conflict. She could see his anger as clear as she saw him now, but there was something more.

He was at war with himself.

He had always protected her, always. From the morning she was brought into that foster home, he had been hers, and she could see it playing a game of tug of war in his mind. She had found his weak point.

"So... You just get to live your life?"

Theo could hear the resentment in her voice.

"You just get to forget about every bad thing that ever happened to you. Every bad thing you did to other people? Well, lucky you, Theo."

He flinched at her words.

32

"I'm trying to move on. All I want to do is live a normal life. A life where the police don't show up every week asking me where I was on some Tuesday at three in the morning because somebody in my neighbourhood is missing their car and they think it was me. All I want to do is wake up, go to work and go home to bed afterwards. I just want a boring fucking life."

She stood quietly for a small moment, assessing, deciding.

And then she looked up at him, sudden heartache flickering across her features. Her voice was quieter this time. Soft.

"I... I don't know what you think of me. I don't even know what you feel for me anymore. But whatever it is, it's confusing. It's *hurting* me."

Theo's eyes angrily searched hers and found nothing but openness and vulnerability. His face fell.

"Theo, all I ever asked for was your help." Her eyes welled up with tears, and she looked to the ceiling as she wiped them before they fell.

He stood still, but she felt the guilt begin to radiate off him in wave after crashing wave.

She was so close.

"I'm just so confused. If— If you don't want me around..." She looked at him, her heartbreak obvious to even the blind. She had hoped she would never have to use this. She had saved it, kept it close, but on some level, she had always known that it's only use now, could only ever be ammunition.

"If you don't want me around, then— why did you fuck me?"

There it was.

The dagger that should have gouged a huge septic hole in each of their chests, but only one had been wounded. She remembered it like it was yesterday. They both did. She had wanted it more than anything for so long, and for one fleeting, uncertain moment in the ethanol haze, he thought he had wanted it too; their shared trauma, their dark pasts. She had told him they were the unlovables, that only the broken could love the broken. She swore like it was as absolute as gravity so often that it was impossible not to believe.

The next morning, she had woken up before him on the dusty warehouse floor, on the bed she had made long ago from drop sheets and stolen pillows. The air had been musky and stale but she hadn't noticed much of anything except the warmth as she settled into the crook of his arm. She had breathed him in, wanting their bodies to become stone, carved into each other for eternity. He was finally hers.

But she had dozed off, wrapped up in her own bliss, and he had woken. By the time her eyes opened again, he had left her nothing but the cold and hollow imprint of where he had slept and no sign of him for weeks, as if he had never existed.

"Okay, fine," she levelled with him, "I won't come here anymore, I don't exactly want to be reminded, either," she paused, her voice breaking. "I just— I need you to help me this one time. I can't do this by myself. I need you."

"Kora, I—"

"Please, just help me move on."

"I can't just—"

"Help me, Theo, please," she pleaded, grabbing hold of the hem of his shirt just like a child would. Just like she had done when she was a child.

She watched him cave to her in slow motion. From the defeat in his eyes, to the slight give of his shoulders and the collapse of his chest. It was like watching a rose burn and crumble like dry autumn leaves.

She had him. He was hers.

"I'm so sorry," he breathed out in remorse, holding his hand out. But he was not reaching for her. He knew what she needed from him. His hands were asking for the clay imprint of the keys.

34

"Let me cut the keys."

FIVE
THE GIRL

Dangling her shiny, freshly cut set of house keys off her finger as she walked, Kora spun them around and caught them in the palm of her hand. She momentarily squeezed them until she felt the small, sharp edges digging into her skin.

Her heated encounter with Theo had left a sour taste in her mouth, and although she had gotten exactly what she wanted from him, something deeper still irked her.

Theo felt guilty. Exactly how she'd made him feel. Exactly how she *wanted* him to feel. But his overwhelming guilt only proved to her that what she was saying, was his truth. That he had intended to throw her away. Now that they didn't need each other, he didn't want her. That he didn't want anything more from her now, than for her to leave him alone. He had truly only helped her out of the guilt she had forced on him. He would never love her on his own.

Her thoughts scratched away at her surface, etching their way deeper into her armour as she continued to pretend she didn't notice.

It was still early in the morning, but the warm rays of the sun created a slight mist from last night's storm. The rainfall had painted cream brick buildings a dirty shade of beige and what were normally ash coloured pavements, a dark grey.

The grey felt like the inside of her mind.

She turned down a quiet, desolate street. Shop windows had been boarded up half-way down and graffiti decorated almost everything in sight, including a tiny, out-of-the-way thrift store. She slowed right down as she walked past it, spying a pair of Doc Martens in the window. Opening hours written on the sign hanging from the window stated that the store wouldn't be open until midday. She pressed her nose to the glass, staring down dotingly at the boots. She would have to steal them later.

She turned away from the window and continued down the footpath. The nude spaghetti strap of her camisole slipped further and further off her shoulder with each step she took but she chose to ignore it. Her mind wandered as she made her way uptown through the near-empty side streets but her thoughts darkened as they flickered back to Theo. His broad shoulders, arms tensing as he gripped her thighs. The soft curve of his lips and the way they felt between her teeth—

"What's your fucking name?"

She came to a halt, interrupted by a man's voice that sounded so menacing it ripped her straight out of her thoughts. She spun around, searching for a face but there was none.

She was immediately wary, but her curiosity won out and she took a few apprehensive steps back in the direction she came. Her eyes furiously searched building doorways for the body the voice belonged to, but there was nothing and nobody.

Hidden between two grey buildings, there was a small walkway. Looking around one last time, she decided it was the only place the voice could have come from. She moved toward the gap in the buildings and peered down the small alley. Littered with bricks and debris, a footpath was clear and sure enough, there stood a man. Kora instinctively moved back behind the wall in alarm. Part of her was not expecting to find anybody. Part of her had thought maybe she imagined the voice.

She turned and looked back down the alley, careful not to attract his attention. The man was tall, boyishly handsome, dark hair with a five o'clock shadow and wearing a moderately expensive looking suit. At first glance, he looked mildly frustrated, but then Kora registered the words that had caught her attention in the first place and furthermore, saw that he stood towering over a girl.

She looked about Kora's age, maybe a little younger. Slight build, creamy porcelain skin, long brown hair and big, round, auric eyes that had in that moment, locked right onto Kora's.

Kora's body went numb as she instantly recognised the look on the girl's face.

Fear.

"Come on *baby*, tell me your fucking name!" The man spat and the girl flinched away from him. She was easily half his size in every aspect.

He grabbed at her arm roughly and pulled her up to his face, sneering. The deep mauve material of her dress rode up as he lifted her arm and frightened, she reached to pull it back down with the other.

Aggression radiated from every inch of the man and Kora's skin began to burn with a mixture of adrenaline and rage. To any normal person, this man would have looked like some type of sleazy businessman harassing a young girl on the street. To Kora, this scene struck a dark and powerful chord somewhere deep within her core.

For a moment, her vision went black as her mind struggled against itself in a game of tug of war. Her own

38

personal little Pandora's Box rattled threateningly in the deep, shadowed corner of her mind, wanting desperately to be opened. Wanting desperately for her to remember.

The darkness edged its way to the forefront of her mind.

"No, baby. Daddy doesn't want to."

"Yes you do, daddy."

"Baby, no..." He laughed.

"Please?" She didn't like this game. She didn't like to beg for something she didn't want.

"It's not right, baby."

He reached for her anyway.

Her hands shook as she forced reality back in, like opening curtains in the morning, forcing the darkness of her vicious box of memories to retreat and lurk in the shadows of her consciousness.

Her eyes focused once again on the pair in the alley. The girl struggled to pry herself out of his grip but to no avail. Kora, all emotions heightened, jolted forward, making a move towards them that she wondered somewhere in the back of her mind if it was entirely voluntary.

"Hey!" She called out as she made her way down to the pair, stepping over the alleyway debris and angrily kicking anything that came rolling towards her as she walked; rocks, bits of wood.

The man turned to her, his overbearing trance momentarily broken in what looked like surprise, as if he had forgotten this was a city, with people, who had eyes and ears. The anger returned to his face and he scowled, letting go of the girl. Kora smiled venomously, baring all her teeth in return.

"Get away from that girl," she growled. She looked around at the ground and picked up a solid piece of wood about the length of her forearm, sitting in amongst the debris.

"You have got to be fucking kidding me." He shook his head at her in what almost seemed like hysterical disbelief. "Back the fuck off."

Kora's rage spiked and she laughed in his face, still advancing on the pair of them. She had completely lost it.

"Likewise, *asshole*." She looked at him, and then pointedly at the girl, who had been backing away from the man in small, almost unnoticeable steps. Realising she was further away than before, he growled, reaching out to grab hold of her. He missed by a slight distance but caught her black satchel strap. Fastening his grip on it, he pulled hard and the girl cried out as she fell towards him.

Kora shook her head.

"*No*."

And with that one word, her face became a darker shade of fury as she ran at him, closing the distance with no more than a few strides. She swung the length of wood directly at his face with such force that it took even her by surprise.

In that moment, everything slowed down.

He turned, flinching and tried to block the blow with his hands, but it was too late. She had already connected with the right side of his jaw and part of his throat with a sickening crack. The connecting shock struck up her arm. His legs crumpled beneath his body as he slumped, unconscious to the ground. His head connected with some stray debris that had been at his feet made up of broken beige brick and rocks of stray concrete. His eyes rolled back into his head and as he let out a strangled gurgle, thick, red blood began to flow from his behind his head.

Blood pounded in her ears. The piece of wood fell in slow motion from her hands and echoed as it bounced off the concrete. The searing flash of adrenaline that had flung itself through her veins had turned to ice cold panic. She couldn't move. The girl, just as pale now as Kora, was still standing against the building wall where the man had kept her, not taking her big, round eyes off her.

Neither of them said a word.

Without breaking eye contact, the girl took a step slowly towards her, holding her hands out with her palms up as if Kora were a wild animal. Kora felt muscles tense and tighten that she wasn't sure she had any control over anymore.

Was this girl going to run, or would she try to restrain her? Attack her?

Kora couldn't feel her legs, her vision was out of focus and she couldn't think clearly. She began to panic. Did she need to run?

After what seemed like an age of indecision, the girl was within arms reach and that was when she finally spoke, breaking the silence and looking her dead in the eyes.

"We have to go." She said. Her voice was soft, light. The ringing in Kora's ears made it sound like bells. "Can you hear me?"

The words echoed and bounced around in Kora's head, not registering or making any sense but she didn't take her eyes off the girl. What was happening to her?

With her hands still up, the girl bent down slowly, and tucking her long brown hair behind one ear, she picked up the piece of wood Kora had dropped. As she stood, she folded it inside Kora's jacket.

Still, Kora didn't move.

The girl pushed the piece of wood a little harder into Kora's ribs, waiting for her to grab hold of it herself and finally, she nodded, understanding. With shaking hands that felt like they belonged to somebody else, she gripped the block of wood tightly and tucked it further into her jacket. The girl nodded back in reply. Tugging lightly on Kora's arm, she motioned towards the street. All at once, the familiar sounds of cars and people only half a street away faded back in as the blood returned to Kora's face. She began to feel her legs once again.

"We have to go." The girl repeated, and she looked back at the man lying motionless and bloodied on the ground. His neck was on an awkward angle and although his eyes had closed, the blood continued to flow.

"I know," Kora's voice cracked. She clenched her jaw and closed her eyes, frustrated. Why was her body responding like this? She desperately needed the fog in her mind to clear. She needed to get out of there, now. She needed to find somewhere to go, she needed to get rid of this piece of wood, and this girl—

Her eyes snapped open as she realised, *this girl was a witness.*

Her senses came flooding back and she kicked into gear.

"Wait," she told the girl, her voice stronger now. The girl regarded her warily but did not move.

Kora turned around and looked at the man's body, sprawled across the concrete in an unnatural position. She walked over to him, eyeing his clothes.

"Do you know him?"

"I really think we have to g—"

"DO YOU KNOW HIM?" Kora barked. It no longer seemed like a question.

"No!"

Kora stared the girl down until she was sure she wasn't going to run. Crouching, she began feeling the outside of the man's pocket with her free hand. Something hard and rectangular was in his left pocket. A cellphone, she presumed. She reached in and pulled it out, instantly finding and holding down the power button to switch it off.

The girl seemed to understand what Kora was doing and stood beside her as she ran her hands over his jacket pockets, but they were flat and empty.

Kora looked up. "We need his wallet."

The girl cocked her head to the side and Kora wondered if she thought Kora wanted to rob the man after knocking him unconscious. She looked back down at him. Unconscious? Or dead?

"Back pockets?" The girl suggested, taking Kora by surprise.

She stole a glance at the girl. She was small and fragile looking. Pretty. This was probably not a situation she ever thought she would find herself in. Kora nodded back at her, reaching underneath the man's body and feeling around with her hands until she felt it. *Voila.*

Wrestling the wallet out from his back pocket, she held it up triumphantly. It was heavy, made of thick, black leather. Kora passed it to the girl who hesitated for a moment before taking it and stuffing it into her satchel.

Standing, Kora tucked the piece of wood back inside her jacket and looked at the girl.

"Let's get the fuck out of here."

SIX

BURN EVERYTHING

Everybody on the street looked like a threat.

The clouds had swallowed up the sun, and with it, the warmth. A bell rang as a woman stepped out of a store with a tray of three styrofoam cups of coffee and Kora could have sworn the woman stared directly at the piece of wood hidden within the folds of her jacket.

The two girls quickened their pace, briskly walking a wide berth around a homeless man. He seemed to be going about his day, digging through rubbish bins on the side of the street, doing what he could to make survival a little more comfortable— bearable. He spotted them out of the corner of his eye as he dug, and turned excitedly toward them.

"*Ladies!*" He cried, hands in the air.

The girls jumped. Kora scowled at the man, whose tattered edges of his faded clothes flailed in the breeze. She grabbed hold of the girl's arm protectively, linking hers around it.

"How much further?" The girl asked, breathlessly. Her nose and cheeks were pink.

"Not far, maybe two blocks."

Her mind was going a million miles an hour. She glanced sideways at the girl whose eyes were glued to the path ahead, and tried to get a read on her. The girl seemed deep in thought. Her lengthy fawn locks bounced around and off her shoulders, almost as if they were dancing in the light breeze their pace had created around them. Kora was momentarily mesmerised but the heavy reminder hidden inside her jacket forced her to regain focus. Could she convince this girl to keep what she had done a secret? Surely, after saving her—no. She couldn't let her just walk away.

Not without some kind of security.

Buildings began to look familiar and she slowed her pace just a touch. The girl felt the change in pace and slowed down to match it. Through their linked arms, Kora felt her tense slightly. She seemed nervous, which, Kora thought, was completely justified given the circumstances.

Of *course* she was nervous.

Kora put her brain to work. She needed this girl to feel comfortable if she was to be convinced to trust her.

To the left, she spotted the entrance to the building she had left only a few hours before. She gently guided them both towards the abnormally large front doors and unlinked her arm to pull one of them open. They each breathed a quiet sigh of relief to be somewhere warm and off the street. After a couple of seconds of tense silence, running her fingers through her wild hair, she turned to the girl.

"I need you to wait in the elevator," she stated simply.

The girl looked at her warily, her eyes searching for an answer to her unasked questions.

"Just for a minute," Kora reassured her. "I need to make sure there's no-one home."

The girl frowned, confused. "Do you live here?"

"Yes—" she stopped herself, answering more honestly. "No. Not really."

She didn't wait for the girl's reaction. She knelt, placing her handbag and the block of wood on the grey, carpeted floor and began moving things around inside her bag, compacting its contents and shoving the block of wood inside before covering it with her jacket.

"Let's go."

Kora walked over to the elevators, pushing the button. There was an instantaneous and deafening buzz and the doors opened. Stepping into the elevator, she stood at the threshold, waiting patiently, but tense. The girl stayed put by the front doors of the building. She seemed unsure and was assessing her surroundings. The buzz rang out again. It seemed to make the girl's mind up for her. She shook off whatever unease she had and closed the distance between them, stepping onto the elevator with a shy smile. Kora relaxed.

The heavy metal doors dragged themselves shut and for the second time today, Kora felt slightly sick as the floor jolted beneath her. The feeling had faded by the time they had reached the top floor, if only to be replaced by uncertainty. She forced her thoughts back to last night, to what little she could remember.

Licking her scarlet lips, she felt feverish and intoxicated as she eyed him flirtatiously. "This wine tastes expensive."

"It should. It was."

They stood in his apartment kitchen as he poured them both a second glass.

"Mmm... Honestly, I'm surprised you have any time for wine at all."

"What makes you think that?"

"Well," she laughed softly, looking around. "Either you make more than you should, or you work some very long, hard hours."

"Both…" He confessed, momentarily distracted by her lips.

His eyes then wandered down to her camisole and she smiled knowingly to herself.

Swirling her glass, she glanced over at the fireplace.

"Are you cold?" He asked her, ulterior motives swimming playfully in his eyes.

She had once learned that if you throw the words *long* and *hard* together into any sentence, it put a halt to a man's lucid and intelligible thoughts with more ease than it should. She liked to distract them from the obvious probing she did to pry information from them. It made them think she was just interested in their net worth and, in all honesty, she had yet to meet a man who cared.

She stepped out onto the top floor and turned back to the girl, who stood still in the front corner of the elevator. Kora gave her a meaningful look, sympathetic yet pleading. The girl slipped her hand out in front of the doors to stop them from closing. Kora smiled gratefully back, relaxing a little as she turned to leave.

"Hey!" She said as she spun back around. The girl jumped.

Kora laughed. "Sorry," she said softly, "it's just— I don't know your name."

She laughed nervously with a smile that didn't quite mask the distrust beneath. "Mila."

"Kora."

The elevator buzzed loudly, giving them both a fright. They collapsed in quiet fits of laughter one after the other, both holding their chests.

"Okay," Kora said, catching her breath, "I'll be back in a minute."

As soon as she was out of Mila's line of sight, her smiled disappeared. Leaving this girl alone to think for herself was not something she had wanted to do. It was an immense risk

47

to leave her even for a moment to consider the situation they were both in. Her mind became completely focused as she began mentally listing every move she needed to make for her to take control of the situation, and everything that could possibly go wrong.

The large, silver numbers loomed. Apartment thirty-three.

Walking up to the cream coloured door, she stood there for a moment as she gathered her thoughts. What if the man from last night had slept in or skipped work? It might not be so far-fetched thanks to their late night rendezvous.

She balled her hand into a small fist ready to knock on the door and practiced letting a sheepish smile play across her lips. She held her breath and knocked a little louder than what would be considered quiet. She didn't want to risk making any mistakes.

She looked up and down the hallway to check for movement from any of the neighbours or other apartment building occupants. Finding none, she moved closer to the door and pressed her ear against it. Letting her hearing adjust, she tried to listen for sounds of life on the other side of the door. Footsteps, perhaps those rattling keys, anything to signal that there could be somebody home.

Knocking again, she could hear nothing but muffled silence. Accepting this to mean the apartment was more than likely empty, she took a step back and swung her handbag around in front of her. Her hands worked quickly as she dug through the bag, sifting through its contents in search of the two keys Theo had cut for her earlier.

All of a sudden a door handle rattled aggressively and a door swung open with a high pitched screech. Her head snapped up and her heart stuttered violently in her chest but to her instant relief, it was not the door she stood in front of.

Down the hall to the right, a woman in a black and silver pinstriped business suit stepped into the hallway. Her blonde hair had been pulled back into a too-tight bun and she spoke angrily into her phone. She was carrying a thermos, presumedly filled with coffee and in the other hand, a sizeable stack of manila folders.

"*Ugh. Hold on.*" She briefly made eye contact with Kora before looking back as she reached to close the door to her apartment with the hand she was using to hold her cellphone. She realised the woman was more than likely too preoccupied to even notice her standing in the hallway. Keeping her head down, she continued to search for the keys in her handbag, careful to keep the block of wood hidden by her jacket.

"*Yes, okay! I'm listening! What is it?*" The woman growled, sounding increasingly frustrated as she passed Kora and headed for the elevator.

The elevator. *Shit*!

She faltered for a second, realising Mila would still be standing in the elevator holding the doors. She listened intently but after a few moments, she heard only the soft drag of the elevator doors closing.

"Mila!" She called in a loud whisper. There was no answer.

Moving quickly, she gave up on finding the keys and tore back down the hallway to the elevator in search of the girl, only to find an empty floor and two closed elevator doors.

Exasperated and strenuously trying to keep a steady heartbeat, she looked up and watched the numbers as they flickered to the ground level. She reached out and pressed the scratched silver button, whirring the elevator back to life but this did not make her feel any less uneasy. She prayed Mila hadn't changed her mind and decided to make a run for it. She eyed the numbers as they slowly climbed back up and silently pleaded that she would be standing in the elevator when it returned to the top floor.

The loud buzz rang out again as the number on the screen showed that it had reached the top floor. The doors slid open at a painfully slow speed, and Kora bit her bottom lip in anticipation. She could feel the adrenaline prickling through her veins, realising with rising panic that she might have to hunt this girl down— but standing there in the corner of the elevator, clutching her satchel, was Mila.

She groaned in relief and clasped both of her hands together as if thanking God. Mila laughed apologetically.

"I'm so sorry, I didn't know what to do! There was a woman—"

"It's okay," Kora reassured her. "I saw her."

Mila stepped out onto the floor, looking up and down the hallways curiously.

"Which one is—" She hesitated, looking at Kora with a slightly confused expression. "Yours? Not yours?"

Kora smiled, amused, and motioned to the right.

All that could be heard as the two girls reached the door was the rustling of Kora's jacket as she moved. With each step that they took, it subtly reminded them both of the secret the jacket was hiding and stole the air of lightheartedness that they were both trying so hard to hold on to.

Finding her keys hidden beneath a glittery mess in the bottom of her bag, she eyed the locks. The deadbolt above the door handle would be first. Picking a key, she spun it around to match the keyhole and pressed forward. The tip slid in easily but it seemed to jam half-way. She wasn't even the slightest bit phased. This always happened with freshly cut keys; the edges were always a touch too sharp in the beginning. She jiggled it from side to side and bit by bit, the key made its way in. Turning the key, they were answered a heavy metallic crack as the deadbolt was thrown back into the wood of the door. She grinned. They worked.

She pushed down on the handle, opening the door. She poked her head in through the door an was greeted by an eerie silence. The nameless man's set of keys no longer lay on the console table and at the end of the hallway, she could see the kitchen counter had been cleared of all evidence. They were alone.

50

Pushing the door back further, she turned and leaned against it, making room for Mila to enter. She bowed and waved her hand inside, as if a doorman. Mila giggled nervously, tentatively stepping over the threshold and into the vacant apartment. She walked down towards the kitchen, looking around as she spoke.

"We're not supposed to be here, are we?"

Kora watched her carefully as she assessed her reaction. "No."

She looked straight at Kora, her toffee-speckled eyes holding no judgement whatsoever. If anything, she felt she came across as naive.

"So why are we?"

Kora nodded her head towards the fireplace and placed her handbag on the counter almost identically to where it had sat earlier this morning. She pulled out the block of wood and the cellphone and made her way into the living room. Running her fingertips along the mantlepiece of the featherstone fireplace, she looked at the items sitting on top. Matches, candles, lighter fluid.

Mila understood, reaching into her satchel and pulling out her attacker's leather wallet, handing it to Kora. Kora picked the lighter fluid up off the mantlepiece and threw both items inside, dowsing them with the fluid. Taking the small box of matches, she turned and offered them to Mila, who timidly shook her head.

"Y—You can do the honours."

Kora nodded. Within seconds a match was struck, lit and thrown into the fireplace.

She looked at Mila who looked back at her.

"You're a part of this now."

Mila nodded solemnly, and they both turned back to the fireplace. They stood quietly together and watched the flames hungrily devour the evidence of Kora's crime.

SEVEN

DEAD OAK

"I'll make you a deal." Kora's coal-like eyes swam with mischief.

The little girl sitting cross-legged across from her cocked her head to the side in playful suspicion, only to break into a beaming grin two seconds later. She loved Kora's games.

It had been six months since Kora had arrived at the foster home. For the first three weeks, her behaviour had been entirely destructive. She never stopped screaming. She screamed at everyone and everything, having to be kept in her room at all hours of the day. She had refused to eat, talk or play with the other children and repeatedly tried to attack anyone who came near her. Although not uncommon behaviour for a troubled child, Naomi had never seen a child so young, so filled with rage.

Then came the day that she noticed Theo. After that, everything changed.

"If you can climb to the top of the dead tree, you can be my best friend!"

Kora and Camilla sat in the backyard in the clearing underneath their favourite thicket of trees.

52

It had rained for almost the entirety of Autumn so far, so spying the afternoon sun, the two girls had decided to chase the rays of warmth while they could.

"But Theo's your best friend," Camilla said quietly in dismay as she scratched away at the dirt with her fingernail.

"Not if you get to the top!" she sang. "If you can get to the top, you'll be my best friend instead!"

Camilla looked up at the treetops, squinting through her shimmering, silver blonde fringe. The last of the day's sunlight danced off the leaves that clung to the oak branches. The largest tree, however, grew nothing. It's stood with its stale branches, barren and cracked and held no life. To two young girls, this made whoever dared to climb it, the bravest.

"We're not even allowed to climb the dead tree."

"I'm not gonna tell. Are you?"

"No way!" Camilla exclaimed, giggling sheepishly.

"Then we can't get in trouble, can we?" she grinned. Her spirit was infectious.

"Get to the top and we'll best friends *forever*. You and me. Deal?" She held out her pinky finger.

"Deal!" She squealed in delight and linked hers around it.

She was a year younger than Kora, making her the baby of the foster home. She was the epitome of warmth and resembled something quite like a little ray of sunshine. There wasn't one person who had come across her that hadn't fallen head over heels in love from the moment she was brought into the home.

Theo and Camilla had been inseparable for the most part. Being the only boy in the household, he had taken on the role of older brother and protector almost naturally. When Kora had become part of the home, he felt he had been given another little sister to guide and take care of; once she had stopped screaming.

Kora peeked back at the weatherboard house, eyeing the windows. Nobody would be bothering to keep an eye on

53

them. They had finished their home-school activities for the day and Naomi and Claire would be in the middle of preparing the evening meal, watching their cooking show from the kitchen together as they did every day. Theo would most likely be upstairs in his bedroom, completely enthralled by his sketchbooks and pencils that were always sprawled across his bed and floor.

They had time.

Sneaking over to the dark and looming dead tree, Camilla hesitated, looking at how high up the lowest branch was.

"I can't even reach it!"

Kora looked at the trunk of the oak, assessing it. She came up with an idea.

"Here, stand on my back."

She knelt down on all fours. She felt the twigs and dirt scratch through her dress as Camilla reached up and grabbed hold of the dry bark and climbed up onto her back. She hoisted herself up onto the first branch and gave Kora a triumphant smile, looking proud of herself.

"You did it! Keep climbing!" Kora whispered excitedly.

She nodded, remembering through Kora's whispers that she had to keep as quiet as possible.

She turned and reached up to the next branch, using her bare feet against the trunk for grip as she swung her tiny body up. Large splinters of dead bark cracked and fell as her toes scrambled to push her body upwards. Kora looked on, watching her find her way up the greyed tree trunk, climbing higher and higher.

Once Camilla thought she had climbed high enough, she hugged the trunk near the branch she was sitting on tightly and looked down at Kora, waiting excitedly for a sign of approval. The air seemed fresher up so high, although colder too, and the skin covering her arms prickled with goosebumps.

Kora shook her head from down below, pointing skywards, signalling for her to climb higher.

She let out an involuntary shiver as a crisp breeze ran through her body but gave a brave thumbs up in return. She was determined to impress her.

Kora watched as she turned around, searching for her next move upwards. The branches were becoming weaker and more brittle the higher she climbed, stretching threateningly towards the ground even under her slight weight.

Back down on the ground, Kora stole a glance at the house. All was still. She took a few steps in the opposite direction, walking around to the far side of the tree and stopping at an unusually placed mound of amber leaves, marbled with deep browns and reds. Bending down, she brushed the leaves away, revealing a pile of rocks and sharp, broken corners of concrete slabs that she had been collecting. Each rock was solid; about the size of a baseball. Running her hands over a few of the rocks, she picked up two of the larger ones and walked back around to where she had stood moments ago to watch Camilla as she climbed.

Rocks in hand and winding her right arm back, she grit her teeth, grinding the enamel down and hurled the first one as hard as she could at Camilla as she reached out for a branch above.

With a soft thud, it hit the branch to the left of her— a little low, and came falling back down to the ground. Camilla jumped as it connected against the bark of the tree, feeling the thump vibrate throughout the branches and not knowing what had happened, she looked down at Kora, confused and frightened.

Kora quickly brought her arm back behind her and took aim for a second time.

Camilla's face was frozen in confusion, not having any understanding of what was happening.

The second rock flew only a few inches to the left of her head and she instinctively flinched, hiding her face in panic.

"Stop! Kora! Stop!" She cried out.

Kora shushed her, bringing her finger to her lips and then pointing at the house.

Tears began to stream down Camilla's face as she looked at the house, and then back at Kora. She didn't know what to do. Kora was her friend. She didn't want to get them into trouble.

She watched in terrified silence as Kora walked behind the tree trunk, out of sight. The branches around her creaked as the wind moved them around and she tightened her grip on the branch above, her knuckles turning white.

When Kora came back into view, she saw she was holding two more rocks.

Her cries caught in her throat, and she choked on her own breath in terror. The third rock connected hard with her cheekbone. The sharp, jagged edge violently tore her skin open.

She was gripping the branch above her head as tight as she could manage but the blow from the rock made her lose her footing altogether. As she scrambled to get it back, the branch below her cracked loudly from the sudden uneven distribution of weight and it broke at the base, swinging down and smacking loudly against the tree trunk.

Her body swung, frantic and helpless as she was left hanging from the branch above by nothing but her small, bony hands. Her cheekbone, searing with pain, swelled quickly as she cried. She could no longer spare the energy to keep quiet, but her cries were so distressed that even if she had called out for someone to help her, nobody would have been able to hear the high-pitched pleas. Tears had completely blurred her vision when the next rock hit her directly in the middle of her chest with brute force. She hadn't seen it coming and unable to brace herself for the impact, her hands slipped from the branch above and her body dropped, plummeting feet first towards the ground.

There was a quiet moment as she fell, where all she could feel was the air. She wasn't sure if she was floating, she wasn't sure if she was falling. The only thing that stopped her from being convinced she was dreaming, was the pain.

All of a sudden, her body bent in half and she felt every bone on the right side of her ribcage forcefully snap as her body landed sideways on a thick branch. The air was forced out of her lungs and she simultaneously threw up the contents of her stomach, most of it getting forced back into her lungs as her panicked brain reached for the air she had lost; the bile burning her from the inside out. After that, it was a short fall to the ground.

Her face hit the dirt first, her chest coming a close second. Everything went black. Her legs lifelessly bounced off one another, sprawled out in different, unnatural directions. One arm lay by her side while the other was trapped beneath her lifeless body.

Kora, vibrating with adrenaline had stood watching the entire scene in awe. Stalking Camilla's body as it lay, she circled her, seemingly uncertain. She knelt down beside her, pausing for a moment before reaching out with her grubby hands to smooth Camilla's hair. She leaned down and breathed in her scent. She smelled like Camilla; like warm honey, but earthy. A dirty, metallic scent was taking over.

Kora whispered in her ear.

"Theo's mine now. Not yours."

She stood up and brushed herself off, scattering the remaining rocks from the pile she had collected as she walked back towards the house.

Stepping both feet inside the door, the life of the house enveloped her. The familiar sounds of Naomi and Claire's voices filled her ears, chatting away happily in the kitchen with the television on in the background. Knives chopped down on wooden cutting boards and Kora found herself breathing in the faint smell of garlic mingled with rosemary. She ducked into the bathroom and climbed up onto the basin, quickly washing the soil from her feet and drying her hands on the pink, floral hand towel that hung on the silver detailed railing. Pulling it down, she dried her feet and hung it back up before heading up the staircase towards her bedroom. At the top of the stairs, she stopped, changing her mind and took the first door on the left instead.

Theo's room.

Theo, with his messy blonde hair and light blue eyes, was sitting on his bed amongst several sketchpads. His pencil scratched away at the paper furiously, his brow furrowed in concentration. He was so focused on his drawing that he almost didn't notice her walk in.

Eventually, he looked up, giving her the brightest of smiles. Without hesitation, he moved his sketchbooks to make room for her to sit down next to him.

"Can I see?" Kora knew Theo loved to show off his sketches.

He picked up the book he had been sketching in and turned it around to show her, his eyes lighting up. The light had caught his messy bed-hair in such a way that seemed almost angelic.

"It's the garage I'm gonna build in my house when I'm older. It's gonna fit like, five cars in it, all American muscle cars." He boasted.

"Which car is mine?" she grinned cheekily, looking up at him.

"How about this one?" He pointed at a scribbly looking car on the far right of the paper. He paused for a second, thinking. "I'll colour it blue, for you."

She beamed back at him, her eyes wide in appreciation. He remembered her favourite colour. She watched Theo as he dug around in his bed covers for his pastel blue coloured pencil and began to add the colour to his masterpiece. His hands were so steady and so sure as line after line appeared under his pencil, one by one. Kora was mesmerised.

He looked almost exactly the way he had when she had seen him for the first time. Focused. Beautiful. She remembered how she had seen him through her bedroom door keyhole, sneaking Camilla into his bedroom across the hallway after lights-out, carrying a bag of chocolate chip cookies under his shirt. She had made the decision then and there to do whatever it took to have Theo.

His head snapped up suddenly as if he had heard her thoughts and he looked over at her, mildly confused.

"Hey, where's Camilla?"

"I don't know," she lied, her voice as sickly sweet as ever. "I think she's playing downstairs."

Theo opened his mouth to reply but Kora quickly pointed out another book, distracting him.

"What about that one? Can I see that one?"

This book was different from the others. It was a smaller, rough looking, lined notebook with Theo's name written on the front, but not written in his handwriting. He shifted a little uncomfortably in his spot on the bed.

"That's the book Dr. Hurley gave me. We're not s'posed to show anybody."

"Oh." Her face fell. She focused her eyes down at her feet in an attempt to hide her disappointment. She frowned, noticing a smudge of dirt on the inside of her foot and using her big toe, she tried to rub it off.

"Don't worry! You're gonna get one too when you meet him," he reassured her. "You're all settled in here now. You'll get to see him pretty soon I guess."

Their conversation was interrupted by Naomi's voice from downstairs.

"Come and set the table, you three! Dinner's ready!"

"Coming!" they called back in unison, as they always did.

They jumped off the bed and raced each other downstairs, laughing hysterically as they tried to leap down more steps at a time than the other. Reaching the kitchen, they stopped to breathe in the dense, rich smell of roast lamb and vegetables. With stomachs rumbling and lungs full of the immaculate scents, they began setting the table.

Kora looked around at the family she had been given, as they bustled around the kitchen and dining room, laying food out on the dining room table and smiled. She could grow to like it here.

Placing the last knife and fork down on either side of a placemat, she turned to Naomi inquisitively.

"Where's Camilla?"

She stopped and looked at Kora. "Was she not with you?"

"Nope, I couldn't find her," she replied innocently, shaking her head.

Naomi walked out of the kitchen and down the hallway.

"Camilla!" She called up the stairs, waiting patiently for an answer. She was met with silence. Taking two stairs at a time, Naomi took to the second floor to search the bedrooms for Camilla, but to no avail. Coming back down the stairs, her face was full of concern.

"When did you last see her, Kora?"

"I thought she went downstairs. I was in Theo's room."

Naomi bit her lip, thinking.

"Maybe she went to play outside?" Claire piped up, hopefully. She was still holding a steaming gravy boat, filled to the brim with rich brown gravy.

Naomi looked towards the front door which was still wide open and instantly moved towards it, stepping outside into the cool evening air.

"Camilla!" She called out again.

Kora, Theo and Claire stood still in the hallway and looked at each other, confusion on each of their faces. As they all began to move slowly towards the front door, a blood-

60

curdling scream lashed through the curious silence and vibrated and echoed through each of their bones. There was no doubt who the scream belonged to.

Naomi.

EIGHT

STAY

"So, if you don't live here, who does?"

Mila rose from her cross-legged position next to the fireplace as the embers slowly began to go out. Kora watched her as she began to circle the apartment curiously, wondering how much of the truth to tell her— or whether to tell her any of the truth at all. Any evidence of the attack earlier that morning had literally gone up in smoke. All that was left were ashes.

As she assessed Mila, she had already come to her first concrete conclusion before they had even entered the building; she was harmless.

"Oh! I've got it," Mila stopped pacing and spun around triumphantly, coming to a conclusion of her own.

"Boyfriend? *Ex*-boyfriend?"

Kora couldn't help but stifle a laugh. Mila looked so proud of herself.

"Ex-boyfriend," she lied, smirking.

Mila grinned, her chin held high in victory.

She spun back around, investigating the apartment further just as Kora caught what she thought was almost a *knowing* look from the corner of her eye. In a strange way, it seemed to Kora like she had understood more than just the conversation they were having.

"Kora, I—" Mila started, nervously fidgeting with her fingers as she faced away. Kora looked up at her from the floor, eyeing her cautiously. Mila was still visibly shaken up.

"You saved me," she said, turning around after a moments silence, a strange look on her face. "Thank-you."

At those words, Kora felt an unparalleled sense of relief that almost immediately spilled over into rogue entitlement. This girl felt only gratitude towards her. She had saved her life. She *owed* her.

Kora stared back at her, searching for a response to give but all she found, surprisingly, was a secret gratitude that equalled what she had been given. Mila had shown no judgement for her, nor the situation they had found themselves in. If she had, Kora couldn't find it. There was something about Mila that made her feel somehow nostalgic; perhaps less alone.

"You saved me, too. I froze—" She stopped herself short. She didn't know how to explain what had happened to her, nor did she want to. Her arms twitched.

Mila held an air of hesitation before crouching beside her. She held out her arms, wrapping them around Kora before her could protest. She immediately tensed, but was answered with a reassuring, tight squeeze. Reluctantly, she relaxed into the embrace, realising only a moment before they broke apart that somewhere deep inside, she was enjoying the pressure of Mila's arms around her. She smelled sweet, of something perhaps resembling toffee, or caramel. It was the kind of scent that felt like a warm, sentimental memory of something she had not yet experienced.

As Mila pulled away from their embrace, Kora felt a pang of embarrassment stemming from her moment of vulnerability. Curiosity hit her full-force, fiercely wondering what Mila had been doing in that alleyway to begin with, and why she didn't seem to have anywhere pressing to be. She felt the urgent need to find out as much as possible about this girl, without giving any more of herself away in the process.

First, she must establish her own authority if she was to trust this girl— only— she had to find a subtle and underhanded way to demand it. Men were simple, but men weren't usually familiar with such simple things as intuition or *The Gift of Fear*. Not in the same way that women were.

She studied Mila's face; the gentle curve of her jaw, the shadows of her eyelashes which cast across the tops of her cheekbones under the light. She paused, collecting her thoughts before putting on her most angelic mask. She needed to come across just as innocent as Mila seemed while she peeled back each layer, dissecting her skin from nerve. She cleared her throat politely.

"Are you new around here?"

Mila smiled sheepishly at her question, playing coy.

"Do I look new around here?"

Kora laughed at her playfulness but took note of her quip. It could have almost been misconstrued as a brush-off, only Mila didn't truly seem the type.

"There aren't a lot of people from around here who would opt to wear a dress in the middle of spring. The weather is pretty temperamental."

"Is it? I've only been here for a couple of days."

Kora smiled but didn't offer anything more in the way of conversation. One of the many things she had picked up from Dr. Hurley when she was younger, was that once you have asked a direct question, you must follow their answer with an expectant silence if you wish for them to keep talking. They will *almost always* continue to keep talking, right through their unintended vulnerability. It all came down to insecurity, inadvertent or otherwise— especially the newly acquainted.

Sure enough, Mila noticed the small silence and continued, flustered.

"I'm actually only here to see my boyfriend. I was supposed to move in with him but we had a huge argument this morning and I think it's kind of over now. I was on my way to the bus station to change my ticket so that I could leave earlier."

"When?"

"Tonight."

Kora mulled this over quickly. It would be easy to have her leave, to jump on a bus and disappear from her life as quickly as she had arrived. But much to her surprise, she felt a tiny knot of sadness somewhere at the back of her throat; a knot so small it could almost have been ignored. She *wanted* her to stay. Mila's company so far had been nothing unfavourable. It had been a while since she had been able to sit down and talk to someone her own age; much less a girl. All Kora ever did was talk to men. Clueless, *clueless* men. There was never any real conversation taking place. All she ever did was play her little seduction games and dig for information about their work schedules, deciding whether or not it would be worth making copies of their keys.

"You should stay," She said suddenly, startling both Mila and herself.

"Stay?" Mila looked at her with a puzzled expression.

If she had had a mirror in front of her, she would have given herself the same look. But the words were out, and she could only use them, not change them.

"I mean, not for him. But you should stay a while, you know? See the city." She forced a grin, her freckled nose scrunching up with vulnerability.

Mila slowly cocked her head to one side, scrunching her own nose up as she considered Kora's idea.

"You are insane," she decided almost instantly and giggled. "Where would I stay? I haven't even had time to find myself a job."

"Well, how much *do* you have?"

Mila dug around in her tasselled satchel, pulling out her purse. She opened it up and counted the notes.

"I have like, a few hundred dollars at best."

"So, let's book you into a cheap little hostel," she shrugged, "I know one not far from here, and you can leave on the bus you were going to leave on in the first place."

Mila smiled a smile filled with pure excitement.

"Really? And you'll show me around?"

"Really."

"Okay, let's do it!" Mila squealed with glee before suddenly growing quiet as the ghost of a thought intruded on her excitement. A look of concern washed over her features and she looked at Kora.

"W—Will you help me collect my things?"

Kora looked at her, confused.

"From my boyfriend's place." She clarified, her brow creasing with worry.

"I can definitely do that," she said, considering the possibilities.

"Really?" Mila asked again, tentatively.

"Is he home?"

"He should be at work, but— with our argument this morning, I don't know," she sighed.

"If you're that worried about seeing him, I can go inside and grab your things. It's really no trouble," she shrugged.

Mila's shoulders relaxed. "God, you really have saved me today," she sighed.

The embers inside the fireplace had finally gone out, leaving a foul stench in the air. Upon inspection, Kora spied several blackened metal pieces leftover from the cellphone.

She stood up and walked to the kitchen and began rummaging around in the cupboards.

"What are you looking for?" Mila piped up, peering over the kitchen counter.

"Plastic bags."

"Okay then," she said with lighthearted sarcasm, clearly mocking the lack of explanation as Kora continued her search, opening and shutting drawers as she went.

"Come on, where are they," she muttered to herself.

"Everybody has a plastic bag full of plastic bags. It's like, the pinnacle of homemaking," Mila laughed.

Kora snorted, amused. The girl had wit.

"Aha!" she exclaimed, holding up a plastic bag that was indeed filled with more scrunched up plastic bags.

Crouching back down over the fireplace, she reached in and moving the ashes around with her fingertips. They were still quite hot, but not hot enough to burn. She dug around and pulled out the small bits of metal she could see until there was nothing left. She dropped them straight into the plastic bag and tied the top into a tight knot before dusting off her hands on her black jeans. Gathering her belongings from the kitchen counter, she looked over at Mila.

"Ready?"

"Ready," she nodded.

Kora held the front door open for Mila once again, who playfully curtsied in a dramatic fashion, giggling as she skipped out the door. Kora smiled to herself, truly enjoying the playfulness. She suddenly became extremely conscious of the way they connected with such ease.

In the elevator, Mila quietly hummed a tune to herself. The tune was familiar, but Kora couldn't quite place it. Her voice seemed ethereal on every note. It was simply charming. It reminded her of a book she had read as a child about sirens; mythical mermaids who sang so beautifully that it lured men on their ships towards the rocks and to their deaths.

The icy air hit them violently as they stepped out onto the sidewalk. Mila shivered, and tiny goosebumps rippled over her skin almost immediately. Kora pulled her jacket over the back of Mila's shoulders. She jumped at her touch and Kora apologised quickly, realising how cold her fingers must be. Mila gratefully slipped her arms inside the jacket.

"Lead the way."

"S—Sorry?"

"To your house," Kora laughed.

"Oh, right!" Mila laughed awkwardly. The laugh didn't quite fit her. It was almost as if she'd attempted *Kora's* laugh.

She looked left, and then right. "I, uh— I have no idea where I am."

Kora laughed again while Mila hid her face, embarrassed.

"Do you have an address? Let's catch a taxi."

Spotting one heading past, Kora signalled the driver. He noticed her at the very last moment and screeched to a halt, pulling over next to the sidewalk. The driver of a silver BMW behind him sounded their horn loudly, and wound down their window. A man poked his head out, his face wearing a furious scowl.

"Hey, moron! The fuck's your problem, pulling over like that?!"

Kora opened the back door of the taxi while Mila quickly jumped inside, cringing at the abuse. Once she was safely inside, Kora turned and hurled her words right back.

"It's a fucking taxi, you zombie. It's *supposed* to do that."

She gave the irate driver her biggest smile and both middle fingers before climbing into the taxi herself. Mila gave the taxi driver the address and they sped off towards their destination.

After a few minutes travelling along the outskirts of the deepest part of the CBD, the taxi pulled up in front of a block of beautiful white townhouses with black painted doors and window sills to match. Kora glanced at Mila, who pointed at the second one from the end, looking tense.

"Don't worry. I'll go inside," Kora soothed. "Where is everything?"

Mila didn't relax as much as she had hoped. For Kora, not only was this an opportunity to help Mila out and strike one up on the board, but it was also another opportunity to be alone inside the house if her boyfriend was at work, like he was supposed to be.

"My things are everywhere!" she cried woefully.

Kora reached out, squeezing her shoulder softly, soothing her. The gesture felt alien to her, but she had had enough practice.

"Are you the only girl in the house?"

Mila eyed her carefully at the odd question, distracted. She nodded.

"It'll make finding your things pretty simple."

She relaxed slightly, then smiled a tiny, nervous smile. She reached into her satchel and dug around, finding a small set of keys and handing them over. Kora winked in return and opened the door, slipping out of the car.

"Give me like, five or ten minutes, okay?" she called to the driver.

"Sure thing," he said in his rough, smoky voice, turning off the car and pulling out a newspaper from his side door. Mila watched as she skipped down the street, keys in hand.

Upon reaching the front door, she silently prayed that whoever this guy was, that he was anything but at home. She knocked loudly, waiting with baited breath; half ready to put on a tough front and collect Mila's belongings for her, and half ready to dig through drawers, happily unsupervised.

No answer. She knocked again.

Turning back to the car, she shrugged, guessing the house was empty.

As she fit the key into the lock and felt it turn, she felt a rising sense of excitement. Her hangover from this morning had finally worn off. The door opened with ease and so she let herself inside closing it behind her, locking it. The inside of the house was not at all what she was expecting from the boyfriend of a girl Mila's age. It was almost immaculate, save for the broken porcelain vase that lay in pieces across the white tiles of the small foyer. She wondered if Mila's break up had been an ugly one.

Sunlight bounced off the walls of the hallway, flooding in through the impossibly large windows that scaled the back of the house directly opposite the front door. She made her way to the set of stairs to her right that lead up to the second floor, assessing everything as she went. Some newspapers were stacked neatly on a console table, a half-empty coffee cup nearby and a flat bowl full of small change. Underneath the table lay a shoe rack with what looked like both Mila and her boyfriend's shoes. She would come back for them. She stopped, quickly counting out the gold coins in the bowl, picking them out and stashing them inside her bra. As she reached the second floor, she found herself with a choice of two doors. Upon inspection, she found that the first door was a home office, with a desk stacked full of paperwork surrounding a laptop. The second door led straight into the master bedroom and ensuite.

The room had a sensual, floral scent. The bed, surprisingly, with it's perfect, crisp white covers and grey throw, was unmade. This seemed out of place, considering the rest of the house was in almost perfect order. It was as though somebody had left in a rush. As she sauntered around the room, she spotted a set of drawers, presumably the ones that Mila had said her clothes were in. Quickly glancing around, she found the wardrobe; surely she would still have some type of travel suitcase laying around if she had only been here a couple of days. Pulling on the door, it clicked open. Clothes hung from coat hangers, mostly men's suits and collared business shirts, but no suitcase in sight. On the floor lay a large black gym bag. She decided it would have to do. She pulled it out and lay it open on the bed. Opening the top drawer, she thankfully found that everything inside clearly belonging to a female. She grabbed it all and dumped it hastily into the bag, doing the same with the second and third drawer. The fourth drawer was filled with a jewellery box, a folder filled with paper and letters. Kora didn't bother looking, she assumed it was all Mila's and shoved everything into the bag.

Moving to the bathroom, she grabbed Mila's toothbrush from a cup next to the sink, the pastel pink one she assumed, and a bag full of make-up. She hesitated for a moment in the bathroom doorway, turning back and also grabbing the toothpaste and a vanilla and peach body wash from the shower.

Zipping up the bag and slinging it over her shoulder, she quickly scoped out the rest of the bedroom, opening each of the bedside table drawers. Finding a mobile phone and charger inside one, she pocketed them both and continued her raid downstairs.

Heading straight into the kitchen, she opened the refrigerator and freezer doors. They were full, and she was *starving*. On cue, her stomach began to rumble. She hadn't eaten in well over a day. She spied a bottle of gin poking out from the back of the freezer and her inner drunk snatched it out, stuffing it into the bag— but her stomach cried for something more substantial. She spotted a half-empty bag of bread rolls sitting over in the corner of the kitchen counter and plucked them from their place like a crow would steal hungrily from the remnants of a carcass, shoving it straight into the bag without a second thought.

She was about ready to leave when she spotted a small cupboard sitting higher up, above the others. Biting her lip as she counted the minutes back, she decided she had time to investigate— but she knew she always did.

On tiptoes, she reached up. Silver pill packets and white bottles full of pills sat messily in a small basket. Pulling them down, she quickly dug through them and pulled out anything that looked remotely inviting, tucking them away into her pockets. She returned the basket and closed the cupboard door. It was time to leave, she just had one last stop to make; Mila's shoes.

Stretching the bag open once more, she crouched down underneath the console table in the front hall. She grabbed every pair of shoes that looked like they even vaguely belonged to Mila. Knowing there was no way the bag would zip back up afterwards, she held the sides as she stood, careful not to drop anything. She stepped carefully over the broken shards of porcelain as she reached for the door handle, pushing in the little silver lock and closing it behind her.

The driver saw her step out onto the front steps and drove up to the letterbox, saving her the short walk. He popped the boot and she threw the bag in the back. She jumped back into the taxi, giving Mila a triumphant grin as the driver hit the gas.

Mila turned and stared quietly out the window, watching the houses as they sped by. Kora didn't need to read her features to know what she was thinking— she knew she was saying her goodbyes.

NINE

HOSTEL CONFESSIONAL

"This place is kind of a dump."

"Because your budget is kind of trash," Kora laughed sympathetically.

"You're not wrong," she laughed back, sighing heavily.

Kora dumped the overfilled gym bag onto the bed and shoes spilled out onto the covers. Mila eyed the bed cautiously, scrunching up her nose as if she could smell something nasty.

Kora had checked them into a cheap hostel on the outskirts of the city, booking in under her own name in case Mila's boyfriend decided to look for her. They had certainly gotten what they paid for. The bed creaked and groaned with obvious age if they so much as *looked* at it. The room itself consisted of a dirty, eroded mirror and a small rusted bar fridge below a wooden bench with a door that hung forever slightly ajar. The bed itself looked suspiciously as though it housed a community of bedbugs— but no credit card or identification was required to stay, which made it a top pick in her books.

She was more than comfortable here— she was more than comfortable anywhere, but she had seen the house Mila had been about to move into, and she knew that the scene around them was a far cry from what Mila was used to.

"At least we managed to get a room to ourselves," she offered, kicking a dust bunny.

Out of nowhere, Mila screamed and she jumped out of her skin, spinning around and searching instantly for a threat, but all she saw was Mila collapsing into a fit of giggles.

"What?!"

"You stole the bread rolls," Mila snickered breathlessly.

Kora relaxed. "Jesus Christ Mila, you scared me," she scolded, rolling her eyes dramatically before pointing at the bottle neck poking out from the bag. "There's also a bottle of gin, for a well-rounded diet," she grinned as she dug out the bottle and found two dirt-smudged glasses in the cupboard next to the bar fridge while Mila rummaged around in the bag, taking stock of everything. Coming across the folder full of paperwork, she had a quick glance through, then closed it and threw it into the bin. Kora, pouring two rather generous glasses, raised an eyebrow at her.

"Not mine," she shrugged. "His sister's."

"Oh. Sorry, I didn't even check."

"That's okay, it's probably just bills and bank statements anyway," she shrugged, reaching out for one of the drinks from her seat on the bed. They clinked glasses and Mila grimaced in anticipation of being faced with drinking straight gin.

"It'll help. You'll learn to like it, trust me."

Mila put on a brave face and lifted the glass to her lips, downing the gin in one go.

"Impressive," Kora nodded as Mila scrunched up her face. Her throat spasmed as she fought to keep the contents of her stomach in place.

"Ugh!"

"Who taught you to drink like that?" Kora tipped her own glass to Mila as a sign of respect before lifting it to her own lips and letting the clear, poisonous liquid slide down her throat. She loved the taste of gin, and she smiled as she felt the blaze of the alcohol spreading throughout her body. She loved the warmth. The warmth had always consoled her, giving her a home wherever she lay her head.

"I feel like we both needed that after today," Mila smiled weakly, her almond-shaped caramel eyes still watering from the searing pain in the back of her throat.

"Another?"

"Please."

Kora's stomach growled again, more aggressive this time — reminding her that she still hadn't eaten in over a day. She poured them both another glass, reaching back into the overspilled gym bag and grabbing at the bread rolls. She was just about to tear open the bag when she felt Mila's eyes on her. She quickly realised what she would look like, devouring nothing but bread, all on its own— Mila would think her desperate. She had to keep up appearances. Without skipping a beat, she turned, placing the bread on the dusty counter top before aptly returning her focus to the two glasses of gin. She passed one to Mila, who sipped on it this time. Kora took a sip of her own, but her mind was still fixated on the bread rolls. The gin left her lips tingling as she tried to calm her frustration. She felt the warm buzz of her first drink slowly take over. She glanced over at Mila and noticed that she too, was swaying slightly on the bed. Her cheeks were glowing, already looking a little bit tipsy. Kora knew that this was her chance.

"I should leave you to it," she suggested tactfully, although she knew she had nowhere to go and she knew exactly what Mila would ask her to do. Nobody ever said men were the only ones with something to offer.

"No," Mila protested instantly, pouting like a child. "Stay."

Kora cocked her head to the side, pretending politely for a moment as though she wasn't sure if she should.

"Stay!" she insisted. "I mean it."

"I mean, if you're sure."

Mila nodded so fast her head looked like it was about the pop off. Kora grinned and grabbed the bottle of gin from the bench. She climbed onto the bed across from Mila and sat, crossing her legs and clinking her glass against Mila's. They both took a large gulp of their drinks in unison.

She could use a free place to stay for a few days. It got tiring sometimes, hopping from bed to bed, having to work her way into them or trudge woefully back to the warehouse to sleep on a bed made up of drop sheets and her own clothes if she failed. Sure, hostels like this one were always an option, but she never knew when she would have money, or when she would run out. Budgeting was not something she was ever taught in the foster system, unlike those fancy schools with degrees and black robes.

"I have an idea!" Mila exclaimed. "Let's play never have I ever."

Kora eyed her warily. "You first."

Mila thought for a second, before raising her glass. "Alright. Never have I ever— drank straight spirits!"

Kora drank. Mila didn't.

"Seriously?" Kora asked in astonishment, mouth wide open.

She shrugged sheepishly and shook her head.

"Well, you'd better drink, because you have now."

She laughed and took another big gulp, the buzz of the alcohol making it much easier to handle the taste now.

"Your turn!"

"Okay, okay. Never have I ever— committed a crime."

This time, they both drank. Kora questioningly raised a surprised eyebrow. Perhaps Mila was not as innocent as she first seemed.

"I helped destroy evidence of a possible murder this morning, actually," she giggled in a slurred, matter-of-fact tone with her nose in the air. Kora's stomach tightened a little hearing the words *possible murder* but she played it off coolly as if the words meant nothing to her.

"Surely you've done something other than that?"

"Mmm, nope," she shook her head. "Why, what kind of crime do you think I'd commit?"

"I don't know, maybe you accidentally shoplifted some lipgloss one time," Kora scoffed. "But you probably went back and paid for it before they put your photo up on their wall of fame. You know the one— the wall full of fellow bad bitches, but ones who actually *meant* to shoplift lipgloss."

Mila shrieked with laughter. The sound bounced gleefully around in Kora's ears, almost like music.

"Maybe I once stole someone's credit card," Mila whispered once she had finished laughing. She covered her mouth, acting shocked at her own criminal admission— but Kora had caught her eyes flicker over to her handbag a second before the words had come out of her mouth. She burst into patronising laughter. She would have to watch her more carefully if she thought she could lie.

"You're adorable."

"Hey!" Mila protested. "I could *so* steal a credit card."

"You couldn't."

"Why not?"

"Because you're, well, *you*."

Mila wore a face of mock defeat. "Well, you're right. I've actually never stolen anything in my life."

She took another sip of her gin and lay down, drunk. She put her head on Kora's lap. Kora, in her hazy state, instinctively stroked her hair while Mila closed her eyes.

"You can still be a badass without stealing people's shit, you know. I mean, you've already spent an entire day committing crimes. I think I can safely say that's enough for one lifetime," she reassured her.

"Kora, can I tell you something?"

Kora's heart beat a little faster in her chest. She hoped Mila wouldn't be able to tell.

"Anything."

"Today has been the most exciting day of my life. I wish I had that kind of excitement every day."

"You want to run around murdering people?"

Mila laughed anxiously. "Not that part, I think I can safely cross that off my bucket list forever. But the rest was exciting, breaking into our ex-boyfriend's houses. We're like Bonnie and Clyde," she gushed, slurring.

"Like Thelma and Louise," Kora corrected.

Mila nodded in Kora's lap, quiet in thought. She then sat up, finding her balance and looking her Kora dead in the eyes.

"Let's do it again."

Kora was slightly taken aback. She thought very thoroughly about her reply before voicing it, even in her tipsy state. She was risking everything she knew, but Mila was so genuine and so *malleable*, she almost couldn't help but want to bring her deeper into her world.

"We can, if you really want to," she offered, finally.

Mila's eyes lit up. Again, in the back of her mind, Kora thought about how much of the truth to tell her, if any at all. She was so caught up in the moment and the soft haze of the alcohol that she almost didn't care— at least, not as much as she might have if she were sober.

"I have to tell you something," she confessed. Mila's eyes widened in anticipation. "That wasn't my ex-boyfriend's house today."

"What do you mean?"

"It was just some guy's apartment whose keys I took." She looked up at Mila guiltily through her long lashes. The dusty

78

ceiling light cast shadows through them onto her lightly freckled cheeks as she watched Mila slowly take in what she had just told her.

"It's a bad habit of mine," she grinned guiltily in an attempt to fill the silence.

"So, wait— we just broke into some stranger's home and used their fireplace to burn evidence?"

"Yes."

She searched Mila's face, expecting to find judgement, disgust or at the very least, disapproval; anything that would let her know if she had said too much. She thought she saw her expression soften, if only slightly.

And then, much to Kora's surprise, she beamed.

"That's genius! We'll never get caught for what we did!"

Kora found it difficult to contain her surprise.

"You thought we might get caught?"

"I mean— kind of." She admitted tentatively.

Kora reached out, squeezing her hand. "We're not going to get caught, I promise."

She was glad that Mila used the term *we* when she referred to what had happened in that alleyway, and not just as though it was Kora all on her own. The more she tangled herself up in it, the easier everything would be.

All of a sudden Mila's head snapped up, her eyes narrow in suspicion.

"What do you mean, *bad habit*?"

Kora hesitated. This was where things could become tricky. But something about the combination of straight spirits and this girl's unexpected intrigue tugged at something inside her; something that bubbled beneath the surface. Something that made her want to share a part of herself she hadn't shared in so long.

She finished her gin and made a decision all in one big gulp. She leaned over, grabbing her handbag, rummaging around inside it for a few seconds. Eventually, she pulled out a large keyring full of keys— there must have been close to five or six different sets. She looked up, catching Mila's expression of awe.

"There were more," she confessed, "but I throw them away when they become, well, redundant."

Mila cocked her head to one side and squinted as if it were a question and she was trying to see the answer written in tiny letters on the opposite wall of the room. The gin had cast a definitive yet soft cloud over her mind. Kora smiled at her confusion.

"Redundant as in, like, they change the locks or get security cameras. It's got to be an eerie feeling, coming home and getting the feeling somebody's been there. I keep the keys of the ones that never catch on," she shrugged in nonchalance.

"H—How do you find all of these keys? Don't they change the locks once they realise they've lost them?"

"Not exactly."

She braced herself for this part of the conversation. She hadn't entirely anticipated where this could go when she had begun her little confession. She could see that Mila knew that she was missing a part of the puzzle piece. Something ticked over in her mind, and then she regretfully watched it click.

"*How do you know where they live?*"

She grimaced, taking a deep breath.

"I got these keys from men I've gone home with, or, I guess, sometimes actually dated. I never actually steal their set of keys, so they never really go missing. I get them copied."

Mila's jaw dropped, unable to hide her shock.

"So you're like," she searched desperately for the right word, but her brain had slowed right down. "You're like, a con artist?"

"No!" Kora objected loudly, catching herself by surprise. Mila jumped.

"Sorry, I— Maybe—I don't know. I really don't." All of a sudden, she felt defensive, like maybe she shouldn't have said anything. Anger crept up her throat like searing hot needles boring holes into the sides of her neck. She felt her face begin to burn.

Fuck this girl. She has no idea what I've been through. Who cares what she thinks.

Mila picked up on the caginess beginning to radiate from Kora's chest and she immediately softened her tone.

"Wait, that's not the right word, at all. I'm sorry," she apologised, eyes full of sincerity. "Please don't be upset! I didn't mean it like that, I—"

Kora shrugged and turned away. She was ready to bow out of this entire conversation.

"Honestly. I didn't mean it like that." Her eyes focused directly on her as she reached out and grabbed her hand, squeezing it just as Kora had done earlier. Mila's skin was soft and warm. Her hand was so delicate; as if it could break so easily.

Kora tucked that little thought away into the back of her mind.

The strangely compassionate tone in Mila's voice washed away at the surface of her anger. She was curious to hear her out.

"I'm just in awe of you, that's all," she said, her voice as soft as velvet. "You saved my life!" she laughed, if only at the incredulousness of it all. "Today was— something else. I envy you. I've always wanted to be a bit bad."

The words stoked at the embers of Kora's ego. Only slightly, but she felt it.

Mila finished her drink and picked up Kora's glass, pouring them another one each.

Kora's wall of defence crumbled altogether; she wanted to laugh. There was no chance on earth that Mila could handle another drink— her head was already tipping too far in each direction as she moved. But she said nothing, keeping the joke to herself.

"So wait," Mila said, handing a glass to her. The bottle now sat empty on the floor.

"If these guys don't catch on, how come you go out and... Take new keys, so to speak."

She thought carefully about her answer. She didn't want to sound as if she *needed* to do this. To sleep. To eat. To survive. The last thing she wanted was to say something that would cause Mila to pity her. The truth was she *did* have to live like this. Her name condemned her. She was a runaway. She could never have a job that didn't pay cash under the table; she could never sign a lease for an apartment— nothing that normal people could do. Not until she could scrape together the money for a counterfeit passport from Theo's contact.

So she shrugged. "It's just a bit of fun."

Mila's eager eyes searched her face, hungry for more information. She knew she would have to elaborate, but without giving away the extent of her place in the world.

"I mean— men use us all the time," she recited suddenly. The resentment in her voice caught her by surprise, but she was not altogether surprised that it was there— not with all her father had done. "They'll tell us whatever they think we want to hear. They use our bodies and then they throw us away when there's nothing left," she continued, repeating what she had once been told. "When we're not *convenient* anymore." A sudden wave of hatred escaped from her lips. Around the edges of her vision, clouds began to roll in around her. "They think we won't figure it out."

She shook her head as if she was shaking herself out of a daze, silently berating herself. She had gotten carried away. She stole a look at Mila to gauge her reaction, who sat still and thoughtful as she sipped on her drink. Kora scrambled to pull the conversation from it's dark path.

"I just mean that they use us all the time and it's fun for them. So I'm just having my own fun in return."

They sat in silence for a moment while she focused on Mila, watching her take it all in. Finally, she looked up with a small grin playing on her lips.

"That's pretty clever, I think."

Kora wasn't sure she was entirely convinced, but almost as if Mila had read her mind, she sat up excitedly.

"So, what you're saying is, we'll do it again tomorrow?"

Kora snickered, relieved. "Eager beaver."

"That's a yes!" Mila punched the air, sending them both into a drunken fit of giggles.

Mila put her glass on the floor and lay down on the bed. She looked at Kora from out of the corner of her eye, and giving her a stupid grin, she reached out and pulled her down onto the bed beside her. Kora's gin spilt all over the pillow, sending Mila into a furious fit of giggles.

"Mila! Oh my g—"

"You can share my pillow!"

"...Gee, thanks!" she rolled her eyes, playfully.

She threw the gin-soaked pillow off the bed and closed her eyes as the room began to spin. She felt warm. She nuzzled her forehead into the warm space between the pillow and Mila's neck. She felt the steady rhythm of her pulse on her cheek. They both lay silent as they listened to the birds begin to chirp in the grey light that had cast itself over the sky. Kora was no stranger to witnessing the sunrise without sleeping; Mila however, began to snore softly. She smiled, feeling at peace for the first time in a long time, and her smile faded as she slowly drifted into a deep sleep.

In what felt like only moments later, Kora woke, uncomfortably hot and covered in a layer of sweat. Her thigh, sprinkled with beads of moisture, was stuck against Mila's, and her head was pounding as if her skull was caving in on itself. The mid-morning sun was facing directly into their room and due to their tight budget, their room was not equipped with an air-conditioning unit. She peeled her leg off of Mila's and rolled over, her stomach tightening with sickness. Next to her, Mila took in a sudden deep breath, as if coming back to life after drowning. She looked as though she were in a similar state to Kora.

On cue, she groaned, rolling over onto her stomach and shoving her face deep into the pillow. Her wavy hair was slightly ruffled and her creamy peach skin held a stronger hue of pink than it usually did.

"There are razor blades in my head!"

The sunlight caught the golden tones in her fawn-coloured locks and Kora gazed at her, mesmerised for just a moment through the queasiness and pain of the migraine that was encompassing her brain. If the weather could occupy bodies, this was a thunderstorm.

She thought back to last nights conversation. Her memory was a little hazy but she knew she had given up more of herself than she ordinarily liked to give— enough to wonder, even with Mila's openness and excitement, if perhaps she had been too loose with her lips. A bigger part of her than she cared to acknowledge, hoped their impending sobriety hadn't changed Mila's opinion. Maybe she wouldn't even remember.

"Okay," Mila grinned, suddenly popping her head up from under the blankets and snapping her from her thoughts. Mila was puffy-eyed, but had nothing but excitement scrawled across her face.

"Show me what you do."

TEN

SEDUCTION

"Go right ahead, ma'am."

The muscular, heavy-set man held a solemn expression as he nodded at Kora. He stepped aside, making way for her— if only by means of the small gap between his gut and the wall. His eyebrow piercing and security badge glimmered simultaneously under the lights of the corridor. She couldn't help but smirk, more so at the fact that his tough-guy stance was so forced than anything else.

She stuffed the stolen drivers licence back into her handbag. The face on the front of the card was not her own, but a similar looking girl she had spied sitting at a bus stop a long time ago. *Jessica Baskette*.

Jessica had had her earphones plugged into her phone with music playing so loud that Kora could hear the distorted static of the tiny speakers. Kora had sat down beside her, coughing, but not bothering to cover her mouth with her hands. *Strategic*. Jessica had turned away, frowning and clutching her phone tight. Unfortunately, in doing so, she had left her purse unguarded and outside the limits of her own peripheral vision. When Jessica's bus had eventually arrived, she had instinctively reached for her purse— grabbing at nothing but air. The seat beside her was empty; no Kora and no purse.

She shimmied past the bouncer's generous muffin top. Her sequinned dress caught on his shirt slightly as she made her way down the scuffed and dirty corridor towards the muffled music. The hair on her arms stood straight up and her skin prickled with anticipation as she pulled one of the heavy, black doors open.

The music hit her, forcing its way through the gap in the door and her eardrums began to pound. She slipped through the gap, leaving the door to drag shut on its own as she let the colourful chaos envelop her.

The club was packed. There were bodies everywhere. The bright, dancing lights, coupled with the deep bass pushed her entire central nervous system to the edge. The almost absolute darkness had her swimming in the ecstasy of her own adrenaline. She felt a flood of eyes on her, from both men and women. This was the rush she so desperately needed. Upstairs, people leaned over the balcony railings, drinks held high as they swayed to the beat. Downstairs, people brushed up against each other, friends were screaming in each other's ears but were still not heard. To the left of the bar was a black staircase with a red velvet rope stretched across it. It lead up to a smaller second floor, covered by a long, red curtain. A black sign dangled from the rope with three golden letters printed on it that she loved to see. *VIP*.

She turned back to watch the entrance as she made her way over to the bar. Every few seconds the doors would sneak open, harbouring a trio of girls dressed like their rent was due in the morning, or a group of young guys nodding their heads to the music like pigeons and giving each other overzealous high-fives. If eye rolls were audible, chances are that her would have been heard even over the deafening music. She had never liked the crowd, only the attention.

Within a few minutes, the doors opened again and in walked Mila. Her lacy dress hugged every inch of her skin to perfection, adding an air of elegance to her down-to-earth poise. She looked so small, standing still and alone in the sea of moving people. She looked graceful and vaguely lost. Her eyes searched for Kora's, and as the light hit her, for a second, Kora couldn't help but feel like she reminded her of someone, or something; maybe even just a feeling she'd had or a place she had been before. The feeling was only fleeting and gone with moments, but it left a lingering residue that made her feel less alone than she had ever felt before.

Their eyes finally met, and the smile that played on Mila's lips swirled with a mixture of relief and excitement. She sauntered over towards the bar behind Kora, but not quite acknowledging her, as per what they had previously planned. Kora kept her eyes low. Mystery was not always what drew men to her and although she knew exactly how to get what she wanted, tonight she wanted to put on a show. Tonight was all about Mila.

She curiously eyed the red velvet curtain that was shielding the VIP area from prying eyes, such as her own. There was no way of knowing who was up there without investigating it further herself. As though on cue, two waitresses carrying empty trays slipped out from behind the curtains and made their way down the stairs. They unclipped the rope, clipping it back in place behind them as they headed back behind the bar. VIP areas usually got bottle service, so she assumed the waitresses would not be back for a while.

She felt Mila brush up against her lightly from behind, simply just letting her know she was there.

"I bought you a drink. It's sitting on the bar," she said loudly over the music, facing away from her.

"You gem!" Kora spun around to the bar and reached for the drink sitting nearest to her on the bar. Taking a sip, she smirked. Gin, soda and lime. She turned to face Mila, who winked at her as she waved her cellphone in the air and moved off towards the dance floor, drink in hand, blending seamlessly into the glittering crowd.

Turning back to the bar, she watched the bar staff serving the crowd. They looked rushed but focused. A raucous group in their early twenties barged their way through the small crowd of people at the bar waiting to be served— this was her chance. The waitresses and bartenders would have their work cut out for them for at least the next fifteen minutes.

Kora took the straw out of her glass and knocked back her drink, leaving it on the bar. She weaved her way through the flood of bodies to reach the velvet rope. Ducking underneath it, she skipped up the stairs, taking two at a time. She took a deep breath and mentally crossed her fingers, hoping that whoever was on the other side of the velvet curtain would be willing to play her game. She pulled back the curtain, slipping inside before anyone behind the bar had the chance to notice her.

The atmosphere in the room was noticeably different from the other side of the curtain; it was driven completely by testosterone and smelled heavily of bad cologne.

She changed her mind. *Maybe not so different.*

She quickly counted out about eight men; all loud, all boisterous and all drunk. They waved their drinks around as they laughed and shoved each other while she stayed still trying to pinpoint the occasion. Most were dressed in suits— untidy and unbuttoned, but suits nonetheless.

She quietly considered herself lucky. Some nights the VIP areas were booked out by hens or couples celebrating birthdays, which were impossible to impose on. Tonight it looked like she had managed to gatecrash a Stag's night.

Nobody had noticed her standing by the curtain yet, so she took the extra few seconds to assess and analyse them as much as she could. She immediately ruled out anybody not wearing a watch, which left four men. She then ruled out anybody not wearing an expensive label, which left two. One man specifically, caught her eye. He held himself differently from the others; he stood taller, he laughed louder. She could feel his ego from across the room. Almost as if he had felt her eyes on him, he looked up and directly over at her.

"Hey! Are you one of the waitresses?" he asked, swaying and stumbling a little as he made his way over. His thick, dark eyebrows and sparkling smile were notably attractive, as was his 5'o'clock shadow and slightly ruffled, dark brown hair. What really caught her attention was the elegant, black and silver Tag Heuer watch that clung to his wrist.

"I'm not," she replied in a shy voice, smiling apologetically. "I—I was actually looking for the bathroom. I'm so sorry, I didn't mean to interrupt your..." she trailed off, but it was all part of her ruse.

She locked eyes with him before slowly letting her eyes travel down to his lips, letting them linger just long enough for him to notice. She then looked back up to his eyes, which were already stealing glances at her body. Her face flushed pink as she felt her body respond. She loved it when she could see the blatant lust on their faces.

"You'd better come in then, before you get into trouble." He winked.

Success.

He led her over to the rest of the group and grabbed an empty glass and a bottle of vodka from the table. A few of his acquaintances noticed her presence and one spoke up in a bullish, obnoxious tone.

"Atta boy, Marcus! Boys, the stripper has arrived!" he laughed, lifting his drink high in the air. The rest of the stags cheered drunkenly.

She stalled. She had not anticipated this, and she was not prepared to play stripper for the night. Perhaps under different circumstances; perhaps if Mila hadn't been waiting downstairs for her she could have played a little game for their cash— but not this time.

"Take it off!" They cheered again.

She gently squeezed Marcus's arm, who seemed oblivious in his stupor as he poured her a drink. He looked at her blankly and then back at his group of friends, who were all looking on expectantly. To her distress, he was slow to catch on. After a couple of seconds ticked over, he finally understood the confusion.

"Sorry boys, she's not a stripper. She's—" He stopped mid-sentence, spinning on his heels. "What was your name again?"

"Honey," she recited.

"This is Honey," he announced. "Honey is not a stripper. I repeat, Honey is *not* a stripper."

A collective groan went around the room like a wave.

"Come on, bro," one protested, clearly disappointed by the lack of female company— as well as the wedding band he wore on his left ring finger.

"We didn't actually hire any strippers," he confessed from the corner of his mouth. He passed her the glass of vodka he had poured while the rest of the group returned to their loud conversations and debates between themselves.

"The bride-to-be forbade it."

"Wow, a law-abiding citizen. Rare," she teased, acting coy. He grinned boyishly back, clinking his glass against hers once she had it in her hand.

"Bottom's up."

"If you're lucky," she winked. He had barely taken a sip when he choked and spluttered in surprise. She wasn't sure if he was the groom-to-be since his left ring-finger lay bare but she had his attention, and if he was willing to take her home, she didn't care.

He recovered quickly. She didn't know how much he'd had to drink but she had his full attention and she knew it. It was time to play.

"So, you must be like, what? Twenty-five?" He looked at least thirty-five.

"I like you," he slurred. "I'm thirty-two, actually."

"You don't look it," she replied in a sultry voice, looking him up and down.

"Well, I..." He involuntarily paused as she slowly bit her bottom lip. She knew he had been expecting to come back with some sort of witty response, but she hadn't given it a chance. She looked up at him through her long lashes, catching his eyes before they looked back at hers. She knew then and there what he wanted; he had been staring at her freshly bitten lips. Excitement snaked its way into her abdomen— she was playing this perfectly.

He threw back the rest of his drink in one gulp and grabbed hold of her hand.

"Do you—" He hesitated for a moment, looking over at his group of friends. They were still shouting and stumbling as they pointed and laughed at one another.

"They all seem pretty preoccupied," she interrupted his thoughts.

"Yeah."

She waited patiently for him to finish what he was going to say, but the alcohol seemed to have dulled his mind and slowed him down. She would need to take the lead on this one.

She leaned in, placing her other hand on his chest and brought her lips to his ear. "Let's go somewhere a little more quiet."

Goosebumps rippled over his skin and the tiny little hairs on the back of his neck stood on end. His arm wrapped around her waist and he turned in so that her lips brushed the teasingly sensitive skin just below his jawline.

"Let's," he said in a low growl.

"I'll call a taxi."

She broke away from him for a moment and grabbed her cellphone out of her bag, searching for Mila's number. She dialled and let it ring once, disconnecting immediately. She dropped her phone back into her bag and walked back over to him.

"On second thought, they'll have a taxi outside." She ran her hands down his torso as he picked up his keys and wallet from the table. She noticed a few of his friends looking over at her but she shrugged it off and chalked it up to curiosity, perhaps even jealousy. *Maybe he has a girlfriend.*

She stood patiently as he went over and said his goodbyes, which consisted entirely of fist bumps and more curious looks. *Eye roll.*

She peeked her head out from behind the curtain in an attempt to spot Mila before they left, but she couldn't pick her out in the crowd; there were just too many people, hundreds of twenty-somethings, stumbling and dancing boisterously with their impaired motor skills and broken moral compasses. She felt Marcus brush up behind her, placing his hand on the small of her back. She grabbed his hand and slipped out from behind the curtain, guiding him down the stairs and towards the entrance. She took one last rushed look around for Mila as he opened the door for her, but she was still nowhere to be seen.

The corridor leading out to the dark street outside already smelled like a mixture of urine and something that perhaps resembled soured beer. Somewhere in the pit of her stomach, the smell niggled at her, inviting a pang of unwelcome nostalgia. The bitterness in the air reminded her of home; the musk of the fluffy greyish mould that grew between the cracks of her floorboards, her pretty dresses smelling of vomit so often that it had been impossible to wash out, the sticky metallic smell of dried blood underneath her ravaged fingernails—

She began to feel light-headed. She swayed violently, her head falling dangerously close to the wall but Marcus caught her just in time, staggering slightly himself.

"Whoa there," he exclaimed. "Looks like you've had more to drink than I have!"

She smiled weakly, waiting for the feeling to return to her legs.

A row of taxis were lined up down the street waiting patiently for couples to finish grabbing at each other long enough to ask the question, tongue-in-cheek; your place or mine?

Leaning against the wall looking at her phone, was Mila. She looked up and her gaze met Kora's, almost as if she could sense her presence. All at once, the knot of uncertainty in her stomach dissolved and the feeling in her limbs returned. She smiled, winking at Mila who gave a small, confident nod back.

All three of them walked towards the taxi stand. Kora and Marcus ducked their heads into the car at the front of the line and Mila in the one behind. While Marcus gave the address to the driver, she fastened her seatbelt and dipped her head to check for Mila in the rearview mirror. She could make out Mila's silhouette gesturing towards their car from the front seat, presumably explaining to her driver that she needed him to follow behind them.

The car took off and Kora felt Marcus's warm, rough hand run slowly up her thigh. She smiled, closing her eyes and tilting her head back. She relaxed, settling into the back seat in escalating euphoria as his hand crept higher and higher.

ELEVEN

TEASE

They didn't make it to the bedroom before he started undressing.

Kora made sure of it.

The second they had passed the threshold of Marcus's front door she dropped her handbag and pushed him up against the hallway wall. Without hesitation, she started unbuttoning his shirt, making him drop his suit jacket onto the floor in the ambush. He didn't protest and she didn't expect him to. She listened for the steady warning beep of a house alarm, but heard nothing.

He grabbed the back of her neck and pulled her roughly into him, letting out a low growl as he kissed along her throat. She pressed her hands up against his chest, brushing them over the front pocket of his shirt which, she found empty. Abandoning the buttons of his shirt, she began undoing his belt. Sliding it off through the loops in his pants, her fingertips fumbled with the button. She looked up at him hungrily and he groaned as he pressed against her, wanting her full attention. The button came loose and she slipped his pants down, letting them fall around his ankles until he stood in nothing but his shirt and boxer briefs. It was now or never.

"Where's the bedroom?" she whispered breathlessly. He stepped out of the legs of his pants, holding his hand out. She took it, and he led her down a hallway full of photo frames she didn't quite have enough time to look at, and into a bedroom.

Still focused on the job at hand, her mind began working overtime; the house was a standalone in the suburbs. Beautiful, tidy exterior and warm and homely inside. There was no way that he didn't have a girlfriend or a wife, and the bedroom decor gave her no different impression. The decorative pillows on the bed were a dead giveaway.

She pushed him back on the soft, diamond quilt bedspread and began to slide his boxer briefs down over his hips, but she hesitated.

"Wait. Wait a second."

"For what?"

"I— I forgot something. I'll be right back."

He sighed and relaxed laying back on the bed, staring straight up at the ceiling. She left the room and made her way quickly back to the entrance hallway where she had taken off his clothes. She opened the front door as quickly and as quietly as she could, placing one of his shoes in the gap to stop it from closing again. Reaching into her handbag she pulled out her phone and dialled Mila's number again, letting it ring once as before, then hanging up and dropping her phone back into her bag.

She sauntered back into the bedroom. Marcus had indeed been patiently waiting for her. He sat up, leaning on his elbows and raised an eyebrow at her. "Where'd you go?"

"I was looking for a condom," she lied, the words dripping from her tongue like cursive written in a silky ink.

"You should have said so," he said as he reached over to his bedside table, opening the drawer and pulling out a string of condoms. Kora took them from his hand and ripped one off, placing it between her lips seductively, straddling him. He lifted up her dress over her head and threw it to the side. It landed on right on the edge of the bed, but slowly slipped off and fell to the floor as their bodies moved. She pressed her hips into him, putting pressure on all the right places. His head rolled back onto the bed in ecstasy as she began to slowly grind, kissing his chest through the undone buttons.

She heard a faint rattle from the front room of the house, and her body tensed momentarily. She looked up to see if he had heard it but he hadn't even opened his eyes. She moaned quietly to cover up any further sounds as she began to grind harder, her soaking wet, silk panties being the only thing between them.

A small thud came from the front room, and she jumped involuntarily. She quickly let out a moan in a feeble attempt to disguise the noise, but it seemed it was too little too late. Marcus gripped her waist roughly, sitting straight up on the edge of the bed. She was still straddled on his lap, but she knew she wouldn't be there for long— He heard it.

Panicking, she tried to push him back down on to the bed, giggling hysterically.

"Stop," he ordered and she froze.

"Take off my shirt," he instructed. "Slowly."

She breathed a massive sigh of relief and obeyed. He pulled her in and kissed her neck as she fumbled with the last few buttons of his shirt. Her hands shook but she managed to pry them apart. She pushed the collar of his shirt backwards and down over his broad shoulders. He took over, slipping his arms out, distracted by her breasts in the dim bedroom light. He kissed them both and she let herself go for a moment, relishing in the sensations pulsing through her. Goosebumps rippled over her arms and breasts like a wave and she instinctively pressed her lips into his. He tasted of salt and skin. His fingertips ventured lower and lower down her abdomen, finally reaching the saturated silk. After what felt like an age, his fingers slipped inside.

A loud creak brought her crashing back down to reality. Marcus's fingers pulled away from her. They both froze; Kora in panic.

"What was that?"

"What was what?"

He growled as he stood, lifting her off him and throwing her back onto the bed— not roughly but not exactly as if she were the love of his life. He stormed out of the bedroom and she got off the bed and followed, tense and apprehensive. Reaching the front of the house completely naked, they both stopped dead in their tracks.

"*What the fuck*?"

His front door was wide open, swinging in the crisp wind that was rushing in from outside. She noticed instantly that her handbag was missing, and she cried out.

"Oh my god, my handbag! Where is it?!"

He walked over to where his suit jacket and pants lay sprawled across the floor, picking them up and rummaging through his pockets, only to find them empty except for his keys. No cellphone, no wallet.

"Fuck!" he yelled. "I'm calling the police."

He stormed into the kitchen, picking up the phone from its stand next to the wall.

"Wait!" she exclaimed, running over to him and snatching the phone from his hand before he even had time to dial.

"What the fuck are you doing? My house was robbed!"

"You can't call the police!" she cried.

"Why the fuck not? Did *you* have something to do with this?" He started on her, reaching for her wrist.

"No! Of course not!"

"*Give me the phone!*"

"I can't!"

"Why the fuck not?" he growled. He was about to lose control. The build-up of sexual tension only intensified his anger.

"You can't call the police— I'm a prostitute," she confessed breathlessly.

He took a second before the words registered in his mind. She watched his face flicker from anger, to disbelief, and then back to anger. This had always been risky. The threat of being caught red-handed flooded her system with adrenaline and heat rushed to her face. Luckily, to him, it looked exactly like embarrassment. Prostitution was illegal and she knew that he knew that they would both be in some serious trouble now if he called the police. For a man with a watch and suit that expensive, she could almost be certain that he didn't want to spend a night in a jail cell trying to argue that he *didn't know she was a prostitute* with police officers. That old chestnut.

"Are you fucking kidding me?" He said the words more to himself than to her.

"I'm sorry, I—"

"You're soliciting me for sex?"

"I— Yes," she answered quietly, placing the cordless phone on the kitchen counter.

He paced back and forth for a few moments, mulling this over. She watched him closely, keeping her terrified expression, but she was almost certain he wouldn't make the call. Not while she was there. She was quite literally banking on it.

He stopped pacing and stared straight at her.

"You need to leave."

"I can't."

He threw his hands up in the air, exasperated. "And why the fuck not?"

"I need my money."

"You're joking."

"No."

He stared blankly at her for a few seconds and she could see he was in two minds. She knew one of those minds was complete and total fury. She held her breath and waited it out, and he finally broke. He held up one finger, signalling for her not to move as he stormed out of the room. She didn't. The thought of running crossed her mind, as she figured he would only be returning with one of two things; money, or a gun. A gun would scare any normal person, but not her, not tonight. She knew he wouldn't shoot her. He wouldn't want to have to explain a dead prostitute in his house when police arrived to investigate a simple break-in.

She heard his footsteps as he returned and braced herself for whatever was about to happen. Somewhere below her cold, naked surface, she was secretly enjoying herself. As he emerged from the hallway she immediately noticed he'd put his boxer briefs back on. He was holding her crumbled, shimmering dress. She flinched as he flung it at her with a look of disgust. The soft material hit her bare chest and fell to the floor. She reached down and picked it up, fumbling—hyper-aware that he was still making his way towards her. He closed the distance between them in only a few strides. When she rose, she saw he was holding a few notes in his hand and struggled not to let out a victorious, shit-eating grin.

"I've never paid for sex before. I don't know what it costs." He glared at the cash in his hands.

"Technically, you still haven't," she offered. Somewhere in the back of her mind, she wondered where she had picked up her sick fascination with pushing other people's buttons; winding them up like little plastic toys until they broke.

"Just get out," he spat as he thrust the money at her and turned around, picking up the phone. He turned, staring at her, waiting for her to leave. She didn't need a second hint. She quickly slid her dress up her thighs and over her hips, adjusting the straps over her shoulders and snatching her high heels from the floor behind her. She took one last look at him, grinning before escaping out the front door barefoot. Poor Marcus had never stood a chance.

She ran out onto the street, the cold pavement underneath her feet. She had done it. *They* had done it.

She looked up and down the street, spotting a taxi parked half-way down the road, still running. It flashed its lights. She almost rolled her eyes as she made her way towards the car; the driver must have told Mila that he would keep the meter running if she made him wait. She folded up the notes Marcus had given her and stuffed them inconspicuously into the string at the back of her underwear.

As she got closer to the car, she heard the low rumble of the engine growl as it began to move toward her. She could see the outline of Mila in the back seat, pointing towards her through the gap between the driver and passenger seats. As the car pulled up beside her she saw her reflection in the dark yellow paint and tinted windows— only, her face and body were monumentally distorted. Her bones jutted out at odd angles and her face was lopsided. Her stomach turned. She looked disgusting. She looked like a monster. She *was* a monster.

It took her a moment before she understood the odd angles of the reflection. It was the bend of the body of the car, not her own. She glanced down over her shoulders for reassurance. They were even, they were normal. It was only her reflection after all. She shook herself from her thoughts and opened the back door of the taxi, climbing into the backseat with Mila who was wearing their victory spread wide across her face. Kora's handbag lay on the seat next to her, slightly more bulged than usual. A flashy cellphone which lay in a few basic pieces could be seen poking out of the top. Mila looked as though she could barely contain her excitement.

"Walk of shame already?" she giggled.

"Get in, get on, get out." Kora winked, and they both burst into fits of hysterical laughter.

The taxi driver cleared his throat, and Mila jumped a little, covering her face with the sleeves of her jacket in embarrassment.

"Squatters' Inc, please," Kora told him.

"Sure thing," he replied, sounding bored, bordering on irritated, but pulling out from the curb nonetheless.

As the taxi wove through the streets of the suburbs and back towards the outskirts of the central city, Kora rummaged through her 'stolen' handbag, pulling out Marcus's wallet that Mila had stuffed inside. It sat wedged between a silver laptop and the tin full of clay she used to imprint keys. She eyed the laptop, and then Mila, impressed with her haul. She pulled out the cash notes from the wallet and then lifted up the back of her dress and pulled out the notes he had thrust at her earlier. She looked up at Mila whose jaw dropped open in astonishment.

"How did you—"

Her question was cut short as they were both blinded by bright lights. They looked up to see silent red and blue lights flashing past them, heading in the opposite direction. Police.

Mila's lips pursed and she began to bite her nails, but Kora grabbed her hand gently and pulled her fingers away from her lips.

"It's okay," she mouthed silently. "We're okay."

She nodded reluctantly. Kora passed her the handful of money. Distracted, Mila flicked through the notes and looked back in astonishment.

"There's got to be like, six hundred dollars here," she said, amazed.

Kora's chest swelled a little with pride. The back seat was electric with the mingling excitement, adrenaline and fear between the two of them.

"I know," she boasted, glancing quickly at the driver before saying quietly, "I'll fill you in back at the hostel."

"Same!"

Kora watched as the bright neon lights flashing above strip clubs and dirty looking late night stores danced across Mila's face through the backseat windows. She was an entire galaxy inside a person. She reached out and grabbed her hands which were still full of notes and squeezed them. They were cold but soft. Delicate. Breakable.

Mila was hers now.

She would never let her leave.

TWELVE

GRIEF AND DECAY

Scratch, scratch, scratch.

Wood chips flaked off underneath Kora's chewed fingernails as she scratched at the edges of the brand new brass lock on her bedroom door. Every bedroom on the second floor of Naomi's foster home had been fitted with locks exactly the same as hers, but Kora took hers personally. It wasn't there to keep people out. It was there to keep her in.

Things hadn't been the same in the foster home since Naomi had found Camilla's body laying lifeless in the autumn leaves. Naomi had been a nervous wreck for weeks, as if the ever-hopeful light inside her had been hopelessly fractured. She would burst into uncontrollable tears, seemingly out of nowhere, upsetting herself so much that no-one dared mention Camilla's name any longer. They all understood her pain, and everyone except Kora felt it with her. For this exact reason, she knew she was being watched closely. She gave nothing away.

It was not long until she had become frustrated with the grim and depressing atmosphere of the house. Grieving, to Kora, seemed tiresome and boring. No, Camilla was not with them anymore, but *she* was, and she wanted things to go back to normal.

As the days dragged on, Naomi began to grow cold. At first, she had been glad. Anything was better than Naomi's muffled cries keeping them all up late at night.

Claire had been the first to mention Naomi's distance, quietly speaking to Kora and Theo one night after dinner as they did the washing up.

"Do you guys notice anything weird about Nay?"

Theo, holding a soggy dishcloth covered with bubbles, looked towards the kitchen door to make sure she was out of earshot.

"Yeah, I do." He replied in a half-whisper. "It's like she don't care about anything anymore."

Claire nodded in agreement, her deep apricot curls bouncing with the movement. "That's what it feels like, doesn't it? Do you think she should talk to Dr. Hurley?"

Theo cocked his head to one side deep in thought. "Maybe..." He trailed off, looking down at his feet with an odd frown. The dishcloth had been dripping all over the floor, but he hadn't noticed until a drip had landed on his toes.

"No," Kora shook her had at them as she put away the dinner plates. "She'll just start crying again. Tell her that things have to go back to normal now."

"You can't just *tell* her that," Theo argued in a hushed but stern voice, but Kora just shrugged back at him nonchalantly.

"Why not? Camilla's not here, but we are. She's forgotten all about us."

"*Kora!*" Claire and Theo hissed in unison, wincing at the sound of Camilla's name.

"What?! It's true."

"What's true?"

All three children jumped out of their skin, hearing her voice behind them. Not one of them had dared opened their mouth to answer her, but that was exactly what had given them away.

That conversation between the three of them that night in the kitchen had begun the slow tipping point for Naomi. One small glass of wine to herself once the children were in bed became three, and then became a bottle. "Bedtime" and "lights out," usually two separate times with a touch of leniency in between, were now at the same time and absolutely mandatory. Home-schooling was a thing of the past and Naomi no longer trusted them. Cutlery and knives were counted after every meal and a closer eye was kept on the children during the day. Strangely enough, although subtle, they noticed they were being discouraged from playing with one another. She would stand in the doorway and watch them, emotionless, until they fell quiet and slinked off to find their own activities to get stuck into alone— eager to create distance between themselves and her uncomfortable stare.

Kora's favourite things were no longer within the realms of what was possible; there could be no more secret trips downstairs into the kitchen with Theo late at night to steal cookies, certainly no more playing outside in the afternoon with the birds in the trees, and no more sneaking into the living room to dig up Naomi's "missing" videotape *Thelma and Louise* from its hiding place.

Kora and Camilla had stolen the tape from Naomi's bedroom one rainy weekend full of boredom-turned-mischief. They had only ever been able to watch it in short intervals, careful not to be caught with it and sliding it back into it's hiding place afterwards.

But things had changed. Naomi had changed. Gone were the nights of sneaking into each others' rooms after dark. If Naomi heard so much as a footstep out of place after bedtime, she would launch herself up the stairs and throw open door after bedroom door to catch them out of bed.

Somewhere deep within Kora's mind, the soundtrack at the start of *Thelma and Louise* began to play as she glared at the lock on her door. It had been hers and Camilla's favourite movie; two girls taking control of the world, making it their own. It was their dream to grow up to be just like them, and last night, that was exactly what she had intended to do; take control of her world.

She had waited until just after lights out. She knew Naomi would be on her second glass of wine, meaning she would be less alert. She had laid in bed and scowled at her door left hanging wide open from across the room, full of resentment. All it had taken was one night of getting caught with her lights on and Naomi had stolen another inch of control with her new "open door policy". Another inch of dignity.

Unlike every child in every movie that has ever run away from home, Kora didn't have a backpack, but she had known that Theo did. It was always full to the brim of sketchpads and notebooks, stashed underneath his bed.

She had put her plan into action and crawled out of her bed, careful not to let it squeak under her shifting weight. She had made her way to the door frame and listened. Music was coming from downstairs; from Naomi's room. She'd smirked, knowing there was no way she would be heard.

Within seconds she had crossed the hallway and had reached the threshold of Theo's bedroom. Cocked her head to one side she'd listened for his breathing, holding hers in. His breathing was light, relaxed. He was not quite asleep yet, but he was close.

Crouching, she sat herself down on the wooden floorboards of the hallways outside his bedroom door and waited. Settling into the darkness, she listened to his steady breaths as they went in and out, over and over. It became hypnotic, lulling her deep into her memories. She closed her eyes and listened. She had learned to differentiate between waking and unconscious breathing patterns from slipping out of her father's grip as he slept. Uneven meant awake, steady meant asleep. Somehow, she could still feel him, his weight, his grip—

Stubble rash blazed across the soft, delicate skin around her throat. Her eyes stung as salty tears threatened to form, but she bit her lip and held them off. The hot, sour breath on the back of Kora's neck swam into the tiny cove of her nostrils, making her stomach turn.

She knew better than to wake her father; the small scar across underneath her eye was enough of a reminder. She quietly held her breath as often as she could, trying not to breathe his in, and she waited.

After what seemed like an age, his breathing slowed and became heavy. She crept out from under his arm and off the edge of the bed. She took a corner of the blanket and tried to wipe the drying vomit from her chest— her own. Blood smeared the inside of her thighs as she limped quietly out of the room, finally letting her quiet sobs free.

Downstairs, a song changed and she was pulled back out of her memories. Theo's breathing was much heavier now. He was finally asleep.

She shook off the sleepiness that had rolled in around her like a storm, and staying as low as possible, she crawled quietly across his bedroom floor. Squinting as she searched the floor in the dark, she looked for his backpack. She had hoped it wouldn't be full of pens and pencils or anything that would make noise. She would have to empty it, and the longer she took, the more chance she had of being caught. She peered under the bed and spotted a dark rectangular mass huddled away in the far corner. Reaching out as far as her painfully thin arm would stretch, her fingertips barely snagged a mesh pocket on the side of it. It was definitely Theo's backpack.

She pulled, teasingly slow until she had it within reach. It was considerably heavy, full of all kinds of books and pens that Theo had accumulated over the past two years he had lived in the home. She gave the bag a quick inspection. Some of the books looked so over-loved that the coloured covers had been worn off. Wrinkled and torn pages hung half out—some had even been taped and folded back in place to save them from oblivion. One book, in particular, grabbed her attention; a small, tattered notebook with his name written on the front, but not written in his handwriting.

Theo's *journal*.

Crouching, she picked up his backpack, struggling a little under the lopsided weight, and hugged it tightly to her chest as she slipped out of his bedroom and back into her own. She began emptying the contents of the bag out onto her bed and replacing them with her own. She stuffed her favourite blue sweatshirt inside, along with various clean pairs of underwear and a pair of jeans. She zipped it up, but she paused. Once again, Theo's journal had caught her eye. She picked it up, running her hands over the top of it. She knew she shouldn't but that was never going to stop her. She opened the tattered front cover to the first page.

Thursday 29th December,
I dunno what to write.

Underneath Theo's first journal entry, he had begun to scribble the outline of what looked like a car on the bottom of the page. She flicked a few pages in, curious to find something of substance, not really knowing what to expect. Theo seemed so *normal*. Why was he living with them? What had he done?

Thursday 19th January,

Today we talked about my family again. I miss them a lot. I miss my sister the most. Dr. Hurley asked me if I remember what I did to them. I don't remember anything anymore. It's all gone. I know I told mama I didn't wanna take my pills so I could stay up to see Santa but I know she said I couldn't. I don't remember killing her at all.

I don't wanna talk about it no more.

Her eyebrows raised in pleasant surprise. She thought Theo was as close to an angel as you could get, but it turns out that the two were more alike than she had ever thought possible. She unzipped the backpack for a second time, sliding his journal down the back behind her clothes before zipping it back up and swinging it over her shoulder.

Back out in the hallway, she skulked past his door. She stopped momentarily to watch him as he slept, shaking her head in disbelief.

What did you do?

She blew him a kiss goodbye and headed down the stairs, careful to move slowly. She checked each step to be sure it wouldn't creak or groan, but her build was so slight that it wouldn't have made a difference if she had flown down the stairs without a care in the world— she was too light.

The further down the stairs she tiptoed, the louder the music got. She could hear Naomi singing along in slightly slurred speech. She had such a beautiful voice, so full of depth and heartache.

As she reached the bottom of the stairs, she eyed the open bedroom door carefully. She had to get past unseen to get to the back door. Once she was there, she was free. Free of the rules, free of Naomi's steadily decaying moods, free of whatever she was supposed to be doing in this house with these people. She would go home.

So she had glimpsed around the corner, looking for Naomi. She was on the far left side of her bedroom, sitting at her painted, antique vanity dresser, writing in a large notebook. *What is it with everybody and their notebooks?*

She peeked around the frame, watching her. She couldn't see Naomi's face in the mirror's reflection, but she knew she was crying. She could hear it as she sung. But if she couldn't see Naomi's reflection, this, in turn, meant that Naomi couldn't see hers. She waited until the chorus of the song. She watched Naomi pause the scribbling in her notebook and begin singing the words loudly. She made a break for it. She flew past the door and ran straight to the back door, hiding around the corner in case Naomi had seen her. Her heart was thumping loudly in her chest and her breathing was shallow, but she could still hear Naomi belting out the chorus of the song.

Once her breathing had returned to a normal pace, she crept out from around the corner to the back door. She turned the handle, twisting it all the way around. She pulled it open, but the door only jolted half a centimetre with a small thud. Staring at the door in confusion, the realisation dawned on her. The deadbolt had been locked.

Out of nowhere, the floor behind her creaked and her stomach dropped. She spun around on the spot where she stood and met Naomi's wooden, featureless face. Her eyes narrowed.

"Fuck this place, right?"

Kora's jaw dropped, hearing her curse. This could not be the same woman who had taken her in, who had nurtured Claire, Theo and Camilla. This was an entirely different creature altogether. Kora stared back at her, stunned beyond words.

"You ungrateful little shit," Naomi hissed. The venom in her words was unmistakable. "You have no idea how *excruciating* it is to act like I don't know what you did— to act like I still want you here. Maybe I should let you leave, hmm?

Leave the home that you single-handedly ripped apart? Would you like that?"

Kora faltered, stuttering. Naomi had her cornered so easily.

"I— Naomi, I didn't... I don't—"

"Shut your fucking mouth," she spat as she zeroed in on Kora and leaned down so that her face was only an inch away.

"*Fuck you.*"

Kora's eyes darkened. She could smell the alcohol on her breath. Not wine, something darker. Something stronger. She scowled. She leaned upwards, drew in the biggest breath she could and spat, covering Naomi's face in saliva.

Naomi screeched, recoiling and wiping the spit from her eyes. She grabbed Kora by the hair on the underside of her scalp and pulled, her fingers instantly tangling in her wild curls. Kora shrieked, reaching up to grab hold of Naomi's wrist in an attempt to break her grip, but she was too strong. Kicking off from the ground, she swung around and latched on to Naomi's forearm with her teeth, biting down as hard as she could. She yelped, and Kora felt her fingers let go of her hair. She tried to run, but Naomi had caught a strap of Theo's backpack. She felt something in the back of her neck stretch and tear as she was yanked backwards towards the stairs.

"You are *never* leaving this room!" Naomi yelled as she dragged her up to the top of the staircase. She kicked her legs out at Naomi trying to escape her grip, but to no avail.

As they approached her bedroom door, Naomi mustered up all of her strength and threw Kora's tiny body as far into it as she could, slamming the door quickly behind her. Kora fell fast, tripping over her own feet. She hit her head on the bed frame with more force than she anticipated, knocking herself nearly unconscious. Dizzy, she tried to sit up but ended up rolling to one side, exhausted. There she had lay, giving up.

Sometime later, she had heard her door creak open. Fully alert, she sat upright, ready to defend herself. Theo poked his head around the door, looking sympathetic. She immediately relaxed but found herself bursting into tears.

"Shh," He cooed as she scrambled to embrace him.

"What happened? Hey—" he paused, noticing both their belonging strewn all over the room. "You took my backpack."

"But I left all your books for you," she offered, sobbing into her sleeves quietly. Theo sat, hugging her tight to his chest and they sat in silence for a few minutes as her shoulders shook with sobs.

"Give Naomi a chance. She's just sad. She used to be perfect, remember?"

"I don't care what she used to be like!" she cried into his shirt, leaving tear stains on the fabric. "Please Theo," she had begged him, tugging on his shirt. She had an idea. He had done it before.

"Please. Let's just kill her."

"No," he told her softly, and so for the second time that night, she gave up.

The next day, Naomi had been extra quiet. Nobody dared speak out of turn, including Kora. After a knock on the door around midday, a man entered the house and went upstairs, fitting new brass door handles with locks to each bedroom door. Locks, like the one which she now stood in front of, scratching at with her fingernails.

The locks were not to keep people out, but to keep her in.

THIRTEEN

NORMALCY

"Oh my god, real food!" Mila squealed, delighted as she stuffed what looked like half of an entire burger into her mouth. She seemed much too hungry to care about proper table etiquette. Kora spat out a partially chewed french fry as she burst into laughter. Mila laughed at herself a second later.

The two girls sat across from one another at a beautiful, up-cycled white table outside a small French café somewhere east of the hostel. Homely white flower pots filled with dainty, pastel pink and white geraniums lined the window sills, breathing life into the atmosphere.

"I'm never taking you out in public again, I swear," Kora said, shaking her head as she took another few fries off her plate, dipping them in ketchup. Mila shook her head slightly in return, almost the way *she* had done it.

Just as she had lifted the fries to her mouth, Mila reached out and pushed her hand right into her face, smearing ketchup all across her cheeks and nose. Kora's jaw dropped in shock while Mila collapsed in a fit of teary-eyed laughter, almost falling out of her seat in the process. Kora glared at her playfully while she reached for a napkin, wiping the streaks of ketchup from her cheeks.

As the bright mid-morning sunlight made it's way slowly up into the middle of the sky, Kora noticed somewhat absentmindedly, that she was genuinely enjoying herself. She felt so carefree sitting across from Mila; eating out at a café like normal people do, on a normal Sunday morning, as if everything *was* normal.

Somewhere in the depths of her mind, a tiny thought tugged at her throat with a force like gravity, sneering; reminding her that nothing about who she was was normal. Reminding her that she would never be able to lead a *normal* life. Her mind tiptoed around the edges of the thought as she tried to ignore it, to push it deeper; fold it into seven tiny halves and bury it so far beneath the surface that it would never be heard. The tiny, ugly thought slowly tightened its grip on her throat and she suddenly felt it move towards her lungs. She inhaled sharply and coughed as hard as she could, forcing it out of her.

Mila stopped half-way through her mouthful and stared curiously at her, amused. "Chew your food," she laughed, ironically with her mouth full of unchewed food. Kora snorted, rolling her eyes. *If only it were that simple.*

Mila finished her mouthful and lowered her voice, leaning in close. "So, what exactly do we do with this clay imprint thing?

"I know a guy," she replied, acting coy.

"Oh you do, do you?"

She grinned, enjoying the way Mila could dish it out almost as well as she got it.

"I do. We grew up together."

Mila perked up at this tiny snippet of information.

"Like a brother?"

"Maybe, at one point." She cocked her head to one side, reminiscing for a fleeting moment. "We had a thing, a while ago. It felt kind of strange after that."

"Wait, with your—"

"He's not my brother."

"Oh, got it. So what happened?"

"Is this lunch or an interrogation?" Kora shot back, deciding she didn't like the questions anymore.

Mila recoiled, covering her mouth. "I'm so sorry!"

"Mila, I'm kidding! Relax," she laughed lightly, poking her tongue out. She felt a pang of guilt for snapping at her, but she hadn't been kidding.

Mila looked down at her plate and began quietly picking at her food. The two continued to eat in silence for a while, while Kora's mind wandered back towards Theo.

It had been the strangeness that she had liked about being with Theo. The forbidden fruit, the longing, the shared past— but most of all, she liked his brokenness.

She liked to think she had control over her mind and the memories she would play out; that she could change what she liked, when she liked. She deliberately forced the elements of her memory of the night they shared together that didn't favour the narrative she wanted at this particular moment in time; namely the deception, the manipulation and ulterior motives that she had used to drive him to her. These tainted her 'perfect' memory and would otherwise paint a different kind of picture. One she didn't like. One where she had known that he didn't really love her the way she wanted him to; that she had worked him over, toyed with him, confused him and guilted him into bed with her. In the end, all it was ever good for was something that she could hold over his head when the time came.

Mila interrupted her thoughts with another question.

"Where did you guys grow up?" Her voice was light, full of innocence. Kora could almost mistake it for *careful*.

"Around here," she shrugged, somewhat irked by her curiosity. Had Mila not just apologised for interrogating her? Chalking it up to naivety, she changed the subject, tucking a curl of hair behind her ear.

"Hey, have you heard from your boyfriend? I haven't heard your phone ring even once."

Mila also tucked a strand of her own hair behind her ear, shaking her head. Kora frowned. Was Mila *copying* her?

"It was pretty clear that it was over. I don't think he'll be contacting me."

"Well, fuck him, anyway," she shrugged. "What's on our to-do list today?"

"Um— Let's see," said Mila, switching into sidekick mode. "Okay, so, we have a laptop and a phone, and a key to cut."

"Just so you know, there's a chance that key won't actually be of any use to us. The guy probably had security cameras installed first thing this morning."

"He was no good, then?"

"Well, the guy deserves *some* respect. He paid for the cow without even getting the milk."

Mila snorted into her food while Kora burst into laughter, both without a care in the world as over-dressed passers-by stared on disapprovingly.

"He might not get security cameras you know," Mila sang in a suggestive tone. Kora raised a curious eyebrow, intrigued.

"Well— I mean, if this Marcus guy makes a habit out of taking home strange women he's known all of, what, ten minutes? He's hardly going to want his wife catching that on camera. Don't you think?"

Kora ignored the *strange* remark and mulled this over. "Sure, but how do we know for certain that he has a wife? I mean, we can't go solely off decorative pillows."

"Here— this is why."

Mila reached into her satchel and pulled out two items of jewellery. The first item being a thick platinum ring with one small diamond embedded on the front. There was no doubt about it— it was a wedding band belonging to a man. The second item was a necklace. The thin silver chain lay in Mila's palm with a small, delicate looking gem hanging from a clasp.

"Are these from his house?" Kora looked at her incredulously, wondering why she hadn't handed them over last night— wondering if she had been keeping them for herself.

"I wanted to surprise you! They were in a bowl on the kitchen counter. I thought you could keep the necklace, as a thank you of sorts..." Mila trailed off, sounding vulnerable and awkward.

Kora hadn't the slightest idea of how to react. Her heart stuttered the tiniest of stutters in her chest. She fought to keep her poker face as concrete as ever. Nobody had ever shown her sincere gratitude. Nothing she hadn't already demanded. Not having felt it before, she had no idea what to do with it. She thought first to shrug it off; throw it away. She began to feel overwhelmed. Her shoulders tensed and she began shutting herself down emotionally, as if her mind was under quarantine. Eventually, she shook her head, convincing herself that the feeling was unwarranted and useless to her in any case.

As she searched Mila's face, she opened her mouth to veer the conversation in another direction, but she stopped herself. Mila's big, almond-shaped eyes were full of sincerity. They flickered to each corner of Kora's expressionless face, confused and not quite understanding Kora's lack of reaction. She looked deeper into them and found they showed something that *was* worth something to her— *Loyalty. Servitude.*

117

"Mila," she started, scrambling to circle back on her initial reaction. What *had* her face expressed? Confusion? Indifference? Dismissal? *Fuck*.

"Mila, it's beautiful. *You're* beautiful. I don't even know what to say. That's the nicest thing anyone has ever done for me," she pouted, acting close to tears. She knew she was only trying to mend the situation for her own benefit, but beneath her dramaticism, she almost knew for certain that none of what she had said was a lie.

Mila let out a sigh of relief, smiling warmly as she carefully handed the necklace over, her curious eyes returning to their swirling marbles of rich chestnut and gold.

"I think it's probably a real diamond," she said excitedly.

"We can ask down at the pawn shop."

The girls finished what they could manage of their food and Kora paid the bill with the money Marcus had shoved at her the night before.

Out on the street, the sun was beating down on the pavement. Kora could feel the heat radiating upwards which should have been a pleasant change for a city with such temperamental weather, if it hadn't been for the bins and bags full of rubbish out on the pavement, waiting to be collected. The smell of warm garbage was the sort that would make your lungs beg you to breathe into your shirt in an attempt to filter out the stink. She scrunched up her nose and kept walking, guiding Mila a few blocks further east. As they rounded the last corner, a pawn shop came into view and she grinned at it's graffiti-splashed, tattered-poster-covered glory. This place was one of the reasons she had survived so well for so long.

"Wait," Mila tugged on Kora's shirt. "Are there cameras?" She glanced around at the store's surroundings, heavy with caution. It wasn't exactly the nicest part of town.

"Not even one."

Skipping up to the door which was decorated with colourfully aggressive graffiti, she pushed it open as if it were home to her. The top of the door hit a small metal bell that rang out through the small shop, sending Mila jumping at the sound. She held the door open for her as she slipped inside without a sound. The shop was cluttered with all sorts of things, some things recognisable and some simply beyond Kora's knowledge of the world and it's possessions and gadgets. The air was thick with musk. Disturbed particles of dust glimmered, catching the light as they hung in the air, floating slowly downwards, in no rush to be anywhere. A large window ran across the front of the shop, separating the counter from the customers; completely bulletproof. In this part of the city, it would be doltish not to take heavy safety precautions such as this.

She waited at the vacant counter while Mila looked around the store. Eventually, a small shuffle of footsteps came from around the corner of an open door frame behind the counter. A small, round woman came scuttling in. She wore brown sheepskin slippers and a loosely fitting maroon dress that looked suspiciously like a nightgown. Without looking up, the woman climbed her way up onto the seat behind the counter, grumbling as she went.

"Buy or sell. How may I help you?"

Kora could never figure out where her accent was from through her broken English. Sometimes she thought she had it pegged, perhaps as Filipino. Other times she could swear the fragments of her accent were from the middle east somewhere. There were no memorabilia nor flags that gave her away, but she enjoyed the puzzle. The little woman finally looked up, her tanned, sun damaged forehead wrinkling as she scowled, recognising her.

"No! No you!" She barked through the holes in the glass, shaking her head and waving her away at once.

"Oh come on," she rolled her eyes.

From the back of the store, Mila craned her head around a shelf to see what was going on.

"No! No more business wi' you!" She said gruffly and she prepared to hop down from her seat grumpily, clearly upset that she had made the effort to climb all the way up there only to end up face to face with her least favourite customer.

"Wait!"

She shook her head and Kora knew then that she had very little time to convince her not to go. This was the only place in the entire city that wouldn't ask for identification to sell goods.

"Look! I promise! Nothing from the warehouse."

She was referring to the warehouse where Theo worked. Between the two businesses, she had become notorious for taking items from one to the other. It didn't take long for Theo to pick up on her petty theft, but it *did* take a while for his boss to realise his and his clients' items were being sold just down the road.

Kora held her hands in the air; a gesture of peace. She slowly reached down and pulled the cellphone and laptop out of her handbag, placing them on the counter. The woman stopped, eyeing the items for a moment, before looking up at her. Scepticism was scrawled across every inch of her wrinkled face, all the way up to her oddly receding hairline. Nevertheless, she shuffled back over to the counter, climbing back up onto her chair.

Even though her frown never left her face, Kora knew she would never be able to resist electronic goods in perfect condition. She reached into her pocket and retrieved the platinum ring, placing it on top of the laptop. The woman picked up the ring with nicotine-stained fingers, full of caution. Kora knew she would accuse her of taking it from the warehouse but this time, she was prepared to let her call them to confirm they were not missing anything. That in itself was a first.

120

"Where you get?" the woman snapped.

"An ex-boyfriend."

"You lie. No boyfrien'. Where you get?"

She sighed and tried again, ignoring the dig at her relationship status.

"It belonged to my ex-boyfriend."

She shook her head from side to side.

"No. This one," she pointed first to the laptop, and then to the cellphone, "and this one, gift from ex-boyfrien'. Yes. No this." She held up the ring again, shaking her head.

"This one, you father. He dead, no money, you sell. OK?"

She caught on quickly, nodding. "Yes, that's right. That's what I meant."

"OK. How much you want?"

"Six-hundred."

"I give you three."

"Bullshit."

The woman grumbled. "I give you three-fifty and I no call police. Final offer."

Kora rolled her eyes. She knew she wouldn't call the police, but she preferred to stay in her good books for future deal-making purposes. Three-fifty was more than enough at the end of the day.

She sighed and held out her hand but instead of shaking it, the woman turned her nose up at the gesture. She turned and jumped down off her chair and hobbled back through the doorway she had come in from. Kora leaned over the counter, trying to see where she had gone. She returned a moment later with a cigar gripped between her yellowed teeth and a handful of cash. She waddled back to the counter and laid out three, crisp, one-hundred dollar bills on the counter and a ruffled fifty dollar note. She reached her hand out to grab them, but the woman grabbed hold of her wrist and pulled her roughly against the glass. She squeezed so tight that Kora could feel the build-up of blood in the tips of her fingers as they began to throb. She tried to pull away but the woman's grip only tightened, like that of a snake.

"If police come here again, I give you to them. Understood?"

"Jesus! Fine!"

With a low growl, she let her go, snatching the stolen goods from the counter and waddling back through the door without so much as a goodbye. Kora took the money and gave her middle finger to the empty doorway before turning around to find Mila. She spotted her almost instantly, peeking around a shelf with widened eyes, full of questions. She had been curiously watching the exchange between the two.

Kora made a face at her, running over to her giggling. She linked her arm around Mila's as they left the store together, three-hundred and fifty dollars richer.

Three-hundred and fifty dollars closer to a new life.

FOURTEEN

THEO

"Kora, seriously?"

"What?!"

Theo stood tall and staunch in front of the half-open warehouse roller door, clearly irritated to a new level. She threw a face full of innocence back at him but he simply shook his head.

"No way."

"Theo," she said in a matter-of-fact tone, secretly wanting to show him that she could act like an adult and use logic and reasoning to get what she wanted, not *just* emotional blackmail.

"It's just one! We probably won't even use it. I just wanted to show Mila what you do."

"It's not *what I do*, Kora."

"It's a part of your job, is it not?"

"Not for free, and not for stolen keys."

"I can pay you, then."

She looked back over at Mila, who was standing awkwardly a couple of warehouses down, barely within earshot. She seemed to be watching the exchange with

123

incredulous amusement. She realised that to her, they must look exactly like siblings; bickering, bargaining siblings.

"Who is *Mila*, anyway? Your new free ride?" he scoffed, looking over her shoulder at Mila. He couldn't deny that she looked pretty from where he was standing. Small and pretty.

She rolled her eyes at him. "Am I not allowed to make friends?"

"Honestly? You shouldn't be allowed to, no," he shook his head.

"Are you really going to embarrass me like this right now?"

"Have you really resorted to whining?" he shot back.

She could see that this was going nowhere, but in a haphazard momentary lapse in his focus, she watched his deep blue eyes linger on Mila for just a second too long. She knew instantly that she had him. She had found the tiny, little, Mila-sized scratch in his armour. She could have rolled her eyes. *Men.*

"You can meet her," she offered instantly, but her voice was too high, too sweet. He glared at her. She adjusted accordingly, bringing her voice down a few octaves to a more casual playing field.

"I can introduce you. She's pretty cute, honestly. Sweet. Not my type, obviously, but you can't just *not* introduce yourself when she's standing right there."

Theo, no longer glaring, cleared his throat quickly, as though he'd had a lump in it.

"What? No! I don't want to meet her. I—I mean, I don't care what your type is." He turned back to the warehouse, faltering, seemingly forgetting how to get in or what he was doing.

She grinned to herself mischievously. He was fumbling. Nervous. He hadn't been around many girls; especially not attractive ones like Mila, not since he was released from prison. Not really since he had left the foster system. It had only ever been Kora, which, to anybody who looked at him and his chiselled jaw-line build from the marble of gods, it would be hard to believe.

"Mila!" she called out suddenly.

Theo spun around, eyes wide with anxiety as Mila began to make her way over to them. "Kora—" he started, but she cut him off.

"Don't be rude," she said playfully, but gritting her teeth as the jealousy began to creep inwards, twisting itself around her internal organs.

As Mila walked towards them, Kora stifled the acidic mixture of her own emotions tearing through the forefront of her chest. She wondered why he had never looked at *her* like that. She looked back at Mila, gracefully stepping over loose gravel on her way over, squinting as the sunlight hit her eyes. She couldn't deny it; she was strikingly beautiful.

Mila smiled as she approached them both. Kora hid her jealousy well, showing off a big, overzealous smile as she introduced them.

"Mila, this is Theo. Theo, Mila."

"Hey," he mumbled, clearing his throat again, and held out his hand awkwardly.

"Nice to meet you," she sang back brightly. "I've heard so much."

"She hasn't," Kora interjected, laughing nervously in his direction.

Mila took his hand and shook it, taking him in as she did so. Kora tried to get a read on her thoughts of him but her face gave away nothing but mere politeness and curiosity. Her eyes flickered quickly from his face to Kora's and Kora realised with a start that she must have been trying to find the resemblance between them. She might have laughed if it were anybody else; Theo's hair was a warm light brown, her hair was wild and dark, full of messy ringlets and secrets. Her skin was at a guess, two or three obvious shades darker than his, sprinkled with dark freckles while his was a soft golden tan. To top it all off, her eyes were almost black. Nothing like his. Different mothers were the only thing anybody could deduce by looking at the two.

"Well, whatever you've heard, none of it's true if it came from Kora." He half-smiled at his poor attempt at a joke.

Kora rolled her eyes and gave him a light punch on the arm before searching through her handbag for the imprint Mila had made of Marcus's key.

Mila smiled back. "Kora's cool," she said simply.

He opened his mouth to disagree but as the wind blew around them, sending leaves and swirling dust up into the air, a small, broken piece of a dead leaf got caught in Mila's hair. It swayed as it begged to be free to fly with the rest of the featherlight debris. He reached out instinctively to untangle it from her strands of hair, unthinking, yet the feeling felt familiar somehow. She immediately flinched and shied away from him. He withdrew his hand instantly and panic surged through him. He looked straight down at the ground. All in a moment he felt an entire galaxy of emotions. He felt terrified, embarrassed, confused. Acidic humiliation burned throughout his chest, lost for what to do next. He looked up at her, apologetic. He opened his mouth to explain himself; not really even having anything to say, but she spoke first.

"Sorry, I—"

"No, I— there's a leaf in your—"

He fumbled with his words just as she did with hers, but her face took on a look of surprise, all at once understanding what he had meant to do. She reached up and began feeling around in her hair for the leaf. He watched, growing more and more embarrassed as she kept missing it by mere inches. She paused, thinking for a second. She looked up at him, her eyes asking him for help all on their own.

"Could you?"

126

Terror surged through him.

"Sure," he answered, not sure at all.

His hands shook slightly as he took a step near her and reached out, taking the leaf between his thumb and forefinger and gently removing it from its trap. The wind suddenly picked up again, and her scent travelled straight through him like a ghost through a wall. Before he had a chance to recognise the sweet, familiar scent, Kora cleared her throat. He looked over at her, having forgotten she was even there. The look of hurt on her face screamed that she knew it. His throat tightened with guilt. He looked down at what she was holding; gripped tightly in her hand, was the familiar, metal box full of clay that she had dug out from her handbag. He grimaced, knowing he couldn't refuse her now. Not after seeing the pain in her eyes.

Kora looked back at him, and then at Mila, who didn't seem to have picked up on their shared moment of pain— or, if she had, she was being polite about not calling attention to it.

"We could help you clean?" Mila offered, voice full of hope. She gestured toward the warehouse.

"S— Sorry?" Theo stuttered.

"Yeah, what?" Kora turned in surprise. "We kind of have *things to do,*" she said through gritted teeth.

"In exchange for cutting the keys, I mean."

Kora peeked behind him, following Mila's gaze. Metal shavings were strewn all over the floor next to the engraving workbench, cardboard boxes and plastic wrappers sat untidily on top and on the floor, surrounding it. There didn't seem to be a lot of floor space at present, and there were even some boxes stacked awkwardly on the stairs leading up to the top floor that were blocking the way up. There wasn't much doubt that he could use the help.

"My boss hasn't been in for a couple of days, I'm just a bit behind, that's all."

"So you could use the extra help then," Mila chirped, walking right past him and ducking under the door.

Stunned, he looked at Kora who shrugged angrily and followed her inside.

The place really was a mess. The girls turned to Theo awaiting instruction.

"Delegate away, boss," Kora said playfully, crawling right back into her suit of armour, regressing back to her carefree, everything-is-fine coping mechanism.

"Uh, okay," he mumbled, not really wanting to be in charge of either of them but he knew he had to take the reins, if only to show Mila he could, embarrassed by his display of awkwardness earlier.

"Upstairs needs to be cleaned, but just like, swept. Uh— Mila, you could do that, if you want. Down here, too, but Kora, you can do that. I'll wipe down the bench and stack those boxes, they're pretty heavy." He gestured to the cardboard boxes on the stairs.

"Sure," Kora shrugged.

"Thanks."

"No problem!" Mila said as she danced her way up the stairs.

Kora laughed, picking up a broom. Mila was like a little Jack Russell; just excited to be there.

"Psst! Hey!" Theo whispered, trying to get Kora's attention as she swept up some stray metal shavings scattered across the concrete floor. "What does she know about me?"

Kora, immediately irritated, paused for a moment before responding.

"Nothing. She doesn't know anything. All she knows is that we grew up together."

He nodded. "Thanks."

She growled under her breath. It's not as if she had gone out of her way to do him the specific favour of not mentioning his past to her, she just hadn't gotten around to it. She didn't even know *Kora's* story yet.

As she swept up the last of the shavings, she considered the fact that for now, it might benefit her more for Mila *not* to know anything about Theo. He had clearly taken a liking to her, and she could use that to her advantage. She began to play around with scenarios in her head, watching him from the corner of her eye.

"You know, Mila's situation is similar to mine."

He stopped what he was doing and looked over at her warily.

"What do you mean?"

"I mean, she's staying in a shitty little hostel on the edge of town. She had nowhere else to go."

"Why not?"

"Her boyfriend kicked her out."

"Her boyfriend?"

"Ex," she corrected.

He was silent as he went back to work with his cloth. She waited. This information *had* to stir up his white knight complex on some level, and like a cherry on top, he now knew she wasn't attached.

Take the bait. Take the fucking bait.

Her thoughts were interrupted by footsteps coming down the stairs.

"Done up here!" Mila sang as she came skipping down to the bottom floor.

"Me too," Kora piped up.

"Alright," he sighed.

Kora high-fived Mila in victory and handed Theo the small tin full of clay.

"Last time," he warned her.

She nodded smugly but once his back was turned and the key cutting machine had roared to life, she turned to Mila and grinned cheekily, shaking her head and holding up her index and middle fingers, both crossed. Mila winked in return and Kora's stomach fluttered. In that moment, it felt like they were the perfect partners in crime.

Sparks and metal shavings flew all over the floor that Kora had just swept as he worked. The sound of the squealing and grinding hurt her ears, but instead of covering her own, she stood behind Mila and covered her ears instead. Kora could feel her cheeks shift, and knew Mila was smiling.

Finally, he switched the machine off and the sounds slowly faded out as the life from the key cutter escaped. He turned, handing the key to Kora but not quite letting go when she took hold of it.

"Last time," he repeated, before letting it go. "And when are you going to take your things?" He asked, pointing at the black rubbish bags still sitting in the corner.

She rolled her eyes as she dropped the key carelessly into her handbag.

"Whatever. I have to use the bathroom, I'll be right back," she declared as she turned and went up the stairs.

The air suddenly thickened with a tension neither Theo nor Mila had been ready for. He nervously adjusted the rolled-up sleeve of his grey collared shirt. Mila watched the waves of nerves wash across his face with intrigue. His eyes were a brighter blue against the grey warehouse walls than they had been outside in the sunlight.

He looked up, catching her eyes stealing curious looks at him through her lashes before quickly looking away. He smiled and quietly cleared his throat.

"Don't let her get you into too much trouble," he said still smiling, if only to take the edge away from his warning.

She grinned cheekily back, lifting her chin slightly with an air of mock-superiority.

"What makes you think *she's* the troublemaker?"

He laughed. Her bravado facade was impossible. She was so much more elegant and angelic than devil-may-care.

130

"Then I guess I've got my work cut out for me with the two of you."

"You sure do."

His smile faded a little. His brow furrowed for a second in thought before reaching into the pocket of his pants and producing a small, white card. He held it out, offering it to her. She took it in her hands and inspected it. It was a business card. 'Engravers' Ltd.' was written on the front in bold black letters and as she flipped it over, she saw that on the back it had two first names, each with a phone number beside it; one of which was his. The other, she assumed, was the name of his boss.

"I mean it," he said, lowering his voice, but gently. "Keep that. Just in case you run into trouble."

She looked up at him. His smile had gone now and his eyes were full of concern. Somewhere upstairs they both heard a tap being turned on and then off again after a few seconds. She nodded and hurriedly stuffed the card into her satchel.

"Let's go!" Kora sang as she bounced down the stairs, linking arms with Mila.

"Thanks, Theo!" Mila waved behind them as Kora dragged her out of the warehouse door and into the sunlight. Mila caught his eye one last time before they skipped out of eyesight.

"What about your stuff?" he called after them, but Kora pretended not to hear.

Once they hit the main road, they unlinked arms and began walking normally. Mila looked at her out of the corner of her eye curiously.

"Are you going to tell me what I missed back there? Between you and him?"

"What did you miss?" she joked, but felt a distinct lump form in the back of her throat, wondering if she had seen that he didn't want her. That nobody wanted her.

They walked in silence for a minute or so before Mila slinked her hand into Kora's, interlocking their fingers.

"You don't have to tell me everything. You have a life outside of our little bubble, I know. I was just curious, that's all," she said. "I like you. I want to know things about you."

The lump in Kora's throat didn't go away. In fact, it grew. Mila had so much empathy within her that she felt as though she could walk the street behind her and slip in the glistening puddles of it that flowed so freely from her body. She silently wished that she could have met Mila a long time before she had. She wished more than anything in that moment, that Mila would stay with her. Without warning, the edges of her mind grew dark and grey. The grey quickly became a hellish shade of black. *Who in their right mind would stay?*

She knew it wasn't a sustainable lifestyle, not forever; petty theft and dirty motel rooms didn't promise a future. Mila *had* to know that. How could she not?

Her breath caught painfully in her chest like ice picks as the perfect picture inside her head came crashing down.

I'm just a phase.

She loosened her grip on Mila's hand, letting her fingers fall free so that only Mila was holding them together. She immediately picked up on her change in mood and slowed her pace, gripping Kora's hand even tighter and pulling her back.

"Hey," she said, trying to read her face but Kora refused to make eye contact, looking anywhere but at her.

"Kora, what's going on? Talk to me."

"What are you even *doing* here?" she blurted out.

"I'm sorry?" Mila's eyes searched Kora's, who was now looking at passing cars as they sped by.

"Aren't you supposed to be going back to your bullshit, fancy life, wherever the fuck you came from?"

"Kora! Where is this coming from?!"

"Why are you still here?"

132

Mila paused for a moment, a look stuck between confusion and disbelief plastered across her face. "Look at me," she said softly.

Kora didn't move an inch, her gaze still focusing on distant traffic, desperately pleading her eyes not to well up with tears.

"Kora!" she demanded, half shouting. She let go of her hand and grabbed her face in both hands, forcing her to look at her.

"Kora, I like you. I don't want to go back to my," she paused, lowering her voice, "*bullshit* fancy life."

Kora, nearly in tears, burst into sudden laughter, surprising both herself and Mila. Tears streamed down her face as she laughed. She knew she looked like she had lost her mind, but she didn't care. She pulled Mila into her arms and let the tears fall freely. Mila laughed too, and began wiping away her tears, kissing her cheeks.

Kora knew then, that she loved her. Here was this girl standing in front of her from a different life, making her feel things— and she couldn't even swear without whispering. Kora decided then and there, that Mila had to be just as crazy as her.

"Mila, you're an absolute idiot."

"But I'm *your* idiot," she laughed into her neck.

"Then I'm never going to let you go. I'm going to hold on to you so tight," Kora said, squeezing her.

"How tight?" she teased.

"Until something inside your body breaks," she whispered.

FIFTEEN

DR. HURLEY

The walls always seemed to creep in on her when they thought she wasn't looking; inch by inch, stealing the smallest pockets of her air; not enough to really notice. Not if you weren't looking for it. Not if you weren't paying attention.

But she was always, always paying attention.

"How are things going at Naomi's?"

Kora flickered her eyes from the walls back to Dr. Hurley, sitting in his comfortable blue chair. His dark, silvery-grey hair had been, as always, routinely styled, but not gelled. Never gelled. The wispy mavericks that had escaped the carefully shaped, side-swept parting of his hair looked ghostly white under the lights. His smile was worn, but welcoming, always creating crinkles around his eyes. It radiated a kind of practiced warmth, accompanied by a combed, greying moustache.

His harmless demeanour made her uncomfortable, distrusting.

What made her the most uncomfortable was that she always found herself, mid-conversation, snapping out of a complacent and relaxed state of which she had somehow allowed herself to be lulled into. This always made her feel as though she had been tricked. This almost always made her look back at the walls, trying to catch them creeping in.

"Kora?" he asked again. He was always patient; never pushing, only ever guiding.

"Things are fine," she replied dismissively, not really wanting to talk about Naomi.

Claire, Theo and Kora had all made a pact long ago not to discuss Naomi with Dr. Hurley, wherever it was possible to avoid it. They had kept her behaviour a secret for two years, now. The older two loved her, but they loved the *old her*. They had been worn down over time, hoping she would wake up one morning and be the old her again. All that had truly happened was that they had grown used to the new Naomi, her change in behaviour, her change in rules. Kora, however, agreed on the pact for a different reason altogether. She decided it was better to live with the devil she knew. There was no telling where she might end up if Naomi was deemed unfit as a carer, and the chance of losing Theo? No. She wouldn't risk it.

"Have you been writing in your journal at all, since we last spoke? It's quite alright if you haven't. I know you don't like to write. It's not for everyone, is it?"

There was that crinkly smile again. The question almost sounded rhetorical, but she looked at the floor and shook her head anyway.

"That's quite alright." He wrote a small, quick note inside his lined notepad.

She opened her mouth but then closed it again, thinking better of it.

"What's on your mind, Kora? This is a safe space, you have always known that."

Her eyes flickered involuntarily towards the video camera quietly whirring away on the tall, maple bookshelf over in the far corner of the room. It made her uncomfortable, as though

135

there was another person in the room, only that person she didn't, and would never know.

He didn't miss a beat. "Now, Kora. You know why that has to be there."

She bowed her head, nodding. She did, in fact, know why she and all of his other patients had to be filmed.

She thought back to one of her first sessions with him; one where he had told her that her release from the foster system and Behavioural Rehabilitation Program depended solely on the progress she made in the home and in her sessions. He'd told her that if she gave him what he asked for, she would progress only that much quicker. This had been where the lines of communication had been severely misunderstood.

She had done the only thing she knew how to do to get what she wanted.

She had tried to seduce him.

He had, of course, firmly and immediately corrected her while simultaneously learning the extent of her damage.

"Why don't I take medication like Theo does?"

"That's a good question indeed." His eyes swam with a mixture of intrigue and confession. "You see, I'd prefer not to prescribe a medication if I think a patient can be treated without it."

"But Theo said you told him medication makes it easier."

"For some."

She squinted over at his notepad from her chair, trying to read from it as she always did. "Why do you make it easy for everyone else except me?"

"It's not always an easier path, Kora. I would prefer to keep you off any kind of medication at this point in time. Your body has been through a tough time battling through the withdrawals of other substances, I wouldn't like to put it through much else. We can most certainly look into it in the future, but not right now."

She scowled, staring at the floor. They sat in an uncomfortable silence for a short minute, before he really got to work.

"So, Kora, can you remember what we talked about the last time you were here?"

She nodded.

"Do you have any thoughts you'd like to share?"

She shook her head.

"Hmm, quite alright." He clicked his pen. "Why don't we pick up where we left off, then?"

Her mind rushed back to the last time she had sat across from him. Her fingers trembled. A knot began to squeeze itself around her lungs. She had no intention of revisiting that feeling, or those memories.

"Breathe," he ordered, albeit in a somewhat soothing manner. She realised in a stuttered breath that she hadn't been breathing at all. Her lungs felt like a furnace.

"Coming to terms with being mistreated by someone we trusted is never easy. You are doing very well, do not forget that."

"He didn't— I wasn't mistreated," she argued, furrowing her brow.

"Yes, unfortunately you were. You're not in trouble. That's why I'm here, to help you understand." he replied softly.

But she knew that *he* would never understand.

"Let's go back," he said, clearing his throat.

Panic rose again. Nothing had ever made her feel so unstable than how delusory Dr. Hurley had made her memories feel the last time they had spoken.

"Back to the last night you spent with your father. We're going to go through some of the behaviours—"

She closed her eyes and shook her head, drowning him out, but the moment her eyes closed, brightly coloured memories ignited before them; and like fire, they blazed to life.

Her paper thin legs were shaking. Her left thigh, a deep shade of blotchy violet and navy, nearly gave out as she stepped tentatively towards him. He was sitting, hunched over on the far side of his mattress on the floor, facing the wall. He held his head in his hands, sobbing. His dirty, matted hair defied gravity in every direction possible. He hadn't slept in a long time; maybe a week. She knew that this was when he was at his worst. His most volatile.

But if she could get him to go to sleep, he would sleep for several days, and she would be left alone.

"Daddy, I—" she started, but he threw his hand out, cutting her off.

She knew better than to disobey him further. She never knew which punishment would come next or if she would be clever enough to avoid it. He had taught her that there was always a way to make somebody say yes, and by somebody, he had meant himself.

"You just have to find a way," he would say.

And so he made her search. But he never liked to make it easy.

She had learned that it sometimes worked for other things too, like talking her way out of punishments— but he hadn't taught her that. She'd had to teach herself; secretly, frantically. Anything not to get poked with the Sick Needle.

The Sick Needle made things beautiful. Sometimes the room glittered as she fell back onto the bed, and the bed was so soft at times that her body melted into it like warm butter. Her silky skin would bubble into the blankets, inviting her into the threads of the mattress. Sometimes it even helped her not to notice the weight of him on top of her, cracking her hips apart.

But it always, always made her sick— so sick she couldn't move her arms or legs. She couldn't sleep, couldn't eat, there were even days she could barely breathe without bringing up the contents of her stomach. During those times, she could not block him out no matter how hard she tried.

That alone, was enough for her to want to avoid the Sick Needle.

"Honey," he crooned. His raspy voice scratched at the inside of her ears, the same way chewing gravel would scratch the enamel from your teeth. Though unlike gravel, it held a particular warmth. It held comfort. It was the voice of her father; the man who raised her, the man she loved— Daddy.

"Honey, you can't keep playing these games with me, you know," he begged.

She felt her voice shake before a word had even fallen from her lips. She knew this game.

"I thought you liked it when I played pretend, daddy," she lied, her voice wrapped in gentle innocence. She took another step towards him, bringing her within arms reach. She felt her stomach tighten. Bile rose and charred her throat, but she managed to keep the vomit down long enough to finish the game.

"I thought you liked it when I said no."

"You thought?"

"I can tell," she corrected herself, manoeuvring into a more adult tone. "I know you like it when I say no."

He looked up at her hungrily from the floor. His tongue flicked over his lips in a poor attempt to wet the dry, cracked wastelands that they were as he looked her up and down. His black eyes, blinking sporadically, had sunken right back into his cheekbones.

With quickness, he leapt at her and reached out to catch her arm roughly, as if he had seen the longing to run in her eyes. He dragged her down onto the mattress. She tried her best not to flinch or shy away but the cry for self- preservation was always stronger, no matter how weak she was or how empty her bones felt.

As he struggled and clawed at her clothes and tore her last, undamaged sundress, she squeezed her eyes closed as tightly as she could, repeating the same thing over and over in her head.

"At least after this, he'll sleep."

"Kora."

Her head snapped up, eyes wide with panic as she immediately took in her surroundings. Dr. Hurley was still sitting in his chair across from her, not having moved an inch — only now he was frowning. A deep wrinkled had appeared on his brow, but it seemed to convey concern rather than anger.

"Did I lose your attention? Where did you go, if I may ask?"

She shook her head aggressively, avoiding eye contact.

He pursed his lips and sat still for a moment, before deciding there was no need to interrogate her. He knew from her reaction exactly where her mind had gone. He wrote down a quick note, choosing instead to move past it and continue with their session.

"As I was saying, this is an exercise I would like for us to do together today. I will begin to go through a list of different types of behaviour you may recognise, either from your father or yourself— only from what we have spoken about so far in our sessions, nothing new. What I would like *you* to do, Kora, is tell me whether the behaviour shows loving behaviour, or bad behaviour. Do you understand?"

She nodded, albeit still distant. He pursed his lips and gave a firm nod back.

"Alright, let's begin." He clicked his pen and cleared his throat. "When you hit the other children in school, were you showing love, or bad behaviour?"

"Bad behaviour," she mumbled, looking down at her shoes.

140

"That's very good. What about when your father hit you at home? Was that love, or bad behaviour?"

She frowned, looking perplexed.

"Kora?"

"None."

"Would you be able to explain your answer for me, so that I can understand?"

She cocked her head to the side, trying to think of the right words. Dr. Hurley spoke to her like an adult and in return, she wanted so badly to explain herself as an adult would.

"It's none, because it was learning. I was bad, so I got a smack. Other kids from school get smacks too when they're bad," she said, feeling as though she had explained herself to the best of her abilities.

"I understand your point. May I explain mine?"

She nodded warily, suddenly feeling defensive.

"You see," he began, "many parents give their children little smacks when they're naughty, you're completely right. The difference between the smacks you received, and the smacks other children received, is that their smacks were *little* ones. The ones you received, usually resulted in injury. Let's see," he flipped back quite a few pages in his notepad, finding one with the notes he needed.

"Ah, here we are. You have had almost all of your fingers broken; eight, in fact. Your ribs have been fractured twice on record, your wrists have had multiple stress fractures in several different places, dislocations of your hips, a fractured eye socket and one hospitalisation for a haematoma on your thigh." He paused as he looked up at her to read her response.

Her fingers twitched as she stopped herself from instinctively lifting her hand to her eye, to touch the groove where the delicate skin had broken under the force of her father's knuckles and left a small, almost unnoticeable scar.

141

She began to feel her body vibrate, deep beneath the rocky surface.

"I don't see children with those kinds of injuries from getting smacks for misbehaving," he said softly. "Don't you agree?"

She nodded her head as she felt the vibrations inside her body grow in intensity, harder and harder until her tiny body felt like home to an earthquake. She closed her eyes, unable to ignore the thunderous bass of each quake as it threatened to rip through her intestines like a tsunami. Tears stung the corners of her eyes but she withheld them with all her might. She had had such good practice at this that it felt like second nature, as though she was merely flexing a muscle. The shaking, however, was almost always too powerful for her to control on her own.

"Kora, you're not in trouble."

She could barely hear him now.

"I know," she whispered.

"Shall we continue?"

"Yes."

He clicked his pen once more. Twice. She wondered how many times he had clicked his pen today. The shaking began to subside.

"When your father injected you with needles containing heroin, was that love, or bad behaviour?"

"Bad behaviour," she said, although she wasn't sure whether she meant her father's behaviour or her own. He didn't notice her confusion, nodding as he ruffled his moustache. He continued.

"When your father made you play games, ones where you were forced to ask him to do things to your body that you didn't want him to do, was that love, or bad behaviour?"

He looked up from his notepad, his eyes then boring into hers, gauging her reaction. Her tears won the silent battle and fought their way through, now spilling over the edges of her eye line.

"Bad behaviour," she answered, her voice shaking in unison with each tremor of her body. Her nose began to run and her vision blurred.

Dr. Hurley reached over onto the table, picking up a box of tissues and offering them to her. She shook her head, recoiling. She pulled down her sleeve, wiping her eyes and nose on the back of it. He gave her a few minutes to calm herself, letting the silence in the room soothe her as she shook. Once she had dried her eyes, he spoke.

"It's quite alright to cry. I'm afraid the next question will be no easier, nor the one after that. This part of the process is necessary so that you can become a strong, healthy and happy girl who will never need to come back here if she doesn't want to. I need you to understand what you have experienced, Kora. Understanding all of this is not easy, and you are doing wonderfully. You are an incredibly clever girl."

She looked at him through her soaked lashes and nodded, sniffling. She began to feel a deep hatred for him and his questions. She wanted to leave. She knew he would never understand and she had no hope of making him try. It was as if they spoke two different languages, only they had the same letters, and the same ugly words.

"May I continue?"

She reluctantly nodded. She was beginning to realise that if she wanted to go home, she would have to finish his game.

"Good girl. Now, when your father touched your body inappropriately, was that love, or bad behaviour?"

"Bad behaviour," she said, obediently.

"Excellent. Last question. When he forced himself on you — or perhaps— let's be a little clearer. Euphemisms can create confusion, can't they?"

She nodded, not knowing what he meant.

"Kora, when your father forced you to have sexual intercourse with him, was that love, or was that bad behaviour?"

She smiled to herself, knowing she had finished the game. That one was easy.

"That was love."

SIXTEEN

ENVY

"Theo's not really the kind of person you want to get too close to," Kora warned.

She emptied the contents of her handbag onto the bed back in their hostel room. Her set of keys, an empty pill bottle and an assortment of different coloured pills spilled out, along with some loose coins. Cash fluttered out as she shook the bag one last time. Mila gave her a quizzical look, not aimed at the contents of her bag, but more so at her statement.

"He seems harmless to me?" she replied, but it sounded more like a question.

"He seemed harmless to his family too, until he killed them."

Mila's jaw dropped. Kora shrugged and gave her a look that said *I told you so*. She sat down on the bed and began collecting the money into her hand, counting it as she did so.

"He's on medication now, of course. It keeps him from losing his mind."

"Shouldn't he be in prison?!"

"Oh, no. He was only a kid when he did it."

The silence was thick with something Kora couldn't read. She counted the money under her breath but her mind was almost solely focused on Mila. She couldn't let Theo steal her. She wouldn't. And all she really had to do, was tell her the truth.

"He seems so nice," Mila said, dismayed. Kora could feel Mila's eyes boring a hole into her. The feeling didn't match Mila's tone at all. Something felt off.

"He is, most of the time. He's just a little bit unstable."

"Do you know how he did it?"

She stopped counting the notes in her hands, biting her bottom lip. Indecision tugged at her chest. She had never told anybody his story before. She had never needed to. But how else was she supposed to keep Mila away from him? How else was she supposed to keep her safe? Things had changed now that she knew she loved Mila.

"Do you really want to know?"

"I— I don't know." Mila bit her top lip with her bottom teeth, making her somewhat resemble a frowning little french bulldog. Kora stifled a smile despite the indecision and guilt that lurked only a few secrets away.

"Do you think he would mind me knowing?"

"Does curiosity really kill the cat?"

Mila thought on that for a second, her sparkling eyes wandering as she leaned against the wall. Finally, she shook her head.

"No, I don't think it does."

Kora sat down on the bed and lay her palms in her lap, still clutching the money. The old bed creaked, even under her slight weight. Somewhere deep within the folds of her mind, she wondered whether the weight she carried from her past had any effect on how much the bed creaked as she sat. She tucked the thought away, knowing that it was an impossible thought— The bed was just old.

She took a deep breath, readying herself to tell the stolen story she had told no-one.

"He strangled his sister on Christmas morning," she started. Mila's eyes widened. She knew then that this story wasn't going to be Mila's cup of tea. She felt the need to cover Mila's ears even though the words were coming from her own lips. It was an odd sensation that didn't sit right; feeling the need to protect somebody from *herself*.

"Why did he— I mean, why—" Mila scrambled, lost for words, but Kora was barely getting started.

"He strangled her until she was unconscious, at first. He thought he'd killed her but she woke up."

"Thank god!"

"When she woke up, he panicked and ran downstairs."

"To get help?"

She shook her head. "No. To grab a pair of kitchen scissors. He stabbed her to death."

Mila covered her mouth with her hands, eyes wide in shock.

"He says he doesn't really remember it, but I think that he does," she said, the words now flowing from her mouth as if they were memories of her own, instead of police reports and old media coverage— coverage that had been dug up during his court trial for the deaths that had occurred due to the cheap car parts he had installed.

"I know he must remember something. He said his sister's name once in his sleep. He was telling her to stop crying," she recalled, her eyes glazing over for just a second before coming back down to earth. "When the police finally came knocking on the door, he'd been left alone for days. They found his sister first, and then they'd found him hiding in a closet, completely catatonic. Their first conclusion was that his mother had killed his sister and run, until they found her body out back in the jacuzzi."

147

Mila had lost all colour in her face and hands. She looked as though she might lose her breakfast. Kora hesitated for a moment, unsure if she should finish the story but the words had been caged inside her chest for so long that they begged desperately to be let out.

"They— They still believed it was his mother for a long time. There had been so many sleeping pills in the bottle of red wine sitting next to her body, that it was nearly impossible not to think that it had been a suicide, but they couldn't figure out why Theo had been left alive and only his sister had been murdered. Theo couldn't talk, so they had to wait for the results to come back from the lab."

"How do they know it was really him who did it?"

"Fingerprints. All over the scissors, the wine bottle and the empty prescription pill bottle that matched the toxicology report— The same ones that killed his mother and the same ones she made him take to stop him from sleep-walking."

"Oh my god," she whimpered.

Kora nodded solemnly and then repeated what she'd read in his journal for the first time out loud. "He'd asked her if he could stay up to see Santa, but she'd said no."

What she didn't tell Mila, was that when the police found his mother's body in the jacuzzi, the jacuzzi was still on. Her skin had softened to a consistency that the police had likened to the soft skin you would find on top of a cooling custard. But nothing could have prepared them for what had happened when it came time to remove the corpse. The jacuzzi was drained, leaving only her soft, malleable body behind. The first attempt at removal had accidentally peeled the skin away from her torso. They said it had slipped off effortlessly, leaving the fat and membranes dragging behind, still clinging to the bones. They had then begun to remove her the only way they could— in pieces, while her muscles fell apart like slow-cooked flesh. The photograph in the newspaper of their home being cordoned off by officials, showed a passerby crossing themselves as they looked on, covering their mouth and nose with a scarf. Nobody had ever mentioned the smell.

"How old was he?"

"I think he was eight."

"Where was his dad?"

"Doesn't have one."

"Poor thing," Mila said sadly before shaking her head as though she were trying to shake something out of her brain. "Ugh, I don't want to think about it any more. I feel sick. He was so young, he probably had no idea what he was doing."

Kora had to rein in an unmistakable look of surprise. That was not at all the reaction she was expecting. Shock and disgust, sure. *Sympathy*? Not quite. She was stunned. Jealousy prickled underneath her skin. He murdered his whole family and Mila actually *felt sorry for him*?

"He knew what he was doing, Mila." The saltiness in her voice was unmistakable.

Mila was immediately silent, having realised she'd said the wrong thing.

"Sorry, I—" she started, but Kora shook her head.

"It's okay. I just wanted you to know."

Mila nodded gently, looking at the floor, drawing patterns in the dust on the floor with her toes.

Kora silently cursed at herself. She knew that without Mila's naivety and strangely empathetic nature, they wouldn't both be here, sharing this dirty hostel room, spending every waking moment together— falling in love. Mila *did* love her, didn't she? She *had* said she was hers, hadn't she?

She looked down at the money she held in her hands and thought about Mila; the beautiful house she had lived in with her boyfriend only a few days ago, the beautiful life she must have had. She then saw the stark and ugly comparison of where they sat now as she looked around, filled with guilt. She bit the insides of her cheeks until her teeth began to sink into the skin and her eyes began to water. She could taste nothing but blood, and she felt in that moment that it was all she ever deserved to taste.

"Mila, we— We have enough to get a better room, you know. Like, if that's what you wanted." The vulnerability in her voice wasn't completely undetectable, and Mila's eyes zeroed in on her instantly.

"We don't have to have a fancy hotel room. I'm happy here, with you."

The words hit Kora like a tsunami. The icy outer shell of her heart began to melt and crack, falling away from her like rotting wood from a decaying tree. Somewhere in the back of her mind, her inner voice screamed *disbelief*! But the raw sincerity in Mila's voice drowned it out. Kora had, in two seconds, offered up everything that she had; her money, her ticket to freedom— just to make Mila more comfortable. Spoil her, if she could. But Mila didn't care about the money, she didn't want the fancy hotel. All she wanted was to be with her.

Kora's system had gone into shock, and Mila picked up on it straight away. Her eyes swam with empathy as she sat down next to her on the bed, disturbing the pills. They both ignored the tiny clicks and taps as the pills rolled off the bed and hit the wooden floors beneath their feet.

"The money could be used for bigger, better things," she said. Kora looked at her with complete curiosity. She searched Mila's face for an answer to questions she hadn't asked, but came up blank. She had forgotten how to do what she did so well.

"Like an apartment. For me and you."

Kora's heart was at its absolute limit. It was redlining into oblivion. She had no words and for once, she didn't even try to speak for fear of her raw, vulnerable emotions spilling out into her world, terrorising it further. But Mila's expression said all that needed to be said. That she *understood*. That

150

each microscopic, blushing vein underneath the veil of peach skin she'd been given, each eyelash that had not yet been caught on the world and torn out, each kaleidoscope shade in each mismatched iris, simply understood.

Mila suddenly rose off the bed, changing the tempo and lifting the mood all at once with her bubbly and bright demeanour. Kora stole her eyes to the floor, hyper-aware of how long she'd been staring blankly back at her. She ruffled her hands through her hair nervously.

"I'm going to have a shower," she sang as she ran her fingers through her own hair, dancing towards the bathroom door. "I swear this room is so cold that I'd shower even if I didn't need—"

Her words continued to ring out, but for Kora, she wasn't listening. Mila's voice had trailed off somewhere inside her head. There it was again; Mila had *mirrored* her movement. Her mind couldn't find an answer for it. She was still trying to comprehend such simple, and such complicated words such as *apartment*.

The bathroom door squealed closed followed by an empty thud. She exhaled a breath she hadn't realised she was holding in and fell back onto the bed, chalking up Mila's little quirk to the sincerest form of flattery.

She hadn't even considered getting a proper house with Mila, but now that it had been said it was all she wanted. She felt a burst of light stream into her mind, as though somebody had opened the curtains and shown her the burning daylight she had been missing. The light fell across parts of her mind that felt as though they had never seen anything like daylight before; parts of her mind that craved a normal, boring life, like Theo had said. She could *almost* picture it— the white walls, beige carpet, two bedroom house just out of the city. *The house she grew up in.*

All in the same thought, the harsh reality set in. It wasn't like she could just put her name down for anything, on an official document. She was a runaway. She desperately needed a new identity. That was *why* she lived the way she did; spending her days laying out the blueprints for the life she needed, spending her nights taking what she needed for it. She was the architect of it all— but for all she knew, she would never make it. She could be a wanted felon, and she would never know until they caught her. She had been wanted for questioning ever since Theo's arrest, and she had attacked a stranger in an alleyway in the middle of the city— that can't have gone unnoticed.

A small vibration coming from Mila's satchel interrupted her spiralling thoughts. She sat up, looking over at it laying on the floor in the corner of the room. Mila's dress from the night before laid crumpled on top and the corner of her cellphone was poking out from underneath. She bit her lip, conflicted. The curiosity was suddenly overwhelming. She realised she knew nothing about the girl she loved. She wondered what kind of life she had outside of the one they had been living over the past couple of days. She never mentioned her friends or her family, she never spoke about home; Kora started to wonder if her ex-boyfriend truly *hadn't* contacted her. She felt sick at the idea of losing Mila. *How can he stand being without her?*

The cellphone buzzed again. She stared at it hungrily, her curiosity begging to be fed. Mila had said it herself; *curiosity doesn't always kill the cat.*

She crept over to the satchel, picking up the phone. There were two unread messages from *Erica*, with only the first three words visible; *You missed your—* and; *I have news!* with an attachment symbol.

As curious as she was to know who Erica was, she didn't dare open it. Not yet. She instead scrolled through the opened messages, but not finding much of interest. The phone seemed fairly old but oddly enough there was not a lot saved on it. She clicked through the contacts curiously, and only found several names— not even her own. As she scrolled somewhat mindlessly, her entire world froze. Acid burned sickeningly throughout her chest when she saw whose number had been added to the list.

Theo's.

Panicked tears of disbelief and confusion stung at her eyes, burning them to no end. Her heartbreak turned to rage so fast that not even she could control its seething overhaul. She stood, tearing the pillows and blanket from the bed, screeching— needing to feed her overwhelming urge to break things. Her entire consciousness screamed and clawed at itself, tearing away the sunlight from its skin. She made up her mind solely and without hesitation in an instant.

Theo had to go.

She had always known that this day might come but she found herself feeling less prepared than she thought she would. She had always loved him, ever since the first day she had seen him, but he didn't love her back, not the way she wanted, and now not only did he not love her, but he was trying to take away the only person who did; Mila.

As she stood, chest heaving, staring at the wall, she devised a plan. It was a plan that she was not entirely at peace with, but she would have all the time in the world to come to peace with it later.

She heard the rusty shower handle being turned and listened to the rush of water dissipate down the drain. She slipped Mila's phone back under the dress on top of her satchel and returned to the bare bed, laying back down and staring at the ceiling.

The bathroom door clicked open and a steamy mist flowed lightly into the room like a soft cloud, bringing with it the luscious scent of vanilla and peach. Mila stepped out in a towel, her hair tied up into a tidy bun. Beads of water decorated her cream-coloured collarbones and lightly freckled shoulders. She looked around at the room in confusion, having been torn apart.

"What the—"

Kora sat up and looked around, realising she had made a mess with no valid explanation. "I was going to make the bed, but I realised we have no fresh sheets," she shrugged.

Mila shook her head, laughing. "Come and take a shower while I get ready," she offered, grabbing Kora's hand and pulling her up off the bed. Her soft hands were still warm from her shower and somehow, even softer than usual. Kora, mesmerised, followed her back into the steamy haze.

She could feel her heart pounding in her throat as Mila let her towel fall around her ankles, her bare skin barely visible in the steamy mirror. Kora fumbled with her buttons, distracted as Mila hummed a familiar tune, wiping away a small window of condensation and effortlessly winging her eyeliner. She turned the shower on, and the water from the faucet sent spurts of water out at odd angles before settling into it's normal, showering pour. She lathered herself in body wash, trying not to watch Mila as she bent over the sink, applying lipstick. She was left feeling oddly naked and hollow as Mila slipped out of the bathroom, leaving her to face her own distorted thoughts. Her body screamed for Mila, but she was too nervous to open her mouth.

A moment later, Mila returned and roped Kora's attention out of her own mind as she twirled, naked in front of the mirror, giggling. She was talking, chattering away excitedly but Kora couldn't make out any of the words. She felt too far away. She turned the shower off and wrapped a towel around her body, feeling achingly self-conscious for the first time in her life.

Mila slipped a black dress Kora hadn't seen before over her head, letting the straps fall into place on her shoulders. She watched as she unfastened the pins in her hair and the picturesque bun sitting on top of her head untwisted itself and fell gracefully in smooth, silky waves down to the small of her back.

She looked ethereal. The inside of Kora's mind itched.

She managed to shake herself out of her bubble long enough to get dressed. As they sat on the bed and waited for the front desk to call their room upon the arrival of their taxi, Kora laid out a new plan for Mila. She needed to drag her further down into the depths of her world— so deep that she couldn't escape. She needed her to feel like an accomplice. She needed her to feel *seen* so that she would feel *stuck*. She needed to up the ante.

"I don't think I can do it," she confessed nervously. "I don't think I can just jump into bed with some strange man. Do we *have* to swap roles?"

Kora nodded, trying to stave off the mental image of Mila laying naked on top of some faceless man, having him paw at her.

"Have fun with it, you'll enjoy it. It's easier than you think."

"Why can't we just go with the same routine as last time?"

"Because last time you nearly got me killed, remember?"

The bedroom phone rang just as Mila opened her mouth to protest. Kora picked up the receiver. Their taxi had arrived. She thanked the desk clerk and hung up the phone, looking at Mila expectantly.

"Grab your shit, let's go."

She stood without question, but Kora could see her mind whirring away.

"What if this— hypothetical man and I don't even leave together?" she suggested suddenly her bright eyes, full of hope.

"As in, we do everything there, before we leave?"

"Could that work?"

Kora paused thoughtfully as she picked up her handbag, realising the only reason she ever went home with anybody was because it gave her a place to sleep. But they *had* a place to sleep.

"I guess— I mean, I don't see why not," she said reluctantly, plans changing in her mind as fast as they had formed.

They grabbed the rest of their things and locked the door behind them, heading to the main lobby to find their driver waiting for them by the front desk looking irritable. Once they had climbed into the backseat of the taxi, Kora gave the driver the name of a different venue from their usual scene. Mila would have looked nervous if she hadn't seemed so excited. She began whispering frantically.

"Where are we going? How do I choose? How do *you* choose? I want to do it just like you would."

Kora's ego rose up from inside her ribcage like a phoenix, stretching its wings. She found her words simply adorable. Of *course* Mila wanted to be just like her.

"I tend to go by a man's watch," she began, matter-of-factly. "But, if they have their wallet and keys on the table, take a look at the keys and pick the one with the nicest car," she winked mischievously.

As they pulled up outside a magnificent, white-pillared building, Mila pressed her nose to the glass of the window, looking out in awe. *The Farryn Hotel.*

"Wow," she whispered breathlessly. Kora smirked before laying out the rules. This was no ordinary hotel. This was a casino with a first class, five-star bar and security team to match.

"I'll meet you at the bar. Don't get drunk. Do *not* choose anybody who is actually staying at the hotel and *don't* get distracted by the high rollers. We're not in some card counting movie. You *will* end up as somebody's prostitute for the night and there is serious security here, so *be careful*," Kora instructed, as she passed the driver some cash and climbed out of the taxi. "And," she added, "look like you belong there."

She walked towards the rotating entrance doors, content with the terrified look on Mila's face as she disappeared past the lavish pillars and past the security team guarding the entrance.

Inside, Kora skulked off and slipped inside the door of the ladies bathroom. Everything was lit up by green lights. Most bathrooms downtown had green lights these days. They were installed as a preventative measure to stop drug-abusers injecting their poison of choice into their veins in club bathrooms. Even some convenience store bathrooms in the downtown and surrounding areas were taking the idea onboard. Kora neither hated nor applauded this new installation. She had never used a needle on herself, but it didn't stop her from checking to see if her veins were visible under the light every time she encountered the green hue. They never were.

She set her handbag on the counter and unzipped her tattered fox pencil case filled with makeup, tampons and loose pills. She dug out five or six pills and examined them closely under the green lights above her. Most of them were painkillers, but two that were stamped, were not. She dropped the stamped pills back into the pencil case, searching for more that matched the ones she kept in her hand. She shuffled them all around in her bony hands before tipping her head back and pouring them all into her mouth. She ducked her head under the tap and waved her hand in front of the sensor until the water begun to fall, taking a sip to down the pills.

She looked up at her reflection in the mirror. Her toasty caramel skin seemed an odd colour against the green lights, greyish, but her eyes were just as dark as they always had been. She noticed her cheekbones were a little less gaunt, and her eyes a little less sunken in. Maybe it was just a trick of the light. Or perhaps she had been eating more. Having Mila to take care of meant a regular eating pattern, of sorts— more than once every couple of days, anyway. She cocked her head to the side, regarding her new face for a moment, before scrunching up her nose and looking away. She zipped her pencil case back up and dropped it into her handbag, swinging it over one shoulder as she made her way out of the bathroom and back into the brightly lit, buzzing high of the casino.

The corridor opened up into a vast, circular, two-storey mecca. Men with jawlines that seemed to stretch on endlessly were dressed to the nines. Glamorous women in embellished gowns with highlighted cheekbones floated gracefully from roulette table to spinning wheels. Ignoring the seduction of the hypnotic violet lights and bells that rang out to her from the slot machines, she made her way past the cheering at the roulette tables and into the bar.

While the music was still of an uncomfortable decibel level, the vibe of the crowd at The Farryn was entirely different from their usual dark and thumping club venues. It had a dress code, for one, but the types who came here were simply just a higher calibre of people. Stage smoke crept from the edges of the dance floor and washed down over the sea of people. There were hints of glitter at every turn.

Her eyes searched the beautifully-dressed crowd for Mila. She spotted her talking to two well-dressed men. Two sets of keys were already sitting on the table next to their drinks; light beer.

A sudden warmth surged through her body, from her belly to her toes, making her fingertips tingle slightly. The pills she had taken had finally softened the harsh edges of her existence. The feeling reminded her vaguely of the warm, glittering feeling from the Sick Needle her father pricked her with when she was younger, but without the sickness or nightmares that followed. She had grown to enjoy the taste of the warmth in her fingertips, knowing she would never take enough herself to make herself sick.

She watched closely from the bar, catching a clear view of Mila every few seconds in between the silky, shimmering bodies that glided around her. She was sitting now, with one of her hands relaxing on the thigh of the man next to her. Her hand crept slowly upwards, higher and higher, and then all of a sudden she stopped. She looked down at his lap, seemingly confused. She leaned in saying something in his ear. He smiled sheepishly, looking down and put his hand in his pocket, pulling out his wallet and phone. He placed them on the table and leaned in to whisper something in her ear in return. She laughed, throwing her head back and resumed stroking his thigh, while his friend rolled his eyes, sniggering in obvious jealousy— Mila *was* gorgeous.

This was Kora's moment.

She walked over to the bar and leaned in, ordering four double shots of whiskey. The barman put the four glasses up on the bar and she motioned to the stack of trays behind him. He nodded, understanding that she couldn't possibly carry four drinks by herself. She thanked him and handed over some cash, waving away the change and downing one of the drinks in one gulp.

As she approached the table, she plastered on a big, fake, customer service smile. The man with his arm draped around Mila's shoulder looked up, confused, while Kora put the tray down and began offloading the three remaining glasses; one for each of them.

"Ah, no. Excuse me, *lady*," he said as he tried to stop her, yelling over the music. Kora could hear several drinks swimming in his voice already. "Those aren't for us."

159

He waved her away, looking over at his friend and scoffing as if she were a waitress who couldn't understand how to do her job.

Kora smiled her biggest smile. *Arrogant.* Mila had chosen well.

"Courtesy of the bar, gentlemen."

And with that, she took her tray, sliding his keys and wallet off the table underneath it and left. She looked back over her shoulder and watched it all play out from the other side of the room as she dropped the tray onto a nearby table, holding onto his belongings.

Mila took a whiff of her whiskey and waved it away, passing the glass to the man she sat with— her victim of choice. His defeated-looking friend, clearly annoyed that he wasn't getting any female attention, pushed his away also. He pointed to his beer when it seemed he was questioned by Mila's victim. She watched her giggle and push her glass, *and* the friend's glass towards him, encouraging. The man threw his head back, laughing and puffing his chest out just a touch more than he had been before. Kora could have read the words from his lips even if she hadn't seen them for herself.

"*What, you think I can't?*"

Kora and the table watched him as he shrugged, feigning nonchalance and bravado. He threw back all three drinks, one after the other, while Mila cheered him on.

Kora took out her phone from her handbag, snapping a picture of the driver's licence inside his wallet. She returned her phone to her bag along with his keys. It wasn't his identity she wanted; it was his address. She waved down the bartender again. As he walked over, she passed the man's wallet to him, motioning towards the crowd of people. She shrugged, he nodded, placing the wallet behind the bar.

Taking one last look at Mila, she strolled back out of the entrance of the bar, past the excitement radiating from the casino and out into the cool night air.

The moon was visible now that the sun had set. It cast an eerie, light that rolled off its own divine curve. She loved the moon. It seemed only ever just to watch over the world and it's endlessly flashing lights and countless people; never judging, never changing its face, just watching. Leaning against the side of the building, she felt mesmerised. By the moon, by Mila, by her own guile.

A hushed commotion from her left stole her attention, distracting her. Several security guards, gripping their two-way radios, left their posts at the front entrance and disappeared inside. Her chest tightened and she checked the time. She had been waiting for over twenty minutes. Her heart began to race as she slid back through the doors in pursuit.

SEVENTEEN

HERS

She desperately scanned the room for Mila as she quickened her pace, hoping to spot her before the security team did. She turned to check behind her in case she had somehow slipped past unnoticed, but saw no one. She absentmindedly bit her bottom lip, turning back around and coming to an abrupt halt, slamming unexpectedly into a large man. She cried out in surprise, nearly toppling over. She tasted blood, and reached up to her lip to where she found she had bitten through the top layer of skin.

"Excuse me, ma'am," a deep voice boomed as she was shoved further out of the way.

Kora looked up angrily, but caught her venomous words right before they spilled from her mouth as she realised she was staring at the same men she had been tailing. She stepped right out of the way as the two security guards bustled out of the foyer with their burly arms hooked around a liquored-up, mess of a man— the same man Mila had been all over not even half an hour ago. She stood, dumbfounded as she watched them escort him out.

But Mila was still nowhere to be seen. She spun on her heels and made a beeline for the bar, hoping she hadn't already been escorted to a security room.

Somewhere above the bass notes of the music, as she was being swallowed by the crowd of nameless, faceless pleasure-seekers, she heard her name.

"Kora!"

She spun around. Mila waved from a booth over the far side of the room, but she was not alone. Two girls sat beside her looking sultry as they sipped on their drinks. Kora growled in immediate distaste as she walked over.

"You came!" Mila squealed, giving her a sly wink as she jumped up.

Kora forced an inviting smile towards the two intruders as she grabbed Mila by the arm and pulled her away from the table.

"Who are *they*?" she snarled through gritted teeth. "I was waiting for you outside."

"That's what I wanted to explain," she yelled excitedly over the music. Her breath held a light hint of alcohol, and so did the pink swirl in her cheeks. She must have disobeyed Kora's rule about not drinking. Her eyes swam with mischief. "I have an idea."

"An idea. Really." She would have rolled her eyes if she hadn't been so agitated.

"Hear me out! What if—" she looked over at the two girls, distracted, who were now waving them over.

"You said pick somebody with a nice car. One of them drives a *Mercedes*. Come on!" She linked arms with Kora and brought her back to the table.

It took all of Kora's strength to keep her expression as fresh and approachable as possible, but inside, the venom she had been so prepared to spit at the security guard earlier, was seeping through her veins and burning her throat raw. This was ambitious of Mila, not to mention presumptuous. She felt unsettled. This wasn't the plan.

They slid into opposite sides of the booth, Kora glaring at Mila. The blonde girl sitting beside Mila leaned over, beaming, and held out her hand.

"I'm Dom!"

Momentarily distracted by the bewitching rose gold tips of her hair, she shook her hand politely in return.

"Kora."

"That's Pagan," Dom motioned to the pale, auburn girl sitting next to her, who gave her a curious smile back that didn't quite meet her eyes.

Damaged, Kora thought as she began internally analysing Mila's chosen company, listing off noticeable things. If Mila was convinced that she would be able to con these girls, Kora would have to obstruct her with a concrete argument as to why she was wrong.

"So, Kora, what do you do?" Dom asked loudly.

Her stomach tightened at being caught off guard. "I'm kind of between places right now."

"Aren't we all," muttered Pagan, seemingly amused. Kora stole a curious glance at her from the side. She had misinterpreted Pagan's demeanour. She wasn't damaged, she was *angry*.

"Ignore her," Dom rolled her eyes, laughing. "She's a nihilist who majored in philosophy."

Mila laughed. Kora stifled an unrecognisable yet familiar feeling. She tried to pinpoint it. She looked around the table as the other three continued to talk amongst themselves over the music. She was the only person at the table who hadn't gone to school. The only person who hadn't lived a normal life.

"I'm going to get drinks!" Mila exclaimed, interrupting her budding insecurities. Dom and Pagan cheered as she left, before turning to each other now completely uninterested in

164

Kora. Stung, she tried to remind herself that she was not trying to charm these girls into bed— in fact, she was trying to do the opposite. Of course they wouldn't be interested in her. She wasn't *trying*.

She took in a deep breath and stared blankly at her feet, just as uninterested in them. She noticed Mila had left her satchel on the ground. She turned to watch her as she stood at the bar, swaying to the beat. She took her chance. She hooked the strap of the satchel around her foot and slid the bag over, unbeknownst to the girls. She reached inside and flipped open Mila's phone.

Not only were there no new messages, there were no messages *at all*. Her entire inbox had been deleted. She felt sick, staring at the screen for a couple of seconds in a state of perplexity and panic as she tried frantically to connect the dots.

Did Theo tell her to delete her messages?

She closed the phone and slid it back into Mila's satchel with such vigour, anybody would assume the phone had burned her. And it had.

Mila returned quicker than she had anticipated and with a tray full of drinks. She quickly tucked her seething rage deep inside her vital organs to fester, beaming up at Mila appreciatively as she took a glass. Mila sat, handing a drink to Dom and giving Kora a knowing smile, almost as if she were giving her a signal. Kora's chest burned. *This was not the plan.*

Pagan, much to Kora's displeasure, slid uncomfortably close and grabbed her own drink from the tray. She rested her deathly white elbow on the table, facing her. The club lights stirred up the dominant emerald green in her eyes, eyes which spoke of nothing but bad behaviour. Her pale, pearl and freckled skin tone made her full lips look freshly bitten and redder than they were. There was something more to this

165

girl than Kora could see on the surface. It intrigued her; it drew her in.

She looked over at Mila, who was already deep in conversation with Dom. They took turns talking in each other's ears and laughing like they had known each other for years, sharing a lifetime's worth of inside jokes. The way she was looking her new companion up and down was immediately recognisable; it was the same way Kora looked at every man she had ever seduced.

She snarled as her blood turned to thick acid. *Who died and made Mila the ringleader?*

She tried to shelve the encroaching theory that was forming in her mind about Mila and her copycat quirks; the theory that maybe Mila didn't just want to be *like* her— that maybe she actually wanted to *be* her.

She turned back to the green eyes that had not looked away, doing nothing but stare back at them. She stared, completely void of emotion. She could see that her enticer took her disinterest as a challenge. Pagan bit her lower lip and leaned in a little closer to Kora, amused as she teasingly slipped her fingertips underneath her shirt. Her fingertips brushed along the sensitive stretch of skin along Kora's side, inching towards the underside of her breast. She could feel the heat of Pagan's body through her fingertips. No words were spoken between the two but she was drawn in so deep that she could swear she could feel her heartbeat pulsing, like it was the steadiest rhythm she had ever felt.

But she had not forgotten about Mila. A sudden bright light from a strobe hit her directly in the eyes, pulling her out of her trance. The bass of the music nipped at her toes with its teeth. Her head snapped up, eyes searching hungrily for Mila.

She would have given anything in the world not to see what she did when her eyes came back into focus— to see her giggling feverishly, as Dom playfully kissed along the outline of Mila's jaw.

What the fuck.

She couldn't sit there, watching this. She felt sick.

She stood, knocking her drink over and pushing away Pagan and her deadly green eyes. She didn't want to be touched, and she sure as hell didn't want to watch Mila get fucked from across the table— she wasn't that type. Her temper flared. Mila was *hers*.

Her glass rolled slowly over the edge of the table, shattering loud enough to catch Mila's attention. She looked up to see what the commotion was about, and her expression immediately changed from exhilaration to caution. Kora stormed around to the other side of the table and grabbed her by the arm. She yanked her to her feet and motioned to her satchel.

"We're leaving. *Now.*"

Mila looked alarmed, but she did not dare argue. She looked over at the two girls who wore expressions of shock, mouthing a polite apology as Kora continued, unrelenting, to drag her away. Her fingers tightened around her arm until red marks began to appear. Finally, the pain became too much to bare and Mila tore her arm away. Kora snapped her head around like she'd been scalded. Mila opened her mouth but before she could get a word out, Kora took a step forward and caught Mila's mouth with her own.

Her cold lips stung as she pressed them roughly into Mila's, as though the harder she pressed, the more she would understand how she felt. There was no spark, no fireworks. There was no epiphanic moment where Kora found herself in that moment not being able to live without her, comparing her to the air she breathed or butterflies devouring her intestines; but there was a deep, burning understanding that she didn't want to live without any of it. Not air, not butterflies, and not Mila.

167

Mila's lips tasted like fire, the ethanol stinging her own as her insecurities faded, being shared, swirling between their tongues. She pinned her hands behind her back and leaned in menacingly.

"You're *mine*."

Mila backed up against the nearest wall, but it was not in fear. She pulled Kora by the waist as she moved, pulling her breathlessly into her body. Kora's hips pressed against her, and she felt Mila's bare thigh brush in between her legs, sending a rippling wave of goosebumps over her skin. Her knees felt weak. She needed more. She needed to be overwhelmed. She needed to sink completely into the sandy depths of Mila's skin.

"Home," she growled into her neck, and Mila nodded desperately.

Kora realised then that she had been wrong about Mila. She was only ever doing what she had taught her to do. It was so *obvious*. She didn't want to *be* Kora, she just wanted to *impress* her.

Mila reached up and touched her bruised lips as Kora pulled her through the club, falling forward into her footsteps obediently. Her fingertips curled around the tips of Kora's as she led her out into the night.

She knew at that moment that she was just simply, and so completely Kora's.

That right now, she couldn't be anything else.

EIGHTEEN

SCATTERED

An ugly screech tore Kora from a restless sleep. She shot straight up in a disoriented panic, only to find it had come from the water pipes in the bathroom. She sighed, rolling her eyes as she lay back down.

"Good morning, sunshine," Mila laughed, holding her pink toothbrush. She squeezed a small bit of toothpaste onto the pristine, white bristles, turning the tap off with another screech.

"What time is it?" Kora croaked.

"Early, like six."

She groaned.

"You're definitely not a morning person, are you," Mila laughed as she shoved her face further into her pillow.

"Hey, so, what I was thinking, after... Well, after last night," Mila's words were so distorted by the toothbrush in her mouth that Kora could only make out the vowels.

Her brain skipped right over her distorted and disarranged night at *The Farryn*. It flashed hot with the fresh, vivid memories that had been burned into her mind in the darkened hours of the morning. She tried to lull the flashbacks back to dormancy as they rushed to the forefront of her mind, burning up her cheeks— Mila's legs tangled up with her own in the throws of the hostel bed, the excruciatingly sensual view from in between the silk of Mila's thighs as she arched her back, involuntarily pushing her hips towards Kora's teasing lips. She could still smell the faint hint of peach that lingered on her skin. She could still hear Mila's breathing as it hastened, whimpering, yet somehow matching the slow rhythm of Kora's tongue as the intensity rose; feeling the desperate, screaming urge of Mila's hips pressing into her, harder and harder as she had dug her nails into the back of her thighs— Then she had woken, feverish and beaded with sweat.

Her neck felt as though it was on fire. She tried to shake herself out of her own thoughts, feeling a sudden warmth rush through her abdomen and down between her legs. She couldn't be sure. She could *never* be sure. Had it really only been a dream? Why could she still *feel* Mila's legs wrapped around her shoulders?

"Hello?" Mila called from the bathroom, toothpaste tracing around the edges of her lips as she looked at Kora in the reflection of the mirror. The way the bathroom ceiling light fell over Mila's hair gave off the slightest hint of a halo.

Kora broke free of the intrusion of her own mind, her ears pricking up like a deer caught in the headlights.

"Did you fall back to sleep?"

"I'm listening, I'm just waiting for you to explain," she lied, propping herself up on one elbow.

Mila eyed her with heavy suspicion, but all Kora could think about was throwing the blankets off her legs and closing the distance between them. She knew she couldn't, even though every cell in her body was trying to break free just to be closer. She felt starved— deprived of something vital, as though she had lived her whole life in the dark and finally, somebody had struck a match. She wondered if this is what it felt like to burn while you're still alive. She wondered if Mila felt the same thirst she did.

"Okay," Mila said slowly, not believing a word. "Well, what if we don't do this whole thing we do with men anymore?"

Kora sat upright and paused, dumbfounded. Her mind scrambled, trying to decipher her words before she was ambushed with an explanation she wasn't prepared for. She felt out of practice. What was Mila asking? Did she want Kora to herself? *Does she feel it too?*

"What— exactly do you mean?" she asked cautiously while her mind began to pace back and forth.

"Well, what about those girls from last night?"

"What *about* those girls?" Her mind tore itself out of her little wonderland, choking.

Mila stopped brushing and spat into the sink.

"I mean, we've been using men. Sure, it works because, I mean, they think with nothing but... Well, you know," she paused, flustered, motioning in between her legs. Kora forced a grin through the sudden pain in her chest. Mila continued.

"But what about Dominique and Pagan? They would have so much more to offer us when you think about it. Clothes, makeup, jewellery— think about it! Keys to their place would be much more suited to *us*, don't you think?"

She nodded, completely numb. She mulled this over for a moment quietly as she let the disappointment take her over. It didn't feel like disappointment. It felt like betrayal. Jealousy seared the inside of her flesh at the memory of Mila with Dom; seducing her, kissing her, touching her. She wanted to be the only one Mila ever thought about.

She knew she had to give her an answer; she had been quiet for too long. She *was* onto something. This only made her jealous in a new way. Jealous that she hadn't been the one to think of it, even after all this time on her own. After all this time, on these same streets, day in and day out.

171

She got up, sleepily leaning against the door frame. She ran through all of the possibilities in her head. Mila watched her in the mirror for a brief moment before she went back to brushing her teeth, seemingly not irked by Kora's slightly off-centre silence.

"At least think about it? I don't bring a lot to the table here, so if I can at least come up with a semi-decent idea—" She shrugged and turned back to the mirror, fixing her hair into a swirling, messy bun.

"Hey," she said softly, walking over to Mila, slinking her arms around her waist. "You bring more than that to this table," and with that, she bent down behind her and sunk her teeth playfully into Mila's left bumcheek. Mila squealed in surprise, jumping away from her and swatting at her backside as though at a fly. She looked shell-shocked. Kora backed off instantly, realising she had crossed a line without thinking. Her cheeks flushed a dark red.

Just a dream.

"I'm just playing," she teased. "Hey, you were all over that guy last night in the bar," she retorted in a hasty attempt to shrug off her little stunt.

"Who? Lucas? *Please*! He was so drunk he could barely stand. His friend had to follow him after security escorted him out. I don't think you're even *allowed* to get drunk in there!"

"How did he get so drunk, Mila?"

"Where are his keys, *Kora*?" Mila shot back, giggling hysterically.

"Okay," Kora called out as she scampered back into the bedroom with her tail secretly between her legs. "I'll think about it."

She forced her embarrassment deep, deep below her surface and eyed the set of keys she had stolen last night. They were laying on the floor, gleaming mischievously in the light. She picked them up, prying the house key from the key

172

ring and dropping the car key into her pocket. She quickly scrawled Lucas' address messily onto a piece of paper torn from Theo's tattered old journal, pocketing that too.

Even after all these years, she had kept his journal from the foster home. It was always with her. It was in worse shape than ever, especially since it was now primarily the place where she stashed her money and secrets. But his journal is how she knew his story; what he had really done. He was not just the mask he wore when he faced the world.

She pulled on a sweater. It was time to put her plan into action. Today was the day she would finally pick up her belongings from the warehouse.

"I'm starving!" Mila called out, all previous awkwardness forgotten.

To Kora, Mila's voice still sounded as mesmerising as the day she had first heard it— a combination somewhere between the softness of a harp, coupled with the purr of a kitten.

She stepped into the bedroom looking immaculate. She had tied her golden hair up with a small ribbon and her skin was glowing and full of life, matching those sparkling eyes of hers. Kora had absolutely no idea how one second she could be brushing her teeth with foam lining the edges of her lips and the next, she looked like a god.

They skipped past the front desk as they left the hostel. The desk clerk looked up from his phone and gave them a bored nod, although it seemed more like an eye-roll than anything else. Kora blew him a kiss, figuring it might give him something to live for. He frowned in return, wriggling backwards into his seat and went back to his phone. She snickered, linking arms with Mila to keep warm as they stepped out into the glacial morning air.

Gravel crunched under their feet as they ducked under the familiar wire fencing and made their way up towards the warehouse. Kora was surprised to see Theo was standing outside so early. He was leaning against the wall taking quick, erratic drags of a cigarette. She squinted and tried to refocus her eyes, just to check if she was seeing it right. He had never been a smoker. As they approached him, he quickly threw his cigarette at the ground, crushing it under his boot.

"Uh, y—you're back," he stammered, clearly caught off-guard at the sight of Mila.

"Hey Theo," she smiled at him, her eyes so full of genuine warmth and wonder that it made Kora feel slightly ill. She tried her best to ignore it, but the image of his name on Mila's phone gnawed at her insides, tapping away at her trachea like rain against a window pane. She was wary about having them meet again. Theo had gone behind her back the first time she had introduced them— who knew what else he had told her while she had been upstairs rummaging around in his bathroom. The only solace she found, was that he wouldn't get another chance to see her. This was the end.

He forced out a smile back at Mila, but looked away quickly— shamefully.

Kora took another look at him; a *real* look. He seemed stressed. His eyes were a little too wild and his hair a little too messy to just have been styled that way. Deep down, She felt a twinge of pain seeing him outside of his usual calm, collected self.

This wasn't the same Theo. What she was looking at, were the edges of somebody entirely different.

"I told you, last time was the *last* time," he growled quietly as he turned to face Kora. The edginess plastered across his face dripped into his voice.

"Don't worry, I'm only here to pick up my things," she rolled her eyes dramatically, but she spoke in a lighter tone than his, careful not to antagonise him the way she usually liked to. She took a small, half-step towards the door, keeping her eye on him. He seemed lost.

174

"Can we come inside?"

"Oh, yeah. You can. Sorry," he muttered.

They entered the warehouse and instantly took in the mess. They had only helped him clean the place up yesterday and already it was back to the same state, if not worse.

"Wow, it gets messy in here fast," exclaimed Mila, sounding surprised.

"Uh, yeah. I, uh, I was looking for something. I guess it just got outta hand." He shook his head and ran his hand through his hair. His fingernails had been chewed right down to the skin.

She had spent countless hours in this building, helping him out from time to time in exchange for being able to sleep there. She knew that this amount of mess was not normal for a day's work. She walked over to the corner where he had *so kindly* dumped her things in cheap, black, plastic rubbish bags. She noticed immediately that they'd been disturbed. The tops had been untied and left gaping, revealing the mess of clothes and shoes inside, whereas she could have sworn the last time she saw them the tops had been tied in tight knots. It definitely looked as though he had rifled through them. He *had* said he had been looking for something. She was almost certain she knew what that was.

She pulled the tops of both of the bags closed, tying them back up without a word. Reaching into her pocket, she fished out the car key, wrapping it in the small piece of paper she had torn from his journal. She placed them carefully on the floor without a sound. She stood, sliding the key underneath the workbench with her foot while at the same time, noisily tossing one bag over each shoulder.

"So that's that, then," she said with a triumphant smile, but a hint of sadness lay somewhere behind her eyes.

"Yeah, I guess that's that," Theo mumbled, distracted.

She glanced at Mila, who gave him a look of sympathy, but she could see that it was riddled with confusion. She realised

175

then, that Mila never hid how she felt; it was always right there, written blatantly across her face.

"Is everything okay?" Kora directed her question at Theo.

"Yeah, just great," he said, his voice heavy with sarcasm.

The air in the warehouse grew stagnant and uncomfortable all too fast, so she nudged Mila and they both made a move for the door. Kora looked up at him in his crazed state.

"I hope you're doing okay, Theo. Call me if you need me."

She leaned up towards him on her tippy toes, still balancing both bags over her shoulders and gave him a small, soft kiss on the cheek. His stubble grazed her lips and she inhaled his scent one last time before turning and leaving.

Mila closed the door behind her with a grating squeal as he muttered something that sounded vaguely dismissive and they stood, just looking at each other. All of the questions in the world swam across Mila's face but all Kora could do is just shrug sadly before she led them away, back down the gravel path to the snaking alleyways.

"That was odd."

"That's Theo," Kora lied. Mila would never have accepted the truth behind why he was acting so different.

They walked in silence for a few blocks before Mila perked back up, shaking off the dark cloud his craze had wrapped them inside.

"Have you thought any more about changing up our game?"

"One thing at a time," Kora said, dangling Lucas' house keys.

NINETEEN

DARLING, LET ME TEACH YOU

Seventeen year old Kora lay flat in the back of the stranger's van as it weaved in and out of streets she had no knowledge of. *Left, right, left, left—* She had lost the pattern long ago.

"*Get in the back,*" the stranger had grunted at her. He was the first man she had ever met— with the exception of her father. He had looked her up and down, snorting at her attempt to threaten him with a rock she had found along the roadside. She had stood in his way of the driver's door at the first service station she had come across after escaping from Naomi, taking her chance when he'd pulled in to fill up his tank.

"Get in. Just *don't touch anything,*" he'd growled, itching his scalp.

Torrential rain bore relentlessly against the windows as the man drove, as if trying to wear the glass down like the sea against rocks. Between the thunderous static and the roaring engine of the van, she could barely hear her own thoughts. She had never been in the back of a van before. The world looked strange at eye-level from the dusty, carpeted floor.

Everything was covered in thick, grey, woollen blankets. With each jolting gear change, a blanket slid further and further down to the back of the van, revealing an old duffel bag within arms reach.

The drive was longer than she anticipated and she was beginning to feel sick, having the floor constantly moving beneath her. Just as she began to feel the bile in her stomach burn its way up her throat, the man spoke.

"When was the last time you were home?"

She sat up, crawling to the front so she could hear him better over the racket.

"Ten," her voice cracked. It had been hours since she'd spoken.

"This morning? You're a long way from home."

"Ten years old."

The man raised an eyebrow. "Ten years old," he repeated to himself as he scratched at his stubble, perplexed. "How old are you now?"

"Eighteen soon."

His lip twitched, deep in thought. "Is that right, honey."

She stared blankly at him.

He raised his eyebrows at her, as innocent as could be. "What're you looking at me like that for?"

"My dad calls me honey."

"Well," he grinned, "a lot of men probably will."

She thought on this for a moment.

"Will they?"

"What?"

"Will they all call me honey?"

He looked back at her confused, unsure of how to answer such a question. "I mean, if that's what you want them to call you."

"And if I don't?"

"Then tell 'em not to," he shrugged as he turned a sharp corner, sending her flying into the wall of the van. "Get in the back and *lay down*. You're gonna get me caught."

She lay back quietly while she watched him drive. His eyes stole glimpses at her in the rear-view mirror every few minutes. He seemed tense. Indecisive. Excited. He looked to be in two minds about something, but she couldn't figure out what. Feeling uncomfortable, she moved away to where his eyes couldn't see her.

"You know, you should really give me something in return for giving you a ride," he said, craning his neck to try to find her in the mirror.

She eyed her backpack. She didn't have anything of any real value.

"What do you want?"

"Well, *honey*," she could hear him licking his dry lips as he spoke, "what've you got that I can have?"

She glanced over at the duffle bag, then looked back at the mirror. She still couldn't see his eyes from where she was. Reaching over, she slowly dragged open the zip and felt around inside. Her hands brushed an envelope. As she pulled it out and opened it up, her heart began to race. Inside, were a handful of tiny, ziplock bags full of what looked to her like yellow rock salt. What had quickened her pulse, was a clip holding together a thick bundle of fifty dollar bills. She didn't know what to make of the salt, and so she quickly stuffed the dollar bills into her pencil case where he wouldn't find them and placed the envelope back in the duffle bag.

"I've got cash."

"Cash? Surely you don't want to spend that all on a ride now, do you?"

"Better than me killing you with a rock," she snarled quietly.

"What was that?"

"I said that's all I've got."

179

"If that's really how you'd like to pay, I guess." He sighed, disappointed. He pulled up onto a curb roughly, bouncing her head off the floor of the van. "We're here," he announced. "Are you sure this is your neighbourhood? It looks pretty rough, kid."

She sat up, rubbing the back of her head and grabbing her backpack. As she began pulling open the sliding door, he grabbed her arm. She jumped out of her skin, letting the door slide closed.

"Nah uh. Not so fast— my money."

She stared back at him, a deer in headlights. Letting go of her, he held out his hand. She immediately noticed a small pattern of dots traced around the soft skin on the inside of his elbow. She would recognise those marks anywhere. *The Sick Needle*. Memories crawled in underneath the blanket of her mind, clawing at her skin. Her vision grew dark around the edges and the sound of his voice bounced through her consciousness, becoming an echo of an echo.

"Payment. In exchange for my services," he reminded her, licking his lips again.

She nodded, dazed. She reached into her bag and slid out a single note from the clip inside her pencil case.

"Thanks for the ride," she mumbled, though it was nothing more than nicely dressed apathy.

"You didn't really give me much of a choice," he snorted as she closed the door on him.

He watched her through the foggy passenger window for a moment as she pushed open the gate to the house, inspecting it as she went as though she didn't quite recognise it. The rain continued to pour, but she seemed unbothered.

"Doesn't seem well," he said to himself, as he put the van in gear and drove off.

Kora walked up to the front door, glad to hear the engine disappear into the storm. She cupped her frail hands up to the frosted glass window pane in an attempt to see inside.

This was definitely *her* house, but it had changed somehow. She ran her fingernails along the seamless paint as sheets of rain soaked through her clothes. Where were the paint cracks she used to pick at during the days when her father slept? Was this paint a different colour? She glanced down searching for the dog door. There it was, in the same place— the same small door that she used to crawl in and out of when she was young.

Crouching down on her hands and knees in the wet, she pushed it open, peering inside. The house was dark. It was different. She slid one arm inside, shimmying one of her shoulders through. It was a much tighter squeeze than she remembered, even with how thin her frame still was after all these years. She pushed the rest of her body through the small gap. The hard plastic scraped at her skin, leaving red and violet streaks down her abdomen as she slipped inside the house.

The walls were a different colour from what she remembered and the floor was spotlessly clean. No mould patches, none of her broken toys lay about where she had left them. She hoped he wasn't so mad at her for leaving that he had thrown her toys away. Thick clouds rolled around her mind. Balancing became difficult.

"Daddy?" she called out, reaching out to the wall beside her for balance.

She heard whispers coming from down the hallway.

"Daddy!" she cried, her eyes welling up with tears of joy as she stumbled towards the voices.

All of a sudden, a man who was not her father stepped out of her father's bedroom, holding a bat.

"*What the fuck are you doing in my house?!*" he shook.

"W—Where's my dad?" she faltered in confusion, backing off as the man advanced towards her. A woman peered around the corner of the bedroom, looking terrified.

"Who's she?" Kora whimpered, mentally disorientated. She covered her face with her hands, trying to make sense of what was happening.

"Who the fuck are *you*?" How did you get in here?!"

"I— I don't—" She turned and ran for the front door, pulling it open and running back out into the furious downpour.

"I'm calling the police!" the man called after her, but she kept running.

She kept running without a trace of an idea of where she was or where she was going. Her lungs burned. Between the rain and her stinging tears, she could see nothing. Dim streetlights all blurred into each other until they became just two, bigger, brighter lights— lights that looked like headlights. The low rumble of an engine crept in around her as the lights got closer and closer, until all she could see through her blurred vision was light. She slowed to a stop, covering her eyes. A door opened and footsteps headed straight for her.

"*You little bitch!*" a familiar voice hissed. The stranger from the van.

She squinted at the light through her fingers, but felt her head snap backwards as he grabbed the front of her shirt, yanking her toward him. She stumbled, falling to her hands and knees. She felt the searing burn of her knees grazing against the asphalt, followed by the warm smear of blood across them, filling in the gashes where her skin had torn. He grabbed her by the shoulders and continued to tow her to the van. In the absence of her fear, the way this man grabbed her felt somehow familiar— her morning routine as a child; waking up every morning to her father's rough, bony hands wrapping around her ankles; dragging her out of her soaking wet bed and across the floorboards; being shoved into the shower with her yellow-stained sheets before the water had warmed— *if* it ever warmed.

Then suddenly, a woman's raspy voice came from behind them.

"Get your hands off that girl."

There was a struggle, but she couldn't tell from where. The man let go of her and she fell, tumbling back onto the street in the darkness. A heavy, solid mass landed near her and just as everything fell quiet, she felt herself being pulled back up to her feet.

"Come with me, darling," the woman said, her voice crackling like fire as she led Kora down the side of a nearby property and out into the garden. A small bungalow sat, overgrown with weeds in the far back corner.

"Did he hurt you?" the woman asked her once they were safely inside. In the flickering light, Kora noticed that she had a scar that cut right through her eyebrow and a long dread that unfurled from behind her ear, almost hidden underneath her untamed hair.

Kora shook her head.

"Did you know him?"

She shook her head again. The woman eyed her curiously as she lit up a cigarette.

"You've been crying," she stated simply. "I'm not gonna make you talk to the cops, don't worry. That's the last thing I wanna be doing."

Kora looked around. The singular room seemed tidy enough; the bed was made, a few candles flickered over on the bedside table next to a pair of plastic handcuffs and a box of condoms. She'd never seen condoms in real life, only ever in movies or on TV. Her cheeks flushed a dark red.

The woman chuckled. "I'm a prostitute, darling. No need to be so polite." She took a long drag of her cigarette with wrinkled lips, squinting slightly as the smoke danced around her eyes.

"So tell me, girl. What is it that has you crying through the streets of this derelict neighbourhood?"

"I'm looking for my dad—" Kora's voice caught in her throat, her eyes stinging. The red rings around her eyes burned with questions she didn't know how to ask.

"Where is he?"

"I don't know. He— we lived here. But our house has changed and there are strangers there now."

The woman nodded, looking thoughtful.

"Tell me about the last time you saw him." She stared so intensely into her eyes that she couldn't look away. Kora's memory swirled in and out before her eyes. Something about this woman's transparency and forthrightness made her feel more like home than she had in years.

"I— I was ten," she began. "I crawled out of the dog door and walked myself to school, because he was asleep again. He used to sleep a lot, after— afterwards." She looked down at her feet, avoiding eye contact. "When I got to school, the teachers were waiting for me. They took me into the principals office and asked me if I had been hurt, why I was bleeding. I said I didn't know. Then the police came in. Daddy always told me never to talk to the police, and I didn't want him to be mad, so I didn't. But they took me away anyway, to the hospital and then afterwards to a big office building."

"Why *were* you bleeding, darling?"

"I don't know," she shook her head.

"*Where* were you bleeding?"

"Between my legs."

The woman stubbed out her cigarette and stood, walking over to her small refrigerator and taking out a bottle of gin from the freezer compartment. She grabbed two glasses and placed them on the coffee table between them.

"Darling, let me teach you a few things. This," she said as she poured them each a glass, handing one to Kora, "will help."

She took the glass, sniffing it and recoiling.

184

"You'll learn to like it, trust me. Now, listen closely. Forget about finding your father. Men are good for nothing," she waved her hand in the air. "They'll tell us anything they think we want to hear. They'll use our bodies and then they throw us away when there's nothing left for them to take— when we're not *convenient* anymore. They'd take our souls, if we'd let them."

Kora stared long and hard back at her, taking in every word and feeling nothing but terror at the world she now knew she faced.

"H—How do we survive?"

"We take what we can from them, when we can. We play them at their own game, darling. Don't ever listen to a word they say. Now," she paused, clinking her glass against Kora's, "drink up."

She woke with a start to a loud banging coming from the door of the bungalow.

"Police, open up!" The banging continued. She sat straight up, her head pounded and her eyes were wide in panic. *Police.*

Over on the bed, the woman groaned.

"Open up, Audrey! We know you're home."

"Alright, alright! I'm coming!" she yelled. "Sons of bitches can't get enough of me," she muttered under her breath.

Kora stood, grabbing her backpack and looked at her in desperation, not knowing what to do or where to go.

"Take a breath, darling," she said. "Climb into the closet if you need to hide," she winked as she slowly made her way over to the door. Kora moved quickly. She opened up the narrow closet door, squeezing herself inside and pulling it closed with her fingertips. She listened as she heard Audrey turn the key, unlocking the door.

"What is it? It's early," she grumbled.

"Audrey, you're going to need to come with us down to the station," a man's voice said.

"What for? I haven't got anybody here," she argued.

"We need to take you in and ask you a few questions about a man who was attacked here last night."

"Well, I wouldn't know anything about that."

"So it's just a coincidence that this man happened to be attacked by a woman of your exact description and was left unconscious right outside your address?"

"Must be."

Kora heard the policeman sigh. "We don't have time for games this morning, Audrey."

"Alright, alright. Let me make myself decent."

She heard the door close and listened to Audrey shuffle back inside. The closet door opened, and Kora looked up at her, scared.

"Now darling," she whispered, "don't you worry about me. Here, hand me my coat. You're welcome to stay until I get back," she smiled, but her smile didn't quite meet her crows feet.

Then all too quickly, she was gone. Kora sat frozen in the closet for longer than she needed to, not wanting to risk being caught. Eventually, when she climbed out she saw that it had grown dark again. Sitting on the end of Audrey's bed, she looked around in the grey light. The room was too quiet. She could hear nothing but her own shallow breathing.

The room grew darker, and she grew more and more uneasy. She had no idea of when Audrey would return, or what to do in the meantime. Reaching over to the bedside table, she turned on the lamp. Light flooded the room and the bottle of gin caught her eye, still sitting on the table from the night before. Audrey's voice echoed in her mind.

This will help. You'll learn to like it. Trust me.

She poured herself a glass, all the way to the top. Pinching her nose, she began to down it, each gulp burning more than the one before it until she gagged, coughing and spluttering. Every cell in her body burned and convulsed. How could she ever learn to like *this?* She lay back on the bed and stared at the ceiling in silence.

Slowly, her toes began to tingle with a warmth she hadn't felt before. It gradually enveloped her, spreading warmth throughout her entire body. She felt the heat in her cheeks. She bit her lip, and found that it was numb. She giggled, enjoying the feeling. She felt happy. Audrey had been right— It *did* help.

Just as she was beginning to enjoy herself, she heard footsteps. She shot straight up, listening to them approach in panic. There was a knock on the door before a man spoke.

"Hello?"

She didn't know whether to answer or stay quiet.

"Hello?" he asked again. "Are you a friend of Audrey's?"

Finding her bravery in the liquor, she replied. "Yes."

"Then you need to vacate the premises. She's been locked up for a long time. She won't be coming back."

"She said I could wait for her here," she replied, staunch.

"I'm sorry, but that's just not possible. Can you open the door, please?"

She furrowed her brow. Something in the depth of her memory scratched away at an old, dusty box— a game she used to play. *Try again.*

She tentatively unlocked the door, opening it just enough to see out. Her features softened. "Please, Audrey has been so good to me," she said gratefully, her eyes pleading with everything she had. "I don't have anywhere else to go," she begged softly. "*Please.*"

He took her in, standing tense and silent for what felt like an age.

"Listen, Audrey called me and said you might be in here," he said finally. "I own the property. She said her rent money for the week is in a case in her drawer, and that you'd leave once the week is up."

Victory bubbled underneath her helpless surface. *This* was what Audrey had meant. Her eyes darted around the room in search of the case he mentioned. Spotting the bedside cabinet drawer, she stumbled over to it. Opening it up, a lump formed in her throat. There it was— *her* pencil case. Audrey must have stolen it from her while she slept.

She unzipped it in disbelief, counting the notes. There was almost nothing left. Flames of betrayal licked at her throat.

"How much is the rent?" she called out, holding back tears.

"Two-hundred."

She counted out the notes as she walked back to the door. Handing him the money, she bit her lip.

"So I can stay?"

"You have a week," he said finally.

"Thank-you," she smiled gratefully, hiding her pain as though she'd done it her whole life.

"One week," he repeated as he walked away. She began to push the door closed when he stopped, turning back to her. "What's your name, by the way?"

She stared back at the man for a few moments before answering.

"Honey."

TWENTY

RECOVERED

"What exactly are we doing here?" Mila asked.

"Waiting," Kora reminded her, blowing warm air on her fingertips to combat the stinging chill in the air.

They sat inside an overpriced, rustic cafe uptown, sipping on organic, vegan coffee. It was early enough in the morning that the steam rose off the top of the almond milk froth as if it had caught fire. Both Kora and Mila hand their hands wrapped tentatively around their coffee cups, careful not to burn their skin but desperately seeking the warmth of the ceramic.

Their feet touched under the table and both of them froze, looking up; each face hiding a different palette of emotions as the rawness of the night before broke its way through the surface. Kora's eyes swam with nothing but content delirium as she looked at Mila, all hostility forgotten and the pecking order restored. Mila's face, however, gave nothing away except a tiny, knowing smile.

The cafe itself gave off a new age, bohemian hippie vibe. The walls were made with old bricks at first glance, but on closer inspection, Kora noticed they were brand new and only painted to look as such. Plants hung from walls, ceilings, even chairs, breathing life into the room. The entire suburb the cafe belonged to seemed obscenely wealthy, and although she would kill to live like the people sitting around them did, as they sat at their up-cycled driftwood tables in their overpriced threads happily chatting away— she hated the coffee.

Mila took a sip and pretended to turn up her nose, mocking her gently.

"Too good for the expensive coffee?"

"It's fucking disgusting."

"Mmm, I love it," she said, taking another sip and wiggling her butt happily in her seat, a newspaper from the magazine rack sitting in her lap. She looked more at home in this setting than she had anywhere else she had seen her.

She had led them for a walk around the block before settling into the cafe. When Mila had asked her where they were going, she had pointed out a house with a black Lexus sitting in the driveway. The same house and the same Lexus that they had stolen the keys to only two nights before. Kora assumed *Lucas* had already had new keys made for both his house and his car but she had doubts that he had changed them entirely. He was more than likely convinced that the keys had just been lost in his drunken stupor, not stolen. In any case, there was only one way to find out.

"So, we're waiting for this guy to leave for work?"

Kora nodded, watching out the window for the Lexus. There were only two routes he could use to get to the city from his house, and taking the road with this cafe sitting on the corner was the fastest and most direct. This particular café had the added bonus of being situated in a spot with a direct view of the end of his street, so that even if he did take the different, less direct route— perhaps to avoid traffic, they would still be able to see his car as it pulled out onto the main road.

190

Kora checked her watch. "You're sure he said he starts work at nine?"

"For the millionth time, *yes*."

She raised an eyebrow at Mila.

"Sorry," she said quickly. "I just don't know why he hasn't left home yet either."

They continued to sip on their coffees, people watching out of the cafe window for a while.

"That's you, surrounded by vegan cafes," said Mila suddenly, giggling and pointing at a woman with a fur coat and oversized sunglasses. They watched as she strut, turning her nose up at almost everything she walked past with the most sour expression on her face that either of them had ever seen. Kora burst into roars of laughter; tears forming in the corners of her eyes. She wiped them with her jacket sleeve and tried to look in the other direction in hopes that she would be able to stop laughing into her coffee.

Then there it was. The black Lexus, sitting at the end of Federal drive, waiting to pull out into the street— only, it wasn't indicating in their direction. She squinted as she tried to get a closer look at the driver. Her eyes widened and her heart stopped dead in its tracks. The face of the man driving was not Lucas from the club, as she was expecting.

It was Theo's.

She choked as she put her coffee down, spluttering as she tried to recover and instantly looking away from the window. Mila looked up, alert. To Kora's relief, she didn't turn to look out the window at all, but instead started laughing and reached for the napkins in the other direction.

"Oh my god, Kora! It's not that bad," she laughed, handing the napkins over. She had assumed that Kora had inhaled her coffee instead of swallowing it with all the laughter.

"Ugh," she coughed, laughing back distractedly. "Bathroom!"

191

She stood, and left Mila rolling her eyes at the table while she made her way to the cafe toilets. Once she had turned down the hallway, she pulled out her phone and immediately dialled for the police.

Her heart was pounding in her eardrums as the line connected.

She checked the time. It was nearing 10 a.m. Perhaps Lucas hadn't taken his car to work at all. Perhaps he hadn't had a new key cut yet; after all, getting a new key cut for a Lexus wouldn't be cheap and it *was* only early on a Monday morning. That would also explain why she hadn't seen the car pulling out of the street before 9 a.m.

"Police, fire or ambulance?"

She dropped her voice as low as she could so that nobody, including Mila, would be able to hear her.

"Hi, yes. Police, please. I'd like to report a stolen vehicle."

The voice on the other end sighed. "This number is for emergencies only. I'll have to transfer you. Please hold the line."

She rolled her eyes and held the phone to her ear while she was put through to the correct line.

When it connected she gave what little details she could about the car to the man on the other end of the line. She gave the address it was taken from, the street it was driven down. She gave a detailed description of the driver; Theo, as though she was a neighbour that had seen him. She stalled as much as could, trying to remember the address of Theo's contact at the garage who would buy stolen car parts from them. There was no doubt in her mind that it was exactly where Theo was heading.

"Plate number?"

"God, I'm so sorry, I don't have it. I should have written it down!"

"Are you sure the car was stolen ma'am?"

"Yes! Why else would a scruffy young man like that be breaking the windows of that expensive car?"

A lightbulb went off somewhere deep inside the trenches of Kora's mind. A phantom memory of a kind of sickness rose up from the depths of her stomach, but this was not the same sickness she felt as a child. She recognised this specific feeling; it was car sickness. She had been there a million times. The garage where Theo took all of his cars was on a street with a complex layout made up of roundabouts, and she remembered feeling sick in the back of the car every single time he had driven around all of the perplexing twists and turns. It was a street well-known for its shady inhabitants and dealings.

Roundabout Lane.

"Do you know," she took a breath, preparing herself for her big finale, "he looked *exactly* like one of those men on TV," she tutted.

"Which men, ma'am?"

"The ones who killed all those poor people using cheap parts for cars last year from that dirty little garage on Roundabout Lane. You know the ones."

Silence ensued for only a moment before the operator finally responded.

"Are you sure?"

"Yes! Exactly like the blond one! Wasn't that awful, what they did?"

"Yes ma'am. We'll definitely send a unit down those ways to check it out. In the meantime, I've written up a report and if you have any more information, I'll give you a number to call and all you have to do is quote the report number. Do you have a pen handy, ma'am?"

She told him she did, and pretended to write down everything he cited. She thanked him and hung up just as he asked her for a name and a contact number, pretending she didn't hear him. Her hands shook as she returned her phone to her pocket.

Approaching the table once again, she strategically checked her watch. "Let's just do another lap of the street in case we missed him."

They got up and grabbed their belongings, making their way out of the hipster-esque venue. Mila stepped off to the side quickly to drop her newspaper back on the magazine rack.

The atmosphere in this small part of the city seemed more relaxed. The people didn't seem to be rushing off to be somewhere— although, Kora noticed; most of the people around were groups of mothers in their expensive leggings and faux ugg boots, pushing their prams together in their cliques, or rocking them back and forth while they sat outside cafes and on park benches, sipping on pink and green smoothies. They looked *looked after*. Kora had considered this option a few times before, but the thought of having a child made her stomach turn, no matter how hungry she was or how cold the nights got.

As they turned the corner onto Federal Drive, the street got even quieter. Trees hung low from both sides of the sidewalk shoulder, decorating the sky with budding leaves and casting flickering shade across the road. Somehow it gave the street a more private, exclusive feel.

Both girls felt the air grow tense as they neared the driveway of number twenty-four. The first thing they both noticed, was that the black Lexus had now gone. It no longer sat in the concrete tiled driveway. The house itself was modern, but simple. Moss had begun to creep along the edges of the odd tile, but it didn't look unwelcome or out of place— just nature making its presence known.

They quickly skipped up the two steps onto the concrete walkway that led to the front door. Kora noticed Mila hanging a step behind and fidgeting nervously with the sleeves of her cardigan. She wanted to reach out and calm her, reassure her, but she instead chose to ignore it in case they were being recorded on some kind of home security system. It wouldn't look right. She continued to move towards the door with her false confidence and Mila in tow. She quickly checked for cameras in the corners above the top of the door and inside the windows facing them. Nothing visible. She gave the front door and doorbell a quick look over. There was an intercom to the right of the door with a tiny camera lens embedded in the top, but she was sure it was the kind that would only turn on if the call button was pressed.

She knocked on the door, hard. Hard enough to be heard throughout the entire house. Simultaneously, she heard Mila hold her breath.

Birds chirped and tittered loudly around them in their own secret languages up in the trees and they heard the rumble of the odd car pass down the street, but the silence that emanated from the house, echoed loudly back at them. To Kora, it was an invitation.

She reached into her nearly empty handbag and produced the front door key, staring intently at the lock that it belonged to. She silently begged it to be one of the same, that he hadn't had the entire lock set changed over the course of the last two days. She pressed the small metal key to the lock, and to her relief, it slid right in with ease. Behind her, Mila let out a long breath. She turned back, grinning at a pale looking Mila.

"You held that for a while," she teased quietly, covering up her own nervousness.

The key turned and she felt the thud of a deadbolt sinking back into the door. She pulled down her sleeves over her hands as Mila had already done and turned the door handle. Swinging the door wide open, she held her arm out in front of her to stop Mila. They were not out of the woods yet.

They could see from the doorway that the house was open plan. Straight ahead, up in the corner of the ceiling sat a small, white motion sensor. A tiny red light flashed on it, detecting their movement. Kora paused, this time holding her own breath, waiting for any kind of alert or signal.

Seconds passed. Silence ensued.

She peeked her head around the doorway and spotted the keypad to disarm the alarm, but it wasn't flashing nor beeping. There was no sign at all that she had set it off.

It hadn't been set.

She let out her breath and took a few tentative steps inside the house, eyeing the keypad like a hawk, but still nothing. She turned to Mila who looked sick with anxiety, giving her a reassuring smile.

"It's okay," she whispered. "Come in."

As Mila stepped inside, uncertainty radiated from her like a deer ready to take off at the slightest of sounds. Kora in that moment wanted so badly to show her that she could protect her from everything bad in the world. She walked over and caressed her cheek, slipping her hand around the base of her neck and giving her a soft kiss on the forehead.

"We're okay. Watch this," she said as she reached into her handbag and pulled out a set of false nails.

Mila looked at her like she'd lost her mind altogether. Kora pried apart the plastic casing and retrieved the nail glue from its plastic pocket, looking up to read Mila's expression for her own amusement. Sure enough, her face still held nothing but confusion. She untwisted the cap from the top of the tube of glue, squeezing it into the keyhole of the lock. She watched Mila's expression change as she blew on the glue to dry it. Her eyes widened and she raised her hands to her mouth in both shock and understanding.

"Now, even if he does come home, he can't get in. We should have enough time to escape out the back."

"Is it okay if I still just hope that doesn't happen?"

Kora laughed sympathetically, giving her hand a tiny squeeze and pushing the door closed with her elbow, careful not to leave fingerprints.

"Let's explore."

They walked around the bottom floor, only looking, not touching. Mila pointed to a laptop sitting on a dining room table, and Kora nodded. She picked it up, careful not to touch anything else, and placed it in her bag as they walked down a small flight of stairs into the living room. Taking note of a key sitting in the lock of a set of beautiful, off-white french doors at the back of the room, she skipped over and with her sleeves still covering her hands, turned the key. It clicked quietly as it unlocked, and she left it as such. This was their escape route in case they had to leave in a hurry and without a sound.

The doors opened up into a small, but unkempt courtyard garden. A tall hedge followed the concrete tiles back around to the front of the house. Small weeds defied man, breaking up through the tiles to thrive.

Moving upstairs they found three bedrooms. Mila entered one of the rooms, too tidy to have been lived in. Kora shook her head.

"Guest room."

The next was clearly a room for storage, full of boxes and old exercise equipment; the kind you'd order from a TV advertisement at 2 a.m. There was nothing that looked as though it was worth anything at first glance so they continued down the hallway to the third bedroom.

The third bedroom most definitely belonged to Lucas. Kora pulled open the bedside cabinet drawers finding an expensive watch, a class ring and a small booklet full of plastic sleeves, each containing a credit card or loyalty card of some sort.

"Jackpot," she grinned. She put everything into her handbag while Mila checked the other drawers. Kora heard her gasp from across the room.

"What is it?"

She held open an envelope, full of cash.

Without warning, they heard a voice right below the window. It belonged to a man.

Lucas. And he sounded furious.

"*Yes, police. My Lexus has been stolen, right out of my driveway. Twenty-four Federal Drive. Yes, I'll hold.*"

Both girls stood frozen and wide-eyed, not daring to make a sound. They listened to him muttering under his breath angrily.

"*Fucking ridiculous! My fucking luck. I only went to get coffee!*"

The blood pounding in Kora's ears was so deafeningly loud, she was worried she might not be able to hear the rest of the phone call— and she *needed* to hear the rest of that phone call. Somewhere in the haze of panic, she felt Mila tugging on her sleeve with a sense of extreme urgency. Kora nodded, but stalled at the bedroom window.

"*Kora!*" she hissed, snatching at her shirt and pulled hard, almost causing Kora to lose her balance.

"Okay!" Kora whispered back, irritated but compliant.

They secured their bags over their shoulders and crept as quickly as they could down the stairs to the ground floor. They checked the windows for signs of Lucas which were clear, and made their way down the second, smaller flight towards the french doors. Kora listened for him talking into the phone as she slid the door handle down as quietly as she could, but could barely make out any of the words now. Both girls stopped dead in their tracks when they heard the unmistakable sound of a key scratching at the front door.

"*What the—*"

A loud bang from the front door echoed off the walls so hard Kora could have sworn she felt the air move. Mila jumped out of her skin.

Kora quickly pushed the door open and let Mila slip out before her. Mila turned to run down the side of the house towards the driveway but Kora saw Lucas' shadow move past a window, headed in their direction. She grabbed hold of her arm before she was out of reach and yanked her back, pulling her down towards the garden. Mila spun around and stumbled, confused, but followed without question. Kora covered Mila's mouth with her hand and pushed her backwards into a feathered gap in the hedge, forcing her right to the back so that she could squeeze in behind her and keep out of sight. Mila's eyes watered in pain. Kora could see sticks from the hedge poking into her shoulders and legs. She mouthed an apology and took her hand away from Mila's mouth.

Footsteps approached the courtyard garden.

Kora caught sight of him through the sticks and leaves, walking up to the french doors. His voice made them both jump. She instinctively brought her hand back up to cover Mila's mouth again, listening.

"*What do you mean it's already been reported and recovered? How is that possible? I've only just—*" He cut his sentence short as he tried the door handle, and it opened.

"*Hey— Listen, send somebody around to my home immediately. I think there's been a break in.*"

Mila's eyes widened in fear, but Kora silently hushed her and shook her head, as if to tell her not to worry. They watched in silence as he warily stepped inside the living room, looking around. She knew it wouldn't take long for him to realise he had been robbed. She waited with baited breath as he walked with caution up the stairs towards the second floor. He moved out of view, which meant they too were now out of his line of sight.

"Go!" Kora whispered, letting go of Mila and backing out of the hedge.

She climbed out and once she was free, they both bolted down the side of the house and down the steps onto the empty driveway. Tearing out onto the footpath, Kora grabbed Mila to slow her down.

"Stop running!"

"But—"

"We've no reason to!"

Mila reluctantly slowed to a walk. Her entire body was tense and her breathing, erratic. Kora hushed her, grabbing her hand and bringing it up to her lips before kissing it as they walked. Mila looked at her out of the corner of her eye, still fearful. Kora's eyes showed no fear in response, only triumph. They were free. After a moment, Mila's shoulders relaxed, her breathing slowed and after a few seconds of catching her breath, she squeezed Kora's hand to let her know she was okay. Kora squeezed back.

"We're safe. We did it," she whispered as they turned the corner, walking back down past the cafe.

But in the back of her mind, the same words played over and over.

"What do you mean it's already been reported and recovered?"

TWENTY-ONE

MILA

Mila's eyes fluttered open, but her eyelashes in the corner of her eyes remained stuck together with crusted rheum. *Sleep dust*, her mother would call it.

She rubbed her eyelashes with her fingertips until they became free. She had been lying awake for some time now, trying to count herself back to sleep— but she had long since given up. There was too much on her mind. Her eyes flickered over to the windows. It was still dark, but the windows were beginning to look a lighter shade of night, which meant the sun would be up in only a couple of hours.

She turned her head to the side, facing a peaceful, sleeping Kora. Her breathing was deep, undisturbed. She wouldn't wake until the late afternoon; evening, even. She wasn't a morning person.

She untangled her leg from Kora's and slipped out from underneath the lumpy blanket, careful not to disturb her as she sat on the edge of the bed. She reached down on to the floor and rifled through her cardigan pocket for her phone, flipping it open.

No new messages.

Biting her lip, she looked around the room, her mind now going a million miles an hour. She spied Kora's rugged pencil case sitting up on top of the bench. Double checking that she was still fast asleep, she inched her way towards it, moving carefully over the floorboards. Picking it up, she looked it over. She'd never really looked at it closely. It was rough, old. There was a fox embroidered onto the front of it, but the material was worn and dirty; frayed from being constantly crushed against other things. She inspected a few loose threads hanging from its ears and paws, wondering how long Kora had held onto this for, and why she had kept it. She unzipped it slowly, cringing as each tooth of the zip clicked open.

Inside, she ignored the makeup brushes and flashy brands. *Stolen*, she figured. But makeup was not what she was looking for, nor did she care whether Kora had paid for any of it. What she *was* interested in, was the empty pill bottle with no lid and torn label. It sat right in the middle, with the assortment of mismatched pills rolling loosely about in the bottom of the pencil case. She pulled the bottle out and inspected the label. It had been torn off right where the name had been. She dug a few of the pills out from the bottom. The majority were a grainy, pastel yellow. On closer inspection, she saw they had a name indented on one side, along with a number.

"S— Seroquel," she whispered slowly, sounding it out. Underneath it, read the number 400.

She flipped her phone back open and opened up the web browser. She typed in the name and waited for the page to load while she listened to Kora's deep, slow breaths. The screen page loaded, edging down slowly from the top. She could make out most of what it said before it finished loading — keywords like *anti-psychotic* and *manic episodes* rang out loudly through the maze of her mind. She closed her phone and returned the pencil case to the bench, quietly zipping it back up as she did so but keeping hold of the pills she already had in her hands.

Hopefully, they would come in handy. Hopefully, they would help.

She slipped on a pair of leggings and threw a sweater over her messy hair. She delicately picked up her boots and her satchel as she passed them, making her way to the door as silently as possible. Slipping out of the room, she closed the door behind her, on a completely unconscious, sleeping Kora.

Pulling on her boots, she high-tailed it down the stairs and out of the front doors of the hostel. The amber light glowing from the streetlights made the empty, grey streets seem less eerie— but they did not altogether charm them into a wonderland.

But she knew where she was going, and she knew how to get there.

She looked up at the sky as she reached the first snaking alleyway, taking note of the amber tone of the streetlights being emphasised by the quickly reddening sky. She wasn't in any rush.

To her surprise, the gate that she and Kora had crawled underneath was hanging wide open. As she walked straight through the gate, it didn't take her long to realise why. A large truck was parked up outside Theo's warehouse with its back door rolled up. Two rough-around-the-edges looking men were unloading boxes and stacking them inside the warehouse. As she approached the truck, one of the men glanced at her briefly, as if he'd just caught something moving out of the corner of his eye. He stopped dead in his tracks, staring, when he realised he *had* seen something in the grey corners of the morning; a young woman nonetheless.

"Der!" He called out over his shoulder. His voice was gruff, as though his lungs had smoked for years longer than he had been alive— and he wasn't exactly youthful.

"Yer got a visitor."

203

'*Der*' came ambling out of the warehouse. He was younger than the other man, but not by much. He looked Mila up and down and screwed up his face, looking away, as if he had looked directly into the sun.

"You aren't that goddamn Kora, are ye?"

Mila was taken aback by this. She shook her head quickly.

"N—No sir. I'm not. M—My name's Mila. I'm looking for Theo," she stammered.

He stared at her with a half-scowl for what seemed like an age before responding.

"He's gone," he grumbled frankly, and he turned back to the warehouse.

Mila, confused, followed him for answers.

"E—Excuse me? What do you mean *gone*? Where is he?"

He stopped and swung around, his face a mixture of emotions. Anguish, anger, pain.

"Whoever ye are, he was doing good without ye! Now he's got himself inter' trouble with them police again, off his pills an' stealin' bloody cars. He won't be comin' out for a long while. Now bugger off, unless ye want his job."

He waved her away as he turned to hide his obvious hurt. He very clearly cared about Theo.

She stood still for a moment underneath the warehouse roller door. She had been right to think the pills Kora had were his. Her mind flashed back to the day she had introduced them at the warehouse, how she had excused herself at the very last second to go upstairs and use the bathroom. A new image burned into her mind as she played another scene back; Theo's pale skin, his sunken eyes and scattered movements.

It was all beginning to make sense.

She turned and trudged back down the gravel way towards the open gate. She knew now what she had to do.

By the time she reached the hostel, daylight consumed the sky. Birds chirped freely, cars with half-asleep drivers waiting for their coffee to kick in ambled along the streets. The city was waking up, only, she hoped, that the city had not yet woken Kora.

Climbing to the top of the stairs, she kicked off her boots and tucked them under her arm. She tentatively twisted the doorknob of their room, careful not to make a sound. Peeking her head in, she saw that not only was Kora still sleeping peacefully, but she hadn't even moved an inch.

She tiptoed over to where she had picked up her boots and her satchel, and laid them carefully back in place along with her clothes, before creeping back into bed. Her bare legs and toes were undeniably polar compared to Kora's, so she was careful to keep her skin at a distance until she warmed up— as tempting as it might have been to warm her toes in between Kora's toasty thighs.

She lay there for a moment, just thinking; listening to Kora's rhythmic breathing. She tapped the back of her fingertips lightly on the mattress by her head, deep in thought as she stared off into space. Suddenly, her nail tapped something hard and cold.

Kora's phone.

It was poking out from underneath her pillow. She eyed it with suspicion for a short moment before slipping it out and opening it up with a click. The blue light glared at her menacingly, hurting her eyes. She squinted, attempting to barricade the light with her long lashes but they did nothing to help her. She flicked through the different folders on Kora's phone before stopping at her recent call list. She opened it up, bracing herself in anticipation of what she thought she might find.

She didn't even have to scroll. There it was, right at the top; an emergency call, made at nine-thirty-ish yesterday morning. The same time they had been in the cafe yesterday. The same time Kora had disappeared to the bathroom while

Mila had had her nose stuck into a newspaper. She finally understood— It was just her and Kora now.

Scrolling through her contacts, she deleted Theo's number before then deleting her own. She closed the phone and placed it back underneath Kora's pillow.

Overcome with a wave of all-encompassing exhaustion as all the pieces fell into place, she stared at the ceiling, letting the cracks in the paint swirl as she let her eyelids grow heavy. She closed her eyes and listened to the birds in between the rumble of traffic. She tried to find a pattern, a language, but her mind could not decipher any of it. She breathed out a laugh to herself for being so silly, thinking she could understand the birds if she listened hard enough. She had soaked this moment up long enough. It was time to go.

She crept back out of bed, gathering her clothes, toothbrush and everything else. She looked around for Kora's tattered notebook, finding it inside her handbag. Opening it up, she took the folded the notes and stuffed them inside her pocket. She grabbed her scarf, wiping down every surface she had ever touched; thankful that it was such a small room. She stood in the bathroom doorway for a moment, just watching Kora as she slept. She turned, leaving one final goodbye on the bathroom mirror before slinging her bags over her shoulder and slipping out of the room, leaving everything almost as though she had never even existed in the first place.

She fumbled her way down the stairs and to the front desk with her belongings, dropping them at her feet. The desk clerk barely looked up from his phone.

Spying his name tag, she smiled. "Riley?"

He looked up, surprised at hearing his own name. His eyes met with hers and he instantly became uncomfortable.

"I was always curious about what your name was."

"Y— You were?" he stammered, cheeks flushing a deep red. He looked around, likely for Kora but she was nowhere in sight.

"Always," she beamed. "Now I know."

He looked nervous.

She gave him a warm smile. "Can I pretty please pay for the next month in advance?"

He stared back at her in confusion. "You, uh, look like you're leaving," he said, motioning to her bags.

She nodded. "It's for the girl I was hanging out with. She's kind of bad news, I think, but I don't want to leave her without a place to stay."

"That's more than what most people would do. Your friend— uh, doesn't seem like the type who would do that for you. Are you sure?"

"I'm sure," she smiled, handing over a credit card. "It's her card anyway."

She rested her hands and face on the counter, staring at him as he put the payment through. She wondered if he had a girlfriend. She wondered who he was outside of this building.

The machine beeped. *Payment declined.*

He looked up, catching her gaze as he handed the credit card back to her.

"Uh, it declined."

She looked surprised, "Sorry! I thought—"

He cleared his throat. "It's OK. Do you want to pay in cash?"

"That's alright. I tried. Would you be able to return that card to my friend when she wakes up?" She leaned over the counter, closing the distance between them, whispering, "Honestly, I think it might be stolen."

"Shit," he muttered, checking the computer screen in front of him. "Uh, sure. Was that everything?"

"Actually, no, there's something else," she let the idea play on her lips, but she knew she had no choice, and she was now running out of time.

"Riley, how much would it cost for you to forget I was ever here?"

207

TWENTY-TWO
CAUGHT

"Let me *the fuck* go!" Kora shrieked.

She stood outside the hostel on the sidewalk, handcuffed and furious. Beads of fresh blood swelled from a cut above her eyebrow, spilling down one by one over the bruising skin surrounding it. Lights flashed alarmingly from an ambulance parked against the curb. Two paramedics stood by looking irritable.

A female police officer with platinum blonde hair pulled back into a too-tight bun stood behind her, holding both of her arms as she continuously tried to wrench her shoulders away from her grip. Another, more official looking officer stood facing her. He wore a dark grey, casual business suit with an identification badge hanging from a lanyard around his neck. He was holding a warrant in one hand and Kora's handbag in the other.

A detective.

"Are you going to explain to me why you have a stolen credit card in your possession, belonging to one, *Mr. Stephen Hayes*?" His voice was deep, masculine.

"Who the *fuck* is Stephen Hayes?!"

She could tell she hadn't a chance in hell that he was going to believe a word she said; truth or not. She scowled and continued trying to shrug out of the police officer's hold.

"I would watch your attitude if I were you. You're in some very serious trouble. We've been looking for you for a while."

"Am I under arrest?"

"You're about to be."

"For *what*?" she spat.

The detective narrowed his eyes. "Let's begin with resisting arrest, credit card fraud, grievous bodily harm, attempted murder and," he paused, looking at his notepad, "identity theft— but we'll have to see about that last one. I mean, this I.D you have here definitely does not belong to you, does it, *Jessica*?" he scoffed.

Her jaw dropped in disbelief. "What the fuck do you mean *attempted murder*?!"

A crowd of people dressed for the clubs nearby had gathered around her, whispering. Some of the braver ones hurled abuse at the police, trying to impress their friends; others looked concerned and had taken out their cellphones to take photos and videos of the scene. This only angered her further as her wild eyes frantically searched the crowd for Mila.

All in the same moment, a movement caught her eye. A flash of red she didn't recognise but long brown hair that she did. She caught small, frantic glimpses of it as it moved away from the hordes of people spilling out into the street to see what all the commotion was.

"There!" She shrieked, taking the police officer by surprise, jumping out of her grasp. "There she is!" The officer moved quickly, regaining control of Kora but very clearly scolding herself for letting her go in the first place.

The detective sighed.

"Who?"

"*Mila!* My—" she faltered, "my *girlfriend*! I was with her all night, she'll tell you!" She stood on her tiptoes, motioning in the direction of the girl in the red coat.

He tried to follow her line of sight as best he could. Her hands were cuffed and she was unable to point in any direction but behind her. His eyes glossed over the faces in the crowd of people, wondering if anyone would stand out.

"Her! In the red!" She screeched frantically, nodding at herds of curious faces towards a slim, brown-haired girl walking away from the crowd.

Spotting her, he gave the arresting officer a look and sighed. "Hold tight."

He placed Kora's handbag on the bonnet of the squad car. He looked up and down the street for oncoming cars before jogging after the girl. The crowd parted to make way for him, muttering abusive one-liners as he passed. He suppressed the urge to roll his eyes. About twenty feet away from the girl, he slowed his pace, calling after her. If she had somehow been involved with his perpetrator, he needed to know.

"Excuse me, miss?"

The girl spun around, surprised to have been followed. She took him in, realising he was an authoritative figure and slowed to a hesitant stop. Her long hair flew up around her, caught in the breeze.

"I beg your apology, miss. May I have a moment?"

"Uh— Sure." Her voice was heavy with uncertainty, but she gave him a polite smile nonetheless.

As he approached her, he watched her eyes search his face for danger. However, he did not interpret this as an admission of guilt. Caution seemed like a natural reaction for a girl having been approached while walking alone in the evening.

"Excuse me for interrupting you ma'am, my name is Detective Declan Parker. We have a situation here across the road and a woman we have in custody claims to know you.

I'm going to need to ask you a few questions." He grimaced at the official-sounding request and then smiled. "If you don't mind, ma'am."

Her face slowly changed from caution to confusion.

"I don't know anybody here." She looked past him at the small crowd gathered in the street, puzzled. "I'm new to the city," she explained.

He regarded her for a moment, absentmindedly noticing how attractive she was.

"Yes, ma'am, I understand. But if you'd humour me for a minute, it would be much appreciated." He gave her a comforting smile.

She gave him a smile of her own in return, nodding.

He watched her carefully as they walked back over to the scene together. She moved gracefully; unlike most people that hung around this end of town. Thankfully, the crowd had begun to disperse without the rising levels of drama to keep them entertained. Kora was still arguing with the arresting officer, motioning in the girl's direction.

"She's bleeding!" the girl said quietly, alarmed as Kora turned to face them.

"Please excuse the scene, ma'am— I should have warned you. She broke free of my partner's grip and ran out into the street. She was clipped by a passing car."

"Oh my god! Shouldn't she be on her way to the hospital?"

He nodded solemnly. "Unfortunately, we already tried. The paramedics made an attempt to clean her up and assess her for a concussion, but she refused medical treatment."

Spotting the ambulance, the girl nodded in understanding.

As they approached Kora, she let out a dramatic sigh of relief.

"Mila! Thank god! Can you please tell these *assholes* they've got the wrong person?"

The girl seemed startled. He watched her taking Kora in. There was blood smeared from her forehead to her chin and her mascara had smudged; mixing in with the dried, red streaks. Her hair was a tangled mess and her knees were scraped and dirty, presumedly from being hit by the car.

This girl looks crazy, she decided.

Kora frowned, confused and desperate as she read her expression.

"Tell them they're wrong! Tell them I didn't do anything!" She began to sob hysterically.

The girl looked at the female officer holding Kora, then at Detective Parker, and then back at Kora with a look of utmost discomfort.

"I'm— I'm sorry. Do we know each other?"

Kora's sobs faltered as though they had never been real. She stared back at the girl, suddenly dead-faced and devoid of emotion. Speaking slowly, her voice began to shake with building rage. Her insides burned with venom.

"Do we fucking *what*?!"

"I— I don't know who you're looking for," the young woman said softly, her eyes full of sympathy.

Kora stared back at her like a caged animal, wild and feral. The girl gave her a look of genuine concern and turned to the detective.

"I'm so sorry, I just don't know who she is. I don't recognise her at all."

She turned back to Kora, catching the last, tiny shred of hope vanish from her expressionless face.

"I'm so sorry, honey. I don't know who you are. I think you're a bit confused."

Kora's face twisted into a mixture half-way between disbelief and fury. "*Don't call me h—*" she started, but the girl gently cut her off.

"I'm sure you'll get the help you need." She smiled, but her face was full of pity as she took a step back.

She turned to the detective once again, speaking quietly this time, to only him. "I think she really needs to be taken to the hospital. It looks like she's hit her head pretty hard."

The detective sighed, exasperated. "I think you might be right, ma'am. I'm sorry for interrupting your evening."

"That's okay. I feel for her. She seems so sure," she paused, looking up at him with concern scrawled across her features. "You will look for her friend, won't you?"

He glanced down at her, taken aback by this stranger's sincerity. It was not something he encountered often in his line of work.

"Yes ma'am. Of course."

All of a sudden, Kora shrieked with rage and lunged at the girl, throwing her entire body towards her, but the officer holding her arms tightened her grip and pulled her back.

"Right! That's enough. You have the right to remain silent. Anything you say can and will be held against you in a court of law. You have the right to an attorney—" Anything more that was said was drowned out by Kora's feral screeches as the officer pushed her head first into the back of the patrol car. The moment her feet had crossed the threshold, she slammed the door closed.

The detective looked on as she struggled. He glanced sideways at the young woman standing next to him, uncertain for just a fleeting moment.

"May I please see your identification, miss?"

"Of course," she nodded. She reached into her satchel, producing her driver's licence.

He looked it over for a second, finally, shaking his head in disbelief.

"Ma'am, I sincerely apologise."

He turned to her, taking off his uniform hat in a polite, gentlemanly gesture. It was not something that was often done in this day and age, and she noticed it. Not only did she notice it but the look on her face said she found it somewhat endearing.

"That's okay," she said, seemingly a little flustered. "I'm sorry I couldn't be of more help to you."

"You've been plenty help."

She smiled shyly. Her long locks bounced off her shoulders and lay fallen around her midsection, resting down by her waist. He tore his eyes away from hers and cleared his throat, standing up a little straighter. "Here's my card, if you ever find that you need it." He reached into his pocket and pulled out a small, official business card with his name and private phone number on the front. "Feel free to give me a call if you happen to remember any information, or if there's anything you need. Just let me know."

She reached out, gently taking the card from him.

"Enjoy the rest of your day, ma'am."

She nodded, smiling gratefully as they parted ways.

As he turned back to the scene, now devoid of the crowd of onlookers, he wondered to himself what she was doing in this part of town. This was the wrong side of the tracks, so to speak. She was in her early twenties, well-dressed and clean. This part of town was no place for a girl like that.

After a few short paces, he turned back to her, his curiosity winning out.

"Excuse me—"

Only concrete stared back; the street was empty behind him. She had already gone.

Kora sat, breathless and shaky in the back of the squad car. The police officer who had held her was standing outside, guarding the car. Her mind was cloudy and throbbing. She was having trouble looking to her left; every time she tried, she saw stars appear around the edges of her vision, feeling an excruciating stabbing pain behind her eye socket. She assumed it was from hitting her head off the concrete when she had tried to make a break for it, running head first into that car.

The pain of betrayal ran through her blood and she fought back panicked and angry tears. She squeezed her eyes shut and bit down, gritting her teeth. It was too much. The walls of her throat seized up as she screamed in silence, caving under the pressure of her emotions. She choked, her lungs knotting, dragging in ragged breaths of air between almost-sobs.

She racked her tangled mind, searching for answers as to why Mila had completely dismissed her the way she had. Where had she been when the detective had woken her, knocking on their bedroom door? Had Mila hidden in the bathroom as she had pushed her way past the detective and bolted down the stairs and out into the street? Slipped out of the room as they had given chase? Maybe she *had* been hiding. Maybe she had a plan.

She squeezed her eyes shut, wondering if she had missed something, *anything*. A code word of sorts, a knowing look perhaps, but she came up empty-handed as her head continued to throb. Her panic loosened its grip around her throat. She took in a long, deep breath, in through her nose and out through her mouth. The air forced itself into her brooding veins, clearing her mind of the stale smoke inside. Dr. Hurley had made her practice this many times whenever she lost control of herself as a child. He had told her it was a practice that was hers to use whenever she liked and that she could practice it at any time, anywhere.

"Don't let your emotions overpower your intelligence, Kora," he had said. A valuable lesson she had forever tossed aside.

The cold, unforgiving metal of the handcuffs pressed hard against her wrists, not wanting to be forgotten. She began to focus on what little she *could* do from the back seat of a police car. Shimmying her shoulders forward, she pushed her cuffed hands under her backside and then further down,

215

under her thighs. Lifting her feet off the floor of the car, she brought her hands underneath them like a jump rope. Having her hands in front of her, although trapped in handcuffs, was unquestionably more comfortable than having them locked behind her back.

Assuming the back door would have a child safety lock engaged, she decided to try it anyway. She knew she needed to exhaust all of her options as soon as possible, and on the one in a million chance the tiny lock had actually been forgotten, she'd never forgive herself if she could have escaped so easily. She flicked the handle. Unfortunately for her, the universe was not giving her one of those chances.

She watched as the detective went back inside the hostel. The grim reality slowly began to creep in, wrapping it's joyless, claustrophobic fingers around her tiny body. There was no escape from the police. For the first time in three years, she would be in somebody else's custody. She would be locked in a building, unable to leave. Unlike the foster system where she knew she could have the choice to stay in the program until twenty-one or leave at eighteen, police custody did not have an age limit and the police did what they liked.

She sat, bug-eyed and unblinking in the back seat. The possibility of being unable to prove her innocence, of never seeing Mila again. Her fingertips shook so violently at the thought that she had to squeeze her hands between her thighs, trying to take solace in the fact that so far, neither the detective nor the paramedics knew her name.

She pressed her nose up against the window as the detective returned. She could see that the streets had cleared of the tens of passersby that had looked on as she had been arrested. Her hot breath fogged up the window as she watched him converse with the paramedics. Not once did they smile. They did, however, seem to agree on whatever idea it was that they were collaborating on regarding her, as once the exchange was over, all three personnel looked toward the car— towards her, and nodded. She could hear nothing but her own heartbeat. The car muffled almost every sound from the outside world and her very real fear of the unknown, crawled deep inside her skin.

She watched each footstep he made towards the car with growing dread. The passenger side door was the first to open, and the car rocked slightly to one side as Detective Parker settled into the passenger seat. He did not turn around to look at her, but she could see his mind working through different ways to approach her as the female officer climbed into the driver's seat.

She watched his every movement carefully, wanting— no — *needing* to learn all that she could about him if she was going to be able to beat him in his own game.

TWENTY-THREE

ONE CALL

Kora screeched, teary-eyed and desperate through the locked door of an interview room in the downtown police station.

"*Fuck you!* I get a phone call!" She thumped her fists against the door. It rattled slightly, but she knew it would do nothing. They had taken the tie-up strap from her jacket, they had taken her heels, her handbag and the silver necklace that Mila had given her. *All for her own safety*.

She scoffed at the thought. If she really wanted to do some damage, they wouldn't be able to stop her. All she wanted was to speak to Mila. *Alone*. If that meant a phone call was her only option then so be it.

She turned around to face the room, resting her back against the door in defeat. The door was cold and sent shivers down her spine. The room itself seemed rather minimalist and yet the air felt clammy. A table sat directly in the centre of the room with two plastic chairs on one side, and one singular chair on the other. In the far corner of the room sat a large, black and silver box, angled towards the table. Near the top, Kora could see the small, circular lens of a camera, and below it, an assortment of different coloured buttons. She glared at it, unsure whether she was already being recorded or whether they had to ask her permission to do so first. There had always been rumours amongst rats, laws and rules the police couldn't break, rights a person in custody supposedly had— but unless you had already been to jail for long enough to decide to get a law degree in prison, nobody who ended up in one of these rooms ever really knew what they were talking about. It was all pipe dream guesswork. She wasn't even sure that she was legally allowed a phone call.

She paced around the room slowly, feeling it out. She didn't want to sit in the singular chair on its own, where she was expected to sit. She settled herself on top of the table with her legs hanging off the floor, facing the door. She stared blankly at it, hostile, until eventually, it opened.

Detective Parker, tall, dark and serious entered the room. Instantly, she noticed him taking note of her and where she sat. He placed a small, polystyrene cup full of water on the table next to her before taking a seat over on the other side of the table. Her eyes followed him the whole way. He cleared his throat, placing a small notebook and a manila folder on the table in front of him without opening either one.

"Would you like to speak with your lawyer?"

"I'm not speaking to anybody until I get my fucking phone call!"

"Would you like to make your phone call before or after I ask you a few questions?"

"*Now!*"

"Sure." He gave a small nod, but she didn't trust him. She could tell he was playing a game, she just didn't know what the rules were yet.

"Would you like me to bring you your cellphone?"

She snorted. So *that* was his game. She was too quick. There was no way she was going to give him permission to go through her phone. *Nice try.*

"Are the police so poorly paid these days that they don't have their own phone line?" she retorted.

He sighed and leaned back against his chair, crossing his arms.

"Look, I can keep you in here all night. More than likely all day tomorrow, too before I even think about getting this over with if you continue not to co-operate. Let's just make this ride as smooth as possible for everyone involved, alright?"

Her temper flared up again. "I'm *allowed* a phone call! Do your fucking job!"

"You just say the word and I'll bring you your phone."

"Give me yours," she shot back.

"Deal. What's the phone number?"

She scowled at him. It was too easy. She didn't like to be played; albeit the idea of getting whatever this was over and done with appealed to her infinitely. She was in two minds as she scowled at the notebook and pen he picked up and laid out in front of her. Her father had taught her never to give the police the information they asked for. She couldn't just *give* him Mila's phone number; she couldn't betray Mila like that. She wasn't even entirely sure if she knew the phone number by heart. There had to be another way. She needed to buy herself some more time.

"Fine," she told him boldly, scribbling a phone number down in the notebook.

He raised an eyebrow at her but she merely shrugged, feigning disinterest— but she could feel the anxiety taking over, squirming its way into each open pore of her body. He gathered the notebook and folder, leaving the room and locking the door behind him. She sat quietly, tapping her fingers on the table in anticipation, deep in thought. Her mind kicked into overdrive trying to devise a plan, and fast.

After what felt like an age, he returned, empty-handed and expressionless. He leaned against the wall next to the door, tutting.

"That number doesn't exist, kiddo. You'd better try again. I'm clocking out soon, and you can be sure nobody else will bother with you until morning."

Her heart sank as hope began to slip through her fingertips. She would have to give him something.

"Call the hostel, cop. There's a phone in our room."

"*Our?*"

"Yes, *our*. Mine and my girlfriend's."

"Ah, right. *Mila*, was it?" he scoffed. She glared at him with everything she had.

He eyed her carefully before opening the door and once again locking it behind him. She ignored him and looked up at the ceiling, exasperated and pleading. *Please just let her be back at the hostel.*

Time crept along slowly. There was no clock in the room; the walls were completely bare. She had no idea how long she had been sitting there. She had moved from her perch up on top of the table and was now sitting in one of the chairs, resting her head in her arms. She couldn't remember how long she had been like that. Her shoulders ached and her head throbbed. The detective had been gone longer than it should take to make a simple phone call and that alone made her stomach twist itself into a plethora of tiny knots.

She closed her eyes, thinking about the first thing she was going to do when she got out of that room. She pictured Mila's face, her soft, perfect cheekbones; the way the light would hit her kaleidoscopic eyes as she threw her head back, laughing when Kora laughed; the way the sun caught the lighter strands of her hair and glittered, giving off the illusion that her cells contained everything mysterious and magical in the world.

She couldn't stand being away from her. She *needed* her.

Somewhere, lost in the depth of her thoughts she must have drifted off, inviting dreams consisting only of swirling marble skin and tangled legs within her sleepy mind.

She woke suddenly in a panic at the sound of the door unlocking. Her head snapped up and turned towards the door as she watched it open, only then registering where she was and what she was doing there.

Detective Parker entered the room along with the blonde police officer from earlier, who watched her quietly from the corner of the room as he closed the door behind them. He cleared his throat, leaning against the wall and folding his arms across his chest.

"Tired?" he asked smugly. She glared sleepily back.

"What took you so fucking long?"

"I told you not to play games with me. I *will* leave you in here."

She was suddenly hit with a wave of indescribable confusion. She looked back and forth between him and the blonde woman.

"What do you mean? I told you to call the h—"

"There was never any need. We thought we'd let you sweat it out in hopes of a confession, but we don't really need one from you. No more games, *Kora*. The desk clerk informed us on site today that the room is definitely under your name, and he had definitely never heard of nor seen anyone who goes by the name of your imaginary friend, *Mila*. Time's up."

Every moving thing inside her body came to an abrupt halt.

He knew her name. He knew who she was.

Her fingers gripped her forearms so tight that she was beginning to cut off her own circulation. She fought back tears through gritted teeth, cursing herself for her stupidity.

"Where's Mila?"

"*There is no Mila*," he snapped, raising his voice well above a comfortable decibel level. Kora stood from her seat bravely, every bone in her body shaking.

"There *is*! She was with me every single day! She *spoke* to the desk clerk!"

"I don't humour liars, Kora. I've seen your file. By some coincidence, Officer Ryall here is somewhat familiar with your case." He took a thick manila folder from the officer's hands and slapped it on the table. "Either you're very sick, or you're very stupid and either way, I'd be very, *very* careful with your next move."

"You can't charge me with anything if you don't have any evide—"

"*I've had enough!*" he roared, cutting her off. He had lost what little patience he had left. "A man was *attacked* in broad daylight. Not only did you just happen to have his credit card in your possession but Officer Ryall and I *personally* inspected your hostel room."

Kora for once was lost for words. She began frantically piecing together what little she could. *The man in the alleyway. But how did—*

"Would you like to know what we found?"

Her blood froze. It felt like flick knives had opened themselves up inside her arteries. She sat silent. Fearful. Guilty and confused.

"Would you like to guess, or should I just give you the cold, hard facts?" The question was clearly rhetorical. He reached into his pocket, flipping open his notepad.

"A laptop, jewellery, watches, a cellphone— all of which match the description of items taken in a burglary earlier this week. Not to mention the necklace you were wearing when we brought you in, reported stolen in a separate break-in before that. Which puts you at the top of our suspect list for a string of burglaries. But the icing on the cake," he paused, shaking his head in disbelief. "The icing was the tiny trophy you kept, sitting pretty on the bathroom mirror. The newspaper article detailing the assault of the man who was attacked. Detailing the crime *you* committed."

She could taste nothing but bile. She had never seen a newspaper article. She wanted to change the narrative— she would talk her way out of this. *They can't prove anything.*

She clenched her jaw and blocked out his words with the only thing she cared about in that moment.

"Where is Mila?" she asked him again, but her voice was weak and it shook violently. She didn't care anymore. She needed to know. Maybe she had thought on her feet. Maybe she had packed everything and left. Maybe she would just return home to her family, at least until she found her. They would start again; save for a home, get real jobs, have a real life together. They would make it this time.

"Oh honey, you're not paying attention," he tutted. "There is no Mila."

"Don't call me honey—" she started, but he cut her off.

"Now, I don't know about your knowledge of the law but here's something I know. Attempted murder carries a heavy, *heavy* prison sentence. So does breaking and entering and believe it or not, so does robbery."

She opened her mouth to argue, knowing her portrayal of innocence was on knife's edge. With a stroke of desperate confusion, she grasped at her defence. In her anxious stupor she could only manage one small, broken sentence.

"I didn't— You can't prove..." she trailed off as he produced a single A4 piece of paper from his own folder, placing it on the table in front of her.

She didn't even need to look at it. She knew from only a half-hearted glimpse that somehow, it had her face on it. She finally tore her eyes from his and looked down at the piece of paper.

There she was.

It was a still-frame of her looking inside a shop window, captured by a security camera. The shop window she had peeked into just before she had heard the man's voice coming from the alleyway.

"That's nothing," she declared boldly, finding her voice. "That's just me looking through a fucking window."

"Let me explain," he began, smirking. Her heart immediately sank at his display of confidence. "That footage was captured approximately twenty-five minutes before a call was made for an ambulance for an unidentified male, *John Doe*, found about twenty feet from that window. You were the only person around. Three days later, another call was made to emergency services to report a man missing, *Stephen Hayes*. A man that matches the description of our victim found in the alleyway. Unfortunately for both him and us, the colleague who came forward to identify him, couldn't, since his face was disfigured beyond apparent recognition. Interestingly enough, we found *your* fingerprints all over his apartment. So you knew him, which makes this premeditated."

His words came crashing down around her like an avalanche of panic. She felt them closing in on the air around her, stealing any oxygen her lungs were desperately trying to grab at. *Why is there no air?*

She suddenly realised she couldn't feel her legs all. *Are they still there?*

She couldn't be sure. Her head felt so heavy, too heavy. She began to sway and her eyes rolled back involuntarily as her eyelids began to close over them.

Officer Ryall rushed to catch her before hit her head on the table. Her breathing was shallow, but Detective Parker wasn't fazed in the slightest. He was already convinced that she was a liar, and a good one at that.

"Time to face facts. You're going to be locked in a concrete room with who knows, for how long."

She tried to clear the fog that was rolling in over her brain. She couldn't see a way out anymore. She was almost too tired to fight it, but she knew that she needed to hear Mila's voice, if only to say goodbye.

"My phone. Her number is on my phone."

He leaned back in surprise. He had been convinced that he had weakened her defence enough to start telling some form of the truth, but he hadn't expected her to stick to her story about her girlfriend.

He knew the entire process would be much easier with a straight-forward confession no matter how much evidence he had stacked up against her. She hadn't asked to speak to a lawyer yet which caused him to pity her. He thought perhaps she didn't understand that she needed to speak with one and was completely within her rights to do so. But she was a criminal, she was guilty, and he had her in police custody. On top of that, she didn't *want* a lawyer, only one simple phone call to a person who didn't exist. And if she *did* exist, she could be an accomplice. Two arrests for the work of one; what more could he want?

"This is your last chance."

She seemed only semi-coherent but mumbled her compliance, nodding her head in defeat. Propping her up, Officer Ryall held her until she stopped swaying. He gave her a firm appreciative nod. He didn't want to risk an injury in his interview room on his watch.

Kora squeezed her eyes shut tight, then she cleared her throat and took a deep breath.

"Please."

He nodded and left the room.

By the time he returned, she had pulled herself together. Officer Ryall was back at her original post in the corner of the room.

She had come to terms with the fact that she was about to try and fight for innocence she didn't have but right now, all she wanted was to hear Mila's voice. Until her, she felt like she had always been alone, and even when she wasn't alone, her company was never real. *Mila* was real. Mila had given her something real to hold onto, to protect; a reason to get out of bed, a reason to want a future. She needed to tell her what was happening; that she was sorry that she couldn't look after her tonight; that she would do everything she could to get out of there and be with her again.

And then she would delete Mila's number and everything else on her phone.

He handed her cellphone over. She squeezed it tight, silently begging for Mila to pick up, wherever she was. She flipped open the phone slowly, and the screen lit up on command. She carefully clicked through her list of contacts, each name a reminder of who she might never see or speak to again; each name, a person who would never know where she had gone. Absentmindedly, she looked at what letter she was up to and saw she had passed Mila's name without realising. She scrolled back up, searching with every ounce of focus she had left, but she found nothing. She was back at the top of the list. Her heart stopped.

"It— It's not here!" she cried out, her voice shaking. She frantically scrolled back down through the list again, this time searching for Theo's name.

Also gone.

"I've had about enough of th—"

"I'M NOT LYING!" She roared. "The number was here!"

He paused, looking at her more closely. The blood smeared across her face had now dried. A violet bruise with hues of blue had formed above her eyebrow. He quietly considered the fact that she may have hit her head harder than they both had realised, that perhaps she was concussed after all. She was agitated, and although he knew for certain she was a liar, as most were in this room, he couldn't find the lie as she spoke now. She was genuinely confused and upset, and it was, in fact, his job to be able to tell the difference.

"Alright," he reasoned, his tone firm, but less harsh around the edges. "The number isn't in your phone. Can you remember it by heart, or should we bring up your phone records?"

She paused in thought, hearing the pity in his voice. She wasn't sure if she knew the number. She wasn't even sure at this point if Mila *was* real anymore. But he was giving her a chance and she was growing desperate. She didn't want to give consent for anybody to look through her phone records— Who knows what he might find. She had to take a chance.

"I think I know it," she said, finally.

He decided not to press her. It would do no more good, and he already had her in custody. She could do no harm. He stood, without saying a word and gave her a small nod.

"Would you like some privacy?"

She nodded and both he and Officer Ryall left the room, locking the door behind them.

"You're letting her take a private call?" she asked.

"We both know she won't be getting out of police custody any time soon and one private phone call won't make a difference, no matter who she calls," he shrugged. "We have her, regardless."

Kora dialled the number tentatively, the way she thought she remembered it.

It rang, and it rang.

She opened the manila folder that had been left on the table. Two faded photographs were paper-clipped to the top page. She stopped dead in her tracks, finding herself looking into the raw, reddened eyes of her six-year-old self. They were photographs of *her*. Her eyes widened as she took a closer look at the first picture. She was sitting on her father's lap; a man whose face she hadn't seen in eleven years.

She felt it happen before she could stop it— A mixture of vomit and bile flushed upward through her esophagus and spilled from her mouth, soaking the files. She gagged, her throat burning, attempting to wipe the warm puke from the photographs but only making more of a mess.

All of a sudden, through her panic, she heard the dial tone click and a kind of graceless silence ensued. She turned away from the photographs, pressing the phone hard into her ear. She could feel a wet smudge of bile trickle from the bone of her wrist, down the inside of her arm. She ignored it, pulling the phone away from her face to check if it was working.

The call had connected. The timer was counting upwards, already at 0:03 seconds.

"Mila?"

A dull, bored-sounding voice on the other end answered.

"Who?"

It sounded like Mila's voice, only not as warm. Nowhere near as inviting.

She faltered for a second before deciding she was probably just cautious.

"Mila, it's me."

Silence.

"Mila, I need you to listen." Her voice cracked and tears stung as she thought of never seeing her again. "I don't know who that credit card belonged to or how I ended up with it. They can't keep me here for long, okay. I'll be out soon," she lied, hoping Mila would believe her through the acidic tears that dug out holes in her throat. "I'll find you. You're not alone."

She pressed the phone so hard into her ear that it was aching. She just needed to hear her voice, to know she understood, but the static silence continued. All of a sudden, the voice on the other end began humming a familiar tune, but she was too agitated to focus on what it was.

"Mila! *Fuck!*"

And then the voice on the other end answered.

"I don't think you know who I am."

The voice was so devoid of emotion it sent shivers down Kora's spine.

"Mila! I know it's you! I can hear your fucking voice!"

"Mm, is it?"

"What the fuck," she breathed. Her heart was beating a million miles an hour. She didn't know whether to hang up or try to figure out what was happening. Panic and confusion were closing in on her as her hands shook violently.

"Let's play never have I ever."

Her brows furrowed, not understanding, but she felt an instantaneous surge of relief knowing that she had been right. It was without a doubt Mila on the other end of the line.

"Mila, what is wrong with you? Did you hear what I said?"

"Never have I ever—" she started but Kora interrupted her, frustration taking over.

"Really? *Now?!*" Her shrill voice was becoming more and more hysterical by the second.

"Never have I ever," she repeated, "taken somebody's brother away from them."

"Wh— What are you talking about?"

"Never have I ever taken somebody's brother away from them," she repeated.

Kora's mind scrambled, connecting what little dots she could. *Brother? Whose brother?*

Her face burned as she considered that fact that she could be talking about the man in the alley. It could very well have been somebody's brother, somebody's husband, somebody's father. What didn't make sense to her was why she would bring it up. Mila was every bit as much to blame as she was. She was there, too. She witnessed it. She *helped* Kora get away. Was— Was that man her brother?

Kora's rambling, spiralling thoughts were interrupted once again by the voice.

"Where's Theo?"

Kora was truly lost. She frantically searched her mind for answers. Theo didn't have a sister; his sister was dead. Theo had killed her— Hadn't he? *Hadn't he?*

Her panicked breaths became quick and shallow. Her chest burned and her eyes stung. The edges of her vision were dark and cloudy, the black edges slowly creeping in on her.

"Mila, stop," she begged. "I'm hanging up."

They both knew it was an empty threat.

"Never have I ever—" but Kora didn't want to hear it.

"MILA!" she roared, but she was interrupted as the voice on the other end of the phone continued fiercely.

"—climbed a dead oak tree— Oh, no. That *was* just me, wasn't it, Kora?"

These words were not a question. They dragged out slowly, as if they were being savoured.

Kora felt her knees go weak. Every part of her body shook in fear. The tune— the tune Mila had hummed on the phone; in the elevator; in the bathroom at the hostel— she recognised it. It was the opening theme to *Thelma and Louise*.

She understood.

She finally understood.

"*Camilla*," she whimpered, breathless and wide-eyed, her voice breaking with such fragility that it was barely audible.

Every part of her body caved in on itself.

And then everything went black.

TWENTY FOUR

RELEASED

"Camilla! How have you been?"

"Oh Erica, I've been so busy! How about you?"

The receptionist lit up with excitement, but before she could get a word out, Camilla gasped.

"Oh my gosh— I nearly forgot! Congratulations on your engagement!"

"Thank-you!" She squealed in delight, showing off the ring sitting snug around her finger. The diamonds glistened, filled with a million secret promises, whispers and kisses. "I couldn't *wait* to send you a message! I wish you'd called!"

Her mouth gaped open wide in complete admiration of Erica's new engagement ring. She tentatively reached out and grabbed hold of her outstretched hand, finding herself mesmerised as the light hit each intricate cut of the diamond.

She heard a door open from behind her and immediately she knew he was there. She had known he would emerge at the sound of her voice in the foyer. She wanted to let go of Erica's hand but she knew she couldn't. Not yet.

"Camilla," Dr. Hurley exclaimed with a ruffle of his moustache. "How delightful to see you, my dear."

She turned around and gave him her biggest smile, letting her hand linger on Erica's for just a second more before letting it go. He had seen the physical contact and that was what mattered.

"Come through, Camilla. Let us talk." He motioned to the door behind him.

She nodded politely, mouthed a quick goodbye to Erica and followed him into his office.

There was a faint but familiar aroma in the room that she had grown accustomed to. It was neutral but homely, as if beige were a scent. It was akin to breathing into a teddy bear you've had your whole life, just to catch the fleeting ghost of a memory you can't quite grasp with your mind's fingertips.

Dr. Hurley made himself comfortable in his aged, blue chair. She could see that time was beginning to catch up with him. His movements were stiff, laboured. He moved with much less ease as when they had first met, but that had been somewhere near sixteen years ago. His hair, that had always seemed to have a touch of grey dancing along the edges, had now been embraced by the wispy colour, although he kept it parted in the same neat style he always had.

He cleared his throat before beginning in a firm, but forgiving tone.

"Now, Camilla. It's good to see you. First of all, thank-you for rescheduling your appointment. Might I ask why you missed our session last week? Surely I needn't remind you that missing your therapy sessions is prohibited?"

"I know, I'm so sorry," she apologised, her voice thick with remorse.

"That's quite alright. I must ask, was there a reason as to why you failed to notify Erica or myself?"

"I— I had an argument with Stephen and we— Well, we ended things. I guess I just needed some time to myself. I'm sorry I didn't call."

"I see," Dr. Hurley said, pausing for a moment. "I'm quite sorry to hear that. How are you coping?"

"I'm okay, actually. It was a mutual decision, for the best— We don't need to talk about it."

"That's very mature of you, Camilla. While I am disappointed you didn't call ahead, I can't say that I don't understand your need to process things on your own, especially before coming in for your monthly interrogation," he chuckled lightly. "Seeing as it is the first and only session you have missed in the long time we've known one another, I am more than happy to let this one go," he winked, smiling warmly before continuing.

"Now," he paused, taking in a deep breath. "In spite of last week, I do have some good news." There was that ruffle of his moustache again. "I would like to confidently say that I am ready to release you from therapy. No more scheduled sessions. Only visiting as you need, whenever you would like. How do you feel about that?"

She smiled gratefully, having known this would be happening any month now. She had worked tirelessly to show him that she could be on her own; responsible and rehabilitated.

"That's wonderful, thank you!" she beamed.

"That's quite alright."

He clasped his hands together and gave her a look that she knew only as pride. She had seen it so many times over the years. The last time she had seen this look was when she had graduated from high school, although it wasn't just any ordinary high school. She had been lucky enough to be enrolled in a four-year residential education program that specialised in helping troubled teenagers with trauma integrate smoothly into society. Without parents or extended family, boarding school had really been her only option after being released from the foster system at eighteen.

Dr. Hurley had been there every step of the way. He was the closest thing to family she could ever hope for. He had seen how far she had come, how hard they had both worked, and now, he sat, staring at the end result.

He was setting her free.

In his eyes, her progress in therapy seemed that it had accelerated tenfold out of nowhere, almost a year ago. Camilla, of course, knew the real reason behind her change of pace.

She had unlocked her most coveted, most repressed memory.

Everybody had wanted to know what had happened that day in Naomi's backyard, down between the oak trees. She had been given vague and varied updates over the years after being re-homed and from what she had been told, had happened to her that day, had ruined Naomi.

Naomi was the first thing she could remember, and she remembered her with such fondness that she could almost feel her warmth. Everything before Naomi had taken a tiny Camilla into her arms, was resounding nothingness. She had no recollection of the reason she had been placed into care. The only thing she could be sure of was that Naomi had looked at her with such sadness at their first meeting, that she had always known it must have been something horrible.

One day, Dr. Hurley had asked her if she would like to know.

"Know what?"

"I feel that it is only fair that I ask, Camilla. You are a young woman now, who has matured into someone wise beyond her years. What I am asking, is if you like to know why we have spent so many years learning the difference between good, healthy displays of affection and behaviour, and bad? Would you like to know the reason we are here?"

For one last, long moment, she considered the same possibilities she had always considered. Deep down she knew what must have happened to her. She had only ever guessed but it was the only explanation that made any sense. The way her skin crawled whenever somebody stood too close— that didn't materialise from just being *abandoned*. But she couldn't remember it, and she didn't want to. She finally decided after all those years, years working through medications, suicide attempts, panic attacks and recoveries, that no, she did not need to know anything more. She wanted Naomi to forever be the very first thing she ever remembered.

Camilla's eyes grazed over his office. Nothing had ever changed. The chairs they sat in had always been the same, as was the wallpaper and the video camera whirring away. The only thing that had been added over the years was a simple photo frame. A frame which cradled a single photo inside it, of Naomi.

The day he had shared with her that Naomi had had a psychotic break would have torn her heart in two— if she had been able to feel anything at all. Claire, the eldest foster child had been released from care, leaving only Theo. Kora had long since run away, never to be heard of or found.

She wanted so desperately to remember what had happened to her that day amongst the trees. She wanted so desperately to be able to help Naomi, but her brain just simply wouldn't let her. She knew she had fallen from the rotting oak tree down at the bottom of the property, but only because that's what she had been told. She couldn't remember climbing it or why she had ever wanted to climb it in the first place, much less alone. It was like the impact from the fall had just knocked the memory right out of her head. Another part of her that the fall stole, was the capability to feel a full range of emotions like love, or happiness.

"*Anhedonia*," Dr. Hurley had told her.

The palette of what she could feel was exceptionally limited and nobody— not doctors nor specialists, knew whether she was able to relearn those lost emotions, or whether they would ever even come back. The mind has always been a secret; an intricate mechanism not altogether understood.

Dr. Hurley had prescribed medication after medication, each one feeling stranger than the one before it. But they only ever dulled her grief for all that she couldn't feel. There was not one pill that ever gave her her happiness back.

The day she had remembered, it was already too late.

She felt a distinct fissure line crack its way down the back of her seat in that office as her entire world shattered around her.

Naomi had taken her own life.

It threw her perception of the earth off its axis in the strangest of ways. They say every cloud has a silver lining, and the silver lining that attached itself to the resounding heartbreak of learning of Naomi's death were the feelings of disbelief, immeasurable helplessness and pain. The exact feelings that matched perfectly with the ones she had felt right before she fell, all those years ago— unearthing some hidden part of her mind. And oh, how she felt them. They ripped through her like nothing she had ever felt, clawing their way out of her pores on fire. Eleven years of darkness and the light had finally broken through the cracks.

She likened it to a coded padlock. Each emotion that terrorised her body violently tore the veil from a different fragment of her memory of the day she fell, each one within only seconds of one another, until all the pieces fit.

And then it was just *there*. As if it had been there all along.

Something deep inside her mind broke away, separating two main things; control and rage. Like two tectonic plates grinding against each other, she struggled to take the reins. The two fell completely away from one another, leaving her with nothing but uncontrolled fury. That, and the overwhelming understanding that she needed to keep her secret buried just beneath the surface until she knew what to do with it. She may have recovered physically to the extent she had after the fall, but she would never recover emotionally, knowing just how many years and moments with Naomi that Kora had stolen from her. Kora should have been the one to be re-homed. Taken away from her family again.

It had taken her weeks of planning. Months of execution. Finding Kora had been the hardest part. She knew that she had disappeared from Naomi's in the middle of the night, sparking an investigation into Naomi's mental wellbeing. She also knew that anybody who had looked for Kora had long since forgotten about her. Prying snippets of information from Dr. Hurley wasn't difficult as long as she was careful not to ask anything of too personal a nature. He had grown such a connection with Camilla over the years that he never grew suspicious. She had eventually asked where Kora had grown up, where she had lived before she had been put into Naomi's care.

"Pearl City, I believe," he had told her.

Just one city over. It was so *easy*.

Each week, she had made herself more and more familiar with the little city, taking the occasional trip between weekly visits to Dr. Hurley but a few days at a time was just *not enough*. She needed more time. She knew she needed to make more progress in her appointments to be able to request that her visits become monthly instead of weekly.

She was no longer a helpless victim, no longer just a foster child with a scar just across her cheekbone and no memory of how it had happened. She knew. She remembered. She was no longer so uncertain of the world around her. All those years of pushing people away, instinctively flinching when they got too close, freezing up entirely if, god forbid, she was ever touched. The years of internally screaming, not knowing why she was the way she was; wondering how other people could be so happy, so carefree. The years wondering how people could stand to hug each other, kiss each other; the claustrophobia, wondering how it never seemed to make their skin crawl the way hers did. Coming to the hopeless realisation that she couldn't ever be loved, not the way she was.

So she learned how to lie.

She told Dr. Hurley about how well she was recovering. She told him about how she had moved in with her old friends from boarding school; the ones who made it out alive and free from their own demons, like Dominique and Pagan. She told him how she would muster the courage to go out with them, how her social life was picking up and how much she was enjoying it. To her, these were elaborate, far-fetched fairytales but to him, this was progress.

She made sure to crinkle the corners of her eyes when she smiled. She taught herself how to throw her head back in laughter whenever he or Erica had laughed— something she couldn't really feel enough of anything to do naturally. She made sure not to forget to brush her hair for weeks on end and to tell him about how she was getting out of bed every day and not just laying there for months like she used to; before she remembered, staring at the wall, feeling purposeless.

She had indeed found her purpose.

The decision was made sooner than she had anticipated. Monthly visits overtook weekly ones, with the all-inclusive option of being able to book an appointment earlier, at any time, if she felt like she wasn't coping. But she coped *just fine*.

After that, she had packed her bags, said her goodbyes to Dom and Pagan, and caught the first bus to Pearl City. She stayed in a low-grade motel that didn't ask for any identification as long as her stay was paid for upfront, cash only. She had saved as much as she could from every disability check she had ever been sent, not able to enjoy much of anything anyway.

Over the weeks, her fixation on finding Kora bordered on obsession. She wasn't sleeping. She grew frustrated. She considered the possibilities of failure; that she might not even recognise her if they crossed paths, that maybe she hadn't returned to her hometown at all.

That's when she had met Stephen Hayes. He was handsome, he was in control of himself and everything around him.

Stephen came from a wealthy, albeit absent family and had worked his entire life away to obtain an incredibly high position at the only bank in the city. He had had no time for relationships nor any real, meaningful friendships. He was a typical workaholic, logical in his approach to things and somewhat lacking in things like physical affection and emotion. Camilla wasn't sure if she adored him or if she simply just wanted to *be like him*. Regardless, she knew that she couldn't give herself completely to him; what little there was of herself to give, and what little of her he had the time for. Finding Kora was her priority.

So she continued to weave herself securely into her web.

She bought a second phone, keeping her own hidden away in a black satchel. She went by the name of *Millie Oaks*— A play on her own name and the very event that had changed her life.

Stephen and *Millie* began dating, or what she felt dating should look like. She had grown a habit of mimicking his behaviour, a habit she could only assume stemmed from the insecurity of knowing that she was missing something crucial as a functioning human being. This routine extended past Stephen and onto anybody she met, adopting alien mannerisms to seem— less alien.

She had listed endless excuses to avoid meeting his family if he had ever happened to ask, as she simply had "no time for herself" with her busy, non-existent career. Although being with him was predominantly a relationship of convenience; a means to an end, she frequently found herself enjoying his company when she did have it. He fell in what little love he had time for and eventually asked her to move in. She fit seamlessly into the slot in his life labelled *relationship*, not needing his full attention so that he was free to continue to throw himself tirelessly into his career. Within weeks she had figured out how to access account information from his home office in search of Kora; her endless rage still burning brightly as fuel for her plight.

But time went on, and she found nothing; there was no trace of Kora, so there was no trace of finding the closure she so desperately sought.

She had never quite settled into Stephen's townhouse. Her belongings were sparse, just two drawers full of clothes and some toiletries. She had never anticipated being in the city for so long. Weeks had turned to months, seasons had changed three times over and Stephen had begun to talk about marriage. She began to think that perhaps this was where she should be. She might not feel love, but she knew of it and knew if she could feel it she would feel it for him. Perhaps that was enough. He wasn't a bad person, in fact, quite the opposite. If anything, he was a perfect fit for her, just the way she was.

There were things she couldn't give him. She knew she would always struggle with intimacy, the smaller, secret moments between two lovers that the world never sees; planting kisses along collarbones and tiny nuzzles in the cold. She figured the best thing she could do for them both was to condition herself. She had fabricated her entire life for months, surely she could do the same with intimacy until it became second nature, and it was *far* from second nature.

With some stroke of luck, intimacy wasn't something he ever seemed to notice was lacking. His work hours were so long, they wore him out as it were.

Subconsciously, she had begun to give up on finding Kora. She had resigned herself, and not unhappily, to where she was, who she was, and what her life with Stephen would look like.

Until one morning, when an empty silence had woken her.

She was a light sleeper, unlike he was. She had opened her eyes, feeling like there was something missing. Some warmth, a sound; his body, his breathing. She sat up in bed only to find it empty, almost. Her small, black satchel full of her most personal things had been tipped out onto their bed while she slept. On the very top, lay her driver's licence— her *real* driver's licence— the one she had kept hidden away along with her other cellphone.

She had been found out.

Thinking fast, she had culminated a plan. She had listened for his footsteps, wondering where in the house he was— if he was even still there. She had grabbed her satchel, replacing her things inside and gotten dressed. She used a scarf to wipe down every surface she had ever laid her fingertips on in both the bedroom and ensuite and crept out of the bedroom. She would come back for the rest of her things later.

The blue glow from his office at the end of the hallway gave away his whereabouts instantly and she had held her breath, readying herself to make a dash past the gap in the door that sat only half-closed. As she did so, she stole a glance into the office and slowed her footsteps to a complete stop.

He was slumped over his desk, asleep in his chair. For how long, she had no idea. The light from his laptop in the early hours of the morning made it easy to make out what was on the screen; an internet search of her alias, *Millie Oaks*.

242

She slipped into the room, grateful that he was such a heavy sleeper. From over his shoulder she deleted his browser history. She had then picked up his cellphone which lay on the desk and deleted her phone number, their entire text message thread, and any photos of her that he had taken, which admittedly were only few. She had then wiped her fingerprints off his phone, the keyboard and the computer mouse with her scarf along with the bannister down the stairs as she continued to make her way down to the foyer.

She scanned the kitchen after wiping it down, pocketing a pairing knife before standing by the front door, reminding herself to breathe. She took a deep breath and knocked his mother's porcelain vase off the console table, flinching as it smashed on the tiled floor. Sharp, triangular pieces danced away from one another as she waited. Then all at once she had heard his footsteps at the top of the stairs.

That had been her moment.

She bolted out of the front door, slamming it behind her, and he followed like she knew he would. He had called after her as he chased her shadow; at first surprised, only wanting answers, but his tone soon took a darker turn. The more questions he asked, the less answers she gave. The faster she walked, the quicker his confusion turned to anger. He pieced what he could together. He accused her of fraud, of identify theft, of being a con-artist. He threatened to call the police if she refused to come clean then and there.

He was *ruining everything*.

He'd followed her as she weaved through the streets, livid, questioning, accusing. Her heart had once again broken. Not because of something he had said, but what she had done. She numbed herself to it as she lead him, knowing what she had to do. She argued for blocks and blocks, feeding him only breadcrumbs of truths; just enough so that he would keep following, one step behind, as always. There is nothing more powerfully enticing than *almost* knowing a truth.

She had spent her entire life knowing that.

She knew the city then, better than he would have ever known it. She led him down streets with no stores, no cameras. She made sure with small glances that there was nobody in sight before turning suddenly down an alleyway. She had planned this out meticulously from the particular streets she took, to this particular alley. Everything.

He cornered her; but really, she had cornered him.

But it had not been meant for him; it had all been meant for Kora.

Kora, who she couldn't find— who she may never have found.

Until *there she was*.

It was as if the universe at that moment had stepped in; whether it was showing her a green light or a red one, she would never know. There Camilla was, standing in an alleyway in between the two people she had trusted, perhaps even loved, and the two people she wanted so badly to kill.

She *had* meant to kill Kora. She had meant to kill them both.

But Kora had moved first, only she had moved in on Stephen with a block of wood and Camilla had been about to use a paring knife.

Camilla had looked on as Stephen bled.

She had looked on as Kora froze.

She still didn't understand what stopped her from killing Kora in that moment, why she hadn't stuck the paring knife right into her throat.

Her mind flickered back over the moment Kora had turned out of the alley, but she had grabbed her arm immediately and dragged Kora in the other direction. If she had let Kora lead them left, only two buildings down, they would have been captured on the security footage by a simple little thrift store, and more than likely every subsequent store after that.

She shook her head in mild bewilderment, somewhat amused. Something so simple as a small, recycled clothing boutique could have been her downfall. She flew back over her memories of the past week, how many moments there had been that could have been her downfall. Moments she had thankfully thought on her feet.

Kora had been protective over her from the beginning, having not understood why she was standing in that alley with Stephen in the first place. She had used that to her advantage. She'd slipped Stephen's credit card out of his wallet while she was alone in the elevator, waiting for Kora; if only at the time to stop her from using it and getting them both caught.

Convincing Kora to collect belongings from Stephen's house— more than likely having left her fingerprints everywhere, had felt as though it were too easy. That was, until she learned of Kora's *bad habits,* as she had so aptly put it. She had quickly gotten rid of the folder full of documents Kora had picked up from the house which were under the alias of Millie, easily passing them off as Stephen's sister's. She was grateful that Kora wasn't even the slightest bit suspicious. She had even kept her cellphone and driver's licence inside the lining of her black satchel so that this time, it would not be found. She was never seen even *speaking* to Kora in nightclubs or places where security cameras lurked in every crack in the wall.

Everywhere except the casino.

She had finally admitted to herself that she was in over her head. She had let Kora drag her in too deep. Reaching out to Dom and Pagan, they had dropped everything to come to her aid. They were, after all, three of the same. Damaged, *angry*. They culminated a plan to lure Kora into a false sense of mastery. A plan where Mila would open up the doorway to Dom and Pagan's home and they could have her arrested, or worse. But it was a plan that never eventuated. Kora's

245

intuition and insecurities were too strong, and Pagan's hatred for her was too powerful to mask.

"*I will fucking kill her,*" Pagan had seethed. But Mila didn't want her dead. Not yet. She wanted her to suffer. Alone.

She had one final idea, the pièce de résistance— using Stephen's credit card to pay for the extra month in the hostel room. It had alerted police while Kora slept, thinking she was king of the world, only to have it all torn apart the moment she opened her eyes.

Camilla thought of moments where she could have run away from all of it, backed out, *gone home*. But her knuckles had itched, seeing Kora in that alleyway. She wanted so badly for her to suffer, to live out the pain of being alive.

She had known all along that Kora was simply longing to *belong*, to be touched, to be loved. All things she similarly longed for but could never have with her brain being damaged the way it was. Things she could never have *because* of Kora.

It wasn't hard to simulate, just like she had with Stephen. She wasn't oblivious to how it was supposed to look, how it was supposed to feel. She did, however, overlook an astronomical difference between Stephen and Kora; Kora, she despised.

Her hands had felt clammy as she had grit her teeth through every touch, every embrace. Her stomach turned. She could still feel her own, unseen grimace in response to Kora's hands as they had covered her ears, while Theo's key-cutting machine fired shrieking, metal sparks into the air around him—

And *Theo*. Oh, Theo.

She had only ever dreamed of being able to see him again. Her stomach had tightened in disbelief when she'd heard Kora say his name; when she'd finally seen his face. His face had changed— he had grown into a man. She realised that she had been so fixated on Kora that she had forgotten he had even existed. She remembered a time where he was her everything. She had waited so long to get rid of Kora, Kora had turned the tables and gotten rid of *him*. Camilla had finally reached out, but it had been too late. It was all her fault. She had to find him again. Something inside her body made her feel as though he was her answer. That he was the cure to her cancerous, soul-destroying sadness.

"Camilla?" Dr. Hurley's voice interrupted her infinite universe of thoughts.

"Sorry," she replied, smiling her irresistibly charming smile. "It's just, I was just marvelling at how far I've come."

"As am I, Camilla. As am I."

On the way out of Dr. Hurley's office, Erica was waiting for her. She stood in front of her desk holding a small bouquet of flowers with outstretched arms.

"Congratulations, honey!"

She squealed, stepping into her arms and giving her a small squeeze. "I'm sure I'll be back to visit."

"I hope so!"

And with a small, knowing nod in Dr. Hurley's direction, she said her goodbyes and stepped onto the elevator, never to return.

As she left the building, she let the flowers fall from her hand and into the nearest bin to mix with the abandoned ash of cigarettes and empty coffee cups. The wind picked up a little, so she wrapped her scarf tighter around her neck. Turning the corner, she took a seat on a nearby park bench, reaching into her satchelled producing Theo's tattered journal. She took Detective Parker's card from between the pages, flipping it over and over in her hand.

She stared off into space, thinking about Theo. He had been her whole world and now, because of Kora, she had almost no one. She would have been completely alone if it weren't for Dom and Pagan. As far as she knew, Theo was in prison and Stephen was dead.

Eventually, she took out her phone and entered the number on the front of the card. She stared somewhat vacantly at the number on the screen for a moment before typing out a message, wondering if she was ready to play with fire with nothing but her raw, bare hands.

She had already come this far.

Detective Parker, it's Camilla Lane.
I was wondering if you could help me.
I'm looking for my brother.

TWENTY FIVE

JOHN DOE

Beep.
Beep.
Beep.

The steady, rhythmic beat of the heart monitor set a dejected and somewhat bleak tone in the room belonging to yet another 'John Doe' in the ICU.

Just by studying his face, any person could tell that this man had been handsome. Underneath the swollen, black bulb that had become his cheek, there was the remnants of what would have been without a doubt, a masculine jawline; Pieces of it now broken and scattered throughout the rest of his cheek like shrapnel.

Old, dried blood spotted the hospital pillowcase and stuck to the white bandage that had been wrapped firmly around his head. It was the only colour to the otherwise dull scene.

Various tubes lay connected to several of his clammy limbs. Smaller ones running into the veins on the underside of his forearms and the back of his hands. A large endotracheal tube ran up the side of his face that wasn't swollen, entering his throat and had been taped to his chin. His chest moved up and down in mechanical intervals, being filled with air by a respiratory ventilator which somewhat stole the feeling of a human being inhabiting the room. The room felt devoid of life, as many of the other patients' rooms in this particular ward did.

Nurses in their light and dark blue uniforms shuffled into the room at scheduled intervals, picking up the clipboard hanging off the end of his bed and combing through the information on autopilot.

Name: John Doe
Date of Birth: Unknown
Blood Type: 0 Negative
Reason for admission: Presumed assault. Blunt force trauma to the left side jaw, multiple fractures to the back right base of the skull, severe muscle contusion to the left sternocleidomastoid muscle.
Attacker unknown.
Condition: Stable.
Notes: Detective Declan Parker is to be notified immediately upon consciousness.

Suddenly, in his empty room, John Doe's eyes tore themselves open. The bright lights on the ceiling burned his retinas and his first instinct was to cry out, squeezing his eyes shut again, but his cries were instantly caught in his throat by the endotracheal tube. He could only splutter in terror. He tried to turn over, but stopped and winced in pain. He reached up to his head, where his fingertips found the bandage wrapped taut.

His eyes searched the empty white hospital room, tearful and panicked. His mind was thick with a fog he couldn't clear. He tried again to call for help but it only made him choke harder. He reached out, knocking his clipboard off the side of the bed and onto the floor.

An older brunette nurse with bright red pursed lips walking by, by some miracle, heard the clanging of the plastic clipboard hitting the linoleum floor and with a start, she looked in. They locked eyes. He was staring right at her. Entering the room with a sense of urgency, her heels clicking as she took long strides straight over to press the emergency call button above his head. He looked up at her with eyes full of panic and confusion. The heart rate monitor beeped at a faster pace and the nurse looked down at him and hushed him softly, trying to calm him as she picked up his chart from the floor, scanning over it quickly. She placed it immediately on the bedside table and pulled two rubber gloves out from a box placed above his head.

"Sir, please nod for yes or shake your head for no. Do you know where you are?"

He shook his head, still as wide-eyed as ever. Tears began to form at the corners of his eyes. She smiled sympathetically in an attempt to calm him.

"Sir, you are in St Margaret's Hospital. You are okay. We are here to help you. I'm going to remove this tube from your throat now so that you can speak, is that okay?"

He nodded his head frantically. The nurse began to remove the tape from around his mouth that had been keeping the tube in place. She then tugged carefully but quickly on the tube, pulling it all the way out. He gagged and dry heaved, wincing in pain. Once his throat had stopped spasming, she wiped the mucus from his chin and pressed the emergency call button for the second time.

"Sir, can you tell me your name?"

He opened his mouth to answer her but frowned, as though he had forgotten; as though he couldn't remember who he was. He looked up at her as his tears streamed down his face in sheer terror. He shook his head from side to side violently as the beeps from the machine that was monitoring his heart beat steadily increased.

"Sir, please, I'm going to need you to try and stay calm for me. You are just fine," she reassured him, pressing the emergency call button again.

"Take some deep breaths for me," she soothed. "In through your nose and out through your mouth, just like this."

She took a big breath in through her nose, flaring her nostrils for dramatic effect, then blowing the air out slowly and loudly so that he could see exactly what she was doing and could follow the movement.

Steady, purposeful footsteps approached from behind the nurse.

"What have we got?"

"Doctor, we need to call in Detective Parker— John Doe number six-nine-one is awake and responsive."

THE END

www.ingramcontent.com/pod-product-compliance
Lightning Source LLC
Chambersburg PA
CBHW021421110726
47901CB00008B/2245